THE ADVENTURES OF CARDIGAN

OF

CARDIGAN

A DIME DETECTIVE™ BOOK

■

FREDERICK NEBEL

Series Consultant: ROBERT WEINBERG

THE MYSTERIOUS PRESS • New York • London • Tokyo

This Mysterious Press Edition is published by arrangement with Blazing Publications, Inc., The Argosy Company, in cooperation with Mrs. Dorothy B. Nebel.

DIME DETECTIVE and CARDIGAN are exclusive trademarks of Blazing Publications, Inc.

The Mysterious Press, 129 West 56th Street, New York, N.Y. 10019

Printed in the United States of America
First Printing: October 1988
10 9 8 7 6 5 4 3 2 1

Library of Congress Cataloging-in-Publication Data

Nebel, Frederick.
  The adventures of Cardigan.

  Contents: Introduction—Murder à la carte—
Spades are spades—[etc.]
  1. Cardigan (Fictitious character)—Fiction.
2. Detective and mystery stories, American. I. Title.
PS3527.E22A67 1988   813'.52   88-5233
ISBN 0-89296-950-4 (pbk.) (U.S.A.)
      0-89296-951-2 (pbk.) (Canada)

CONTENTS

■

THE
ADVENTURES
OF
CARDIGAN

CARDIGAN

BY ROBERT WEINBERG

While a number of fictional detectives appeared on postage stamps, and one such character regularly receives mail at a certain London address, none of those famous sleuths ever financed a publishing empire. That honor was the unique legacy of a nearly forgotten, hard-boiled pulp-magazine investigator named Cardigan, ace investigator for the Cosmos Agency. Appearing in more than three dozen novelettes in *Dime Detective Magazine* in the 1930s, he helped propel Popular Publications to the top of the cheap-paper magazine field.

Harry Steeger and Harold Goldsmith started Popular Publications in 1930, using ten thousand dollars borrowed from relatives. Working mostly on credit advanced against their cash reserve, the new company issued four pulp magazines—one each in the western, action, air war, and detective fields. Of the titles, only *Battle Aces* made money right away. However, both Steeger and Goldsmith felt that the pulp field was ripe for new titles. People wanted cheap entertainment during the Depression and the pulp offered hours of reading at bargain prices.

Following the advice of their distributors, Popular began a series of magazines using the word *Dime* as part of the title. The first of these was *Dime Detective*, which began in November 1931. Soon after came *Dime Western, Dime Mystery, Dime Sports,* and *Dime Adventure*.

In the pulps, imitation was the standard method of business. Steeger, who served as editorial director for all the Popular magazines, looked to the most successful detective pulp of the period for inspiration for his new magazine. *Black Mask*, under the brilliant editorial hand of Captain Joseph T. Shaw, had a circulation of over a hundred thousand copies a month, making it the best-selling publication in the detective genre.

Started in 1920 as an English-style mystery magazine, *Black*

Mask had evolved over the years into the leading publication featuring the hard-boiled detective story. By 1931, Dashiell Hammett was no longer writing for the pulp (succumbing to the lure of big bucks in Hollywood), but it regularly featured stories by Carroll John Daly, Erle Stanley Gardner, Frederick Nebel, Raoul Whitfield, and other leaders in the tough-guy genre. *Black Mask* had a stranglehold on the pulp detective field.

Steeger broke that grip by a series of brilliant editorial decisions. *Black Mask* featured static covers—usually only one or two figures against a white background. With dozens of pulps competing for space on the newsstands, cover art often sold a magazine. Hot colors appealed to male buyers and so the covers for *Dime Detective* were done in bright reds and yellows. A large *10¢* in yellow, with a red circle highlighting it, was prominent next to the title, emphasizing the magazine's low price. Even the spine of the magazine was bright yellow. Each issue featured a garish cover painting by William Reusswig illustrating the wildest action scene in the issue.

However, while covers might attract browsers, contents sold issues to the general public. Big names sold big quantities. In a bold move, Harry Steeger offered the best-selling authors writing for *Black Mask* a penny *more* a word than they were being paid by that magazine if they would contribute to his new publication. He put only one condition on his offer—series characters created for *Dime Detective* could appear only in that magazine—thus insuring reader loyalty to the pulp.

Long novelettes and short novels by hard-boiled favorites filled the pages of *Dime Detective*. Steeger wisely stayed away from serials, and instead had his authors concentrate on continued series characters. The most popular writers for the new magazine were Erle Stanley Gardner, Carroll John Daly, and Frederick Nebel.

An accomplished pulp stylist who had been writing since 1925, Frederick Nebel was one of the most popular contributors to *Black Mask*. Incredibly prolific, he contributed two excellent series to the magazine. The MacBride and Kennedy stories featured a tough cop and an ace news reporter investigating crimes in a corrupt big city. Donahue was a tough ex-cop who worked as a private investigator for the Inter-State Detective Agency. Nebel was a good friend of Dashiell Hammett, and while his stories rarely matched the Continental Op adventures in plot or style, they were equally hard-boiled.

For *Dime Detective*, Nebel created Cardigan—a new character combining the best of his two *Black Mask* heroes. A hard-as-nails Irish detective, the operative for the Cosmos Agency solved mysteries using both his brain and his fists. He prowled a city filled with corruption and casual violence, where the dividing line between right and wrong was stretched exceedingly thin.

Nebel wrote in a terse, staccato style that perfectly suited the fast-paced action of the Cardigan adventures. They were tough-guy fiction at its best. The series was an immediate hit and established *Dime Detective* as a top detective fiction pulp. Early issues of the magazine prominently displayed Nebel's name on the front cover, with Cardigan's name boldly listed on the contents page directly above the featured story.

Harry Steeger's gamble paid off. The new series stories by top-name authors sold his magazine. Even with the high cost per story, *Dime Detective* immediately earned a profit. Within a few years it became a biweekly, and rivaled *Black Mask* in circulation.

The tremendous success of *Dime Detective* financed future expansions at Popular Publications. Within ten years, the chain grew into the largest pulp-magazine publisher in the world. *Dime Detective* continued to lead the Popular lineup, which at one time featured over forty different magazines a month.

Frederick Nebel also moved on to bigger and better things. In 1933, his first novel, *Sleeper's East*, became a best-seller and was made into a motion picture. Within a few years, he left the pulps for the better paying "slick" magazines. He became a regular contributor to *Cosmopolitan, Liberty, Good Housekeeping*, and other similar publications, writing contemporary romantic fiction. Suffering from high blood pressure, Nebel died in 1967 at age sixty-three.

Surprisingly enough, only one collection of Nebel's short stories has ever been published. When the mystery pulps died in the 1950s, interest in reprints from the magazines died with them. The Cardigan stories have remained untouched and forgotten until now. When first published, they were considered among the best hard-boiled detective stories ever written. Fifty years after their initial appearance, the Cardigan stories still rank among the best.

MURDER
À LA CARTE

■

BY FREDERICK NEBEL

Hardesty was as dumb an egg as they come—but boy how that baby could pitch ball. So when he tangled himself all up in a murder net it was up to that big dick from Cosmos to pick the knots. Or else— But there just wasn't any "or else." Cardigan had laid too much hard-earned dough on the Series to permit his favorite hurler to fumble himself into the hot seat.

ONE

THE GIRL IN ROOM 1205

■

The jangling of the telephone wakened Cardigan at seven, and he turned over, scowled at it, considered the clock, the dim daylight coming through the open window and remembered that he had told the hotel operator not to ring him before eight. He had mixed drinks the night before, got in late, and his head felt like a balloon—loaded with lead. When his scowling at the phone failed to stop its ringing, he ripped out an oath, grabbed the instrument, hauled it back into bed with him, and growled upward into the mouthpiece.

"Yowssuh!" He nodded to himself, bared his teeth and droned, "Oh, so it's you. Maybe you're on Chinese time or something. . . . Oh, no; you didn't wake me up. Go lay an egg!"

He slammed the receiver into the hook, set the instrument back upon the table, and yanked the covers over his head. He had begun to breath normally, and was slipping back to sleep, when the phone jangled again. He sat bolt upright, kicked the covers over the bottom of the bed and grabbed the instrument, yelled into it.

"Listen, you fathead! There's no use ringing me, because I'm

7

not civilized until I've had eight hours sleep! . . . What?
. . . Well, that's just too bad. Try using your head for a change. I
tell you, Sam— Now listen; I don't give a damn who— Huh?
. . . Who? . . . Well, why don't you know? . . . Oh, you
were cockeyed drunk, eh? Suppose Carmicheal found out his ace
pitcher was hitting the bottle a week before the World Series?
. . . I should think you would! . . . Of course, I've taken a
drink in my day. Last night I took seventeen, but what's that to
you? . . . Oh, I know, I know. Good old Cardigan, good old
horse's neck Cardigan. . . . Well, I suppose I may as well, if
you're going to keep this phone hopping all morning. . . . Soon
as I can.''

He hung up, got out of his wrinkled pajamas, and went into the
bathroom growling, "Damned fool!" He showered as cold as he
could take it, groaning, grunting, and gasping meanwhile. He used
all the towels in the bathroom to rub himself dry, then dressed,
removed bills, change, penknife, and watch from the bureau and
shoved them into his pockets. He looked at himself in the mirror.
He didn't, he saw, look so swell.

Downstairs in the restaurant, he ordered a full pint of tomato juice
and into it he put a tablespoonful of Tabasco. It burned its way
down like fire. Then he ate wheatcakes, two lamb chops, fried
potatoes, three rolls—and drank two cups of black coffee. He felt a
little better by the time he reached the lobby, but not yet equal to a
cigar. He compromised on a cigarette and set out on foot. Sam
Hardesty's hotel was not far distant, and Cardigan reached it in
fifteen minutes, kicked his way through the swing door.

A green elevator hoisted him to the fifteenth floor, and he went
down a corridor long-legged, his tie a little to one side, a few
superfluous dents in his fedora, his vest buttoned wrong, and his
face not jovial.

The door of 1510 was opened by a tall, muscular man who held
an ice bag on his head and looked the worse for wear and tear. He
grimaced. Cardigan made swearing movements with his lips.

"Hello, Jack," Hardesty gulped.

"Hello yourself. If you think misery loves company, you're
screw-loose." He strode in, scowling, and went on into the large
bedroom while Hardesty closed the door and followed like a man
in the first stages of the bends.

"Hell, Jack, I'm in a tough spot, I think."

Cardigan sat down, keeping his hat on, and thrust his hands into his pockets, shot his legs out straight, crossing them at the ankles. Hardesty was drinking Canadian ale as a pick-me-up, and he sat down painfully on a chair, holding the bottle in his right hand, by the neck. He looked worried and pale and sallow; not at all like the famous pitcher and speed king the baseball diamonds had come to know.

"Jack, I got tangled up last night. I couldn't think of anyone to call but you, seeing as how we went to school together, played as kids together—"

"Chuck the album, Sam, and get to the point. You may have a hangover, but I've got one myself and it's a pip."

"Well, it's like this, old sock. I went to a nightclub, met a jane, took her to her flat, and then things happened. And that's the trouble. I can't remember what happened. Usually if I get awful tight, I write out a lot of checks."

"Did you write any last night?"

"That's it! I don't know! I carry the blanks loose around in my pocket and I can't remember how many I started out with. Usually I mark down what I write out, but sometimes I forget. Honest, Jack, I haven't been tight since I was married last year. I'm scared as hell. Marjorie gets the bank statement each month, and if she sees a big withdrawal—Hell, maybe I even wrote a check for everything we have! O-o-o, am I in a spot!" He touched his head, took a long swig at the bottle of ale.

"So what?" said Cardigan.

"Look, can't you do something? You're a private dick. You know your way around."

"Who's the jane?"

"I don't know."

"Where's she live?"

"I"—he swallowed—"don't know."

"Oh, I see. You don't know if you wrote out a check to a jane you don't know at an address you don't know. That's what I call a swell lead for me to start on."

"That," breathed poor Hardesty, "is just about how it stacks up, you might say."

"I might say! That's a good line, too." Cardigan leaned

forward, shed his air of sarcasm, got down to business. "Can't you remember just something of what happened?"

"Uh-uh. It was dark and raining and I remember where we got out. I was pretty tight then, Jack, but it was in her apartment I got blind, and I remember kind of dimlike there were some guys there. I couldn't tell you what they looked like. Then all's a blank till I wake up here at five this morning." His face was working. "I tell you, Jack, something happened. I feel it in my bones. I didn't mean any harm. I was just lonesome and I danced with the jane and— Listen, if I wrote out a check, Marjorie'll see it. I've got to get that check back. If I have to pay, I'll get cash. I can hock myself to get the cash—"

"Wait a minute, Sam." Cardigan was calm now. "Take it easy. Don't get all steamed up. Let me think. . . . See here, one thing you must know. What nightclub was it?"

Hardesty nodded. "Yes, I remember that. It was the Club Medallion; it's up in East Fifty—"

"I know where it is. They charge a buck and a half for a cocktail you can get in the Forties for four bits, and you get charged ten percent extra because the waiters, all of them South Brooklyn dagoes, say 'Merci, monsieur,' instead of plain 'Thank you.' . . . D' you remember anybody there?"

"A tall guy, with silky gray hair. He got me to write an autograph on a menu—"

"McQueston. He runs the scatter. He collects autographs. Usually keeps a stiff eye on his place. Well"—Cardigan stood up—"pull out of the hangover and for crying out loud lay off the booze. You've got a couple of World Series games to pitch and I," he added sententiously, "have bet a couple of centuries on any game you pitch."

"Honest, Jack, it was the first time I fell off the wagon since I was married. I'd go nuts if Marjorie thought—if I hurt Marjorie. And if Carmicheal finds me like this—"

"Listen," Cardigan cut in slowly. "Take this key. Go down to my place and sleep it off and you'll be okay by tonight." He chuckled. "Hell, you look funny, Sam."

"Funny? If you knew how I felt . . ."

Cardigan was on his way to the door, saying, "By the way, do you remember her name?"

"I—I think it was Priscilla."

"I suppose she wore curls and old lace and lisped and supported a rheumatic mother in Hoboken who had to take in floors to scrub." Cardigan laughed raucously, rasped out, "Mammy!" and left the room.

He left the hotel by a side door.

Ben McQueston was eating breakfast at a card table in his living room overlooking Central Park. He was an unusually tall man with a pink-cheeked pale face, aluminum-colored hair, neatly parted, and fragile nose glasses. His small, neat mustache matched his hair. He looked very dignified, almost like a minister; and his apartment had a rarified atmosphere, with its books, its framed autographs, and its good paintings.

McQueston never showed surprise. "Oh, hello, Cardigan. Haven't seen you around the Medallion in ages. Well, I guess you weren't around. That's what I thought. Have an egg."

"Uh-uh."

"I suppose you came up to look at my collection of autographs."

"No."

"I didn't think so. Lovely day, isn't it?"

"I wouldn't like it even if it was nice."

"*M-m-m!* Indigestion, huh?"

Cardigan flopped down in the divan, slapped his hat on his knee. "You run a nice joint, Ben. You soak a guy four times what anything's worth, but that's okay. Your liquor's pretty bum, but they forget that when the girls come out in tights and the lights go low and somebody hauls off with a torch song. So it's pretty funny when a guy walks in, has himself a good time, and is dragged home by a pickup."

McQueston blinked brightly. "Go on."

"I am looking for an autograph, Ben. An autograph on a check."

"I'm still interested."

Cardigan leaned forward. "Sam Hardesty was in your place last night."

"The baseball player? Sure. I got his autograph, Jack, but not on a check."

"I'm talking about the jane who took him out of your place."

McQueston put knife and fork neatly together on his plate and dabbed at his lips with a napkin. He kept his small blue eyes intently on Cardigan, compressed his lips and reached for a cigarette.

He said, "If you're intimating that I've a flock of chiselers in my scatter, you're off your trolley, boy. I charge like hell for everything I sell, and I get people who can pay out, but outside of that any guy's as safe in my place as he is in church." He lit up, tilted back his fine head, and eyed Cardigan levelly. "Come down to brass tacks, Jack, or politely pick up your hat and take a walk."

Cardigan grinned. "I'm looking for the jane took Hardesty home last night."

"I'm sorry, Jack. When I got his autograph, he was alone."

"I don't give a damn what he was when you got his autograph. A jane took him home. He got liquor somewhere after he left your place and it was hopped up. He was pretty tight when he left the Medallion, too, because he doesn't remember the address the jane took him to. He thinks he signed a check, and if he did, then there's chiselers running loose in your place and if you don't want headquarters to get wind of it, stop looking down your damned nose at me and talk sense!"

McQueston puffed. He did not take his eyes off Cardigan, and for a long moment he made no reply. Then he rose, went across the room to a telephone saying, "Chiselers, eh? I'll call my head-waiter." He put through a call.

A moment later he said, "Louie? . . . This is Ben. Listen. Hardesty—you know, the baseball player—was in last night. You remember? . . . He came in alone, didn't he? . . . Okay. Who'd he leave with? . . . Do you know her name? . . . Did she come in alone? . . . Who'd she come in with? . . . Three guys, eh? Well, what about the guys? . . . Don't know, eh? Well, it's a hell of a fine state of affairs when you don't know who's coming in these nights! . . . Shut up! Call Otto. See if he put them in a cab and if he got the address. If he didn't, see if he remembers who drove the cab. . . . Never mind. You heard me. Do what I say and call me back."

He slammed the receiver back into the prong, swiveled. There was higher color in his cheeks, and he said, "Chiselers, eh? Not while I know anything about it!"

Ten minutes later the telephone rang and McQueston grabbed it, talked for several minutes, and then hung up. "Okay," he said, turning. "We don't know who the jane is, but Otto, the doorman, remembers Hardesty and remembers putting him and a jane in a taxi. The driver asked Otto where he should take 'em and Otto stuck his head in back and asked them and the jane said the Drexel Tower. That's in West Sixty-fifth Street. . . . Now look here, Cardigan. I'm sore. I'm going to fire Louie. My joint's always been on the up-and-up—"

Cardigan rose. "I know, Ben. That's why I came around."

McQueston took off his glasses, blinked his eyes. "I don't want this to get in the papers."

Cardigan was on his way to the door. "It won't."

He went downstairs, walked out into the street, and climbed into a taxicab. It took him up Fifth Avenue, through the park by way of a transverse, and westward through Sixty-fifth Street to the Drexel Tower. The building was tall, narrow, white, with a short glass marquee. The lobby was rectangular, with a small desk at one end, and behind the desk a very young man with a dazzling haircomb.

"How do you do," said the clerk, without looking up.

"How do you do," said Cardigan, disapproving of the haircomb.

He laid his identification on the desk and lit a cigarette while the clerk perused it with lifted eyebrows.

Then Cardigan said, "This is kind of funny. Last night a woman resident here called up the agency and asked to have a man sent up this morning. The clerk who took the message lost the memo, and all he could remember was that the address was this and the first name of the woman was Priscilla. So I don't know her full name, but I don't think you'd have a flock of residents here all named Priscilla."

"We have one," said the clerk quietly.

"I'd thank you to tell me her whole name and her apartment. It'd look bad for the agency if I fell down. The guy was dumb to lose the memo, but we all make mistakes."

"There is a Priscilla Ferne in 1205," the clerk said. "Shall I ring?"

"No. She told us to come right up."

He thanked the clerk and swung his long legs across the lobby, entered a small elevator, and was hoisted noiselessly to the twelfth floor. He got out and slapped his big feet down the corridor, shooting out his shaggy head to read the door numbers as he went past. He came at last to 1205, listened with an ear pressed to the panel, and hearing no sound, worked the brass knocker. He waited, tapping his foot, and then knocked again; and when no reply came, he took out a bunch of skeleton keys, and the fifth try gained him admittance to a large, opulent apartment. He went from the foyer into the large living room, noticed that the shades were three-quarters down. Listening, he moved across the living room and reached the bedroom doorway. His scalp tightened.

A girl lay on the floor beside the bed. She wore sheer blue silk pajamas, and bronze hair streamed out on the rug. The light was bad, so he pulled up one of the window shades, and now he saw that her face was discolored, but not so much so that he could not be certain of her beauty. She was, he saw, very beautiful. And she was also dead. Strangled. . . .

He drew down the shade again, shaking. He thought of Sam Hardesty, who could not remember what had happened, and a thin chill knifed through the flush that had welled up in him. His own breathing, thick and heavy now, was the only sound in the room. He turned on a light and bent to study her face closely, and then he switched the light off and returned to the living room.

He wrapped a handkerchief around his hand and searched her purse and the desk, thinking of Hardesty's check. But he did not find it. However, he found Hardesty's card, and shoved it into his pocket. He saw an empty glass standing on a tray, and wiped off the glass. Hardesty would have written out the check at the desk, so Cardigan wiped off the desk. Then he went around clearing chair arms, tables, the bedposts, of possible fingerprints. At last he returned to the door, wiped his own prints off the knobs, outside and in, and left, locking the door. Heat throbbed in his chest, and when he reached the lobby he said to the clerk, "I guess she's not in. I'll try later."

TWO

MURDER À LA CARTE

■

When Cardigan swept into his own hotel room, he found Sam Hardesty on the bed.

"Hell," said Hardesty, "I can't sleep. I can't—"

"You won't now, sweetheart."

Hardesty did not miss the hard note in Cardigan's tone. "What—what—"

Cardigan took off his hat and whacked it into the nearest chair. "No, you won't sleep now, Sam, and that's a fact. Now I want it straight." He slapped his hands on the bedpost, and his big face was dark, tight-drawn, and his dark eyes bit down at Hardesty. "The jane's dead," he said suddenly.

"Dead!"

"Don't yell."

"But good God!"

"I know, I know. I know all about that. Lay off the third-act cracks. Tighten up. Keep your pants on and sit quiet. The jane's dead. That's a fact. We know about it. And we know that you were so lousy drunk last night that you can't remember what happened.

15

You think you signed a check, and off I go waltzing to do my stuff—and what do I run into?

Hardesty stood up, suddenly grim. "Listen, if you think I knew she was dead when I sent you there, you're nuts!"

Cardigan looked bored, and waved a hand. "Don't get tough, Sam. I believe you didn't know she was dead, but still that doesn't help matters. She's dead. You were there—drunk or drugged or something—and next morning, tra-la, she's dead."

"My God, I didn't do it!"

Cardigan muttered soberly, "How do you know?"

"How do I know! You know as well as I do that I wouldn't go around killing people!"

"You forget, Sam, that for a little while you were blotto. Maybe she teased you. Maybe you were blind drunk and let her have it. It's possible. Now hold on—pipe down. We'll say you didn't kill her, just for the sake of argument. Still, where are you? When the cops land on you, where are you? You can't remember a thing. You see, you can't remember a thing. Cram that in your pipe, smoke it, and sit quiet."

Hardesty slumped back to the bed, his mouth slack. "I get you, Jack," he muttered. "I get you."

Cardigan went on. "I searched the place. I didn't find any checks authored by you. I wiped off all the furniture, a glass, and the door—for fingerprints. Understand, I used a master key to get in the place. I left and told the clerk I didn't get an answer and that I'd try later. I thought of calling in the cops, but I wanted to think things over, and talk with you, and I knew the cops would haul me eventually anyhow."

"You?"

"Sure. The clerk will remember I stopped by. Now you and I don't know if you killed her or not. I believe you were tricked, and the point is, whether you murdered her or not, we've got to get you out of it. We can't even have them suspect you did it. I don't believe you'd kill anybody, Sam, but the odds are against you and we've got a tough row to hoe."

Hardesty got up and tramped the length of the room. "Hell, Jack, if I'd thought I'd be hauling you into a mess like this—"

"That's done. I'm in for it. If this thing breaks up your alley, you're out of the World Series, you're out of baseball for good. And if you're out of the Series, that ball team of yours is going to lose two games—and the pennant."

"What could I tell my wife? What could I tell Carmicheal? How could I make them understand?"

Cardigan heaved a dark sigh. "I don't think you could. Sam, you're in a spot—a tough one, and no fooling. And I'm in a spot. I'm in a spot because the cops are going to call me in and ask me things and I'm going to have to shadowbox all over the place to keep you out of it."

"Nix. I'm not going to drag you in, Jack. By God, I'll go right over now and make a clean breast of it!"

Cardigan was sardonic. "A clean breast about what? You're going over and tell the cops a bedtime story. You can't remember a thing. What can you tell them?"

Hardesty groaned and held his head in his hands.

Cardigan spoke with a hard calm. "Get back to your hotel and act natural. Leave this to me. You're not in it yet. McQueston won't talk because surer than hell they'd close up his club. We're safe there. And McQueston can shut up the taxi driver that took you and this jane to her apartment. So far, you're safe. The thing we don't know about is the check. And we don't know who the guys are you said you thought were there. They must have been friends of hers. They must have been the guys brought her to the Medallion. So you see what we can bank on, and what we can't. Who are these guys? What part do they play? If one of them was her boyfriend, and she double-crossed him by giving you the boudoir eye, he might have strangled her. But I can't see it that way because they were all there when you were there. . . . Okay. Dress and shoot back to your hotel."

Cardigan saw Hardesty off in a taxi, and then took one to the Agency office. Pat Seaward and George Hammerhorn, the chief, were in conference, but Cardigan broke in and said, "Excuse the interruption, but this is important."

Hammerhorn said, "Indicating, I suppose, that what Patricia and I are talking about isn't."

"Honest, George. This is hot, red-hot. Listen, both of you." He slapped his hands on the desk, bracing his arms. "Sam Hardesty is a friend of mine. We grew up together, and he went his way and I went mine, and every now and then we'd run across each other in some city and go on a bender together. Sam could never hold a lot of liquor—"

"Comparing him with yourself, of course," Pat put in, smiling sweetly.

Cardigan inhaled, looked down at her. "You'll please keep that affected humor to yourself, precious orchid—"

"Now, now," George Hammerhorn said. "None of that. Get on with your story."

Cardigan did, and gradually Hammerhorn and Pat leaned forward, their interest growing. Cardigan finished and his listeners sat back and Hammerhorn, reaching for a cigar, said, "So what?"

"So it goes on the record that this Priscilla Ferne called up last night and asked us to send a man up early this morning. The memo was lost, but the man on duty here remembered her first name was Priscilla and that she lived at the Drexel Tower. I went up and talked to the clerk as I've explained. Then I couldn't get an answer from Priscilla's apartment, so I left, intending to come back later."

Pat said, "I never saw a man like you! Always getting into hot water on somebody's account but your own! Phooey!"

Hammerhorn was frowning. "Little irregular, Jack."

"Of course it is. But I've got to be cleared! I can't drag Sam's name in it! I've got to keep him in the clear, too!"

"How do you know," Pat said, "he really deserves it? How do you know he didn't kill her?"

Cardigan rasped, with gestures, "How do I know! How do I know!" And he leaned forward, asking, "How do I know that you're really Pat Seaward? Can I prove it? Can I prove that's your name? No! I only know it because you told me! How do I know Broadway is Broadway? How do—"

"Oh, dear me, now you're off again; now I've started something. Let's call it a day."

Hammerhorn, broad, placid, fanned himself. "Well, well, children, I'm glad recess is over."

Cardigan suddenly hit the desk so hard that a glass cover jumped from an inkwell; and he shouted, "By God, I've given the best years of my life to this Agency, and if I can't get help to lend an old pal a hand when he needs it—"

"Damn it!" roared Hammerhorn. "This is no hall! This is an office! My office!"

Pat held her ears.

The phone rang and she pulled it toward her and said, "Yes, this is the Cosmos Agency. . . . Oh, hello, Lieutenant O'Mara. . . . Yes, this is Pat Seaward. . . . Oh, you old naughty mans, you. . . . I beg your pardon? . . . Why, yes. That is, we had a call, but the memo was lost, but the clerk remembered the first name and the address, so we sent up Cardigan. He phoned back to say there was no one in, and Mr. Hammerhorn ordered him to try again, later. I'm sure he'll turn up any minute. . . . Thank *you*, Lieutenant O'Mara!"

Hammerhorn sighed, leaned back, lit his cigar. "Well," he said, "so I guess it's in the records."

"But," said Pat, sliding the phone to the middle of the desk, looking up meaningly, "there's a fox on the case."

There was a great amount of activity in the Drexel Tower apartment when Cardigan arrived. Some reporters were there, a police photographer, a man from the D.A.'s office, half-a-dozen uniformed policemen, Detective "Knucks" Hermann, loud-mouthed, dramatic, and dumb. All these men had something to say to one another, and the result was a continuous babble, worse than a debutante party. In a far corner of the room, remote, looking slightly absent-minded, sat Lieutenant Chauncey O'Mara; he sat on the arm of a wing chair, small, slight, debonair, with black hair, a black mustache, a thin bony face with high, red cheekbones, and a good-humored mouth.

"Ah!" roared Knucks Hermann above the general uproar. "As I breathe and live, if it ain't not Cardigan. Hey, Chauncey; look what the wind blowed in!" He grinned widely, chewed on a great wad of gum.

"You look well, Knucks," Cardigan said drily.

"Yeah? I don't mind if I do."

O'Mara had not moved, though he began swinging his leg idly. "Hello, Cardigan," he said, his blue eyes twinkling. He nodded to the bedroom. "Looks like a case of beauty and the beast."

"What happened?"

"Take a look. She's in there."

O'Mara rose and sauntered into the bedroom, and Cardigan and Hermann followed. O'Mara closed the door against the babble in the living room, lit an Egyptian cigarette, and looked down vacantly at the body.

Hermann advised: "She was choked."

"I see," Cardigan said. He said no more, determined to let O'Mara take the lead.

O'Mara did. "I hear the Agency sent you up to see her this morning."

"If she's Priscilla Ferne, yes."

"She is."

"I came in and— You see, the mug down at the office lost the memo with her name on it. She called the Agency last night. All I had was her first name and the address. I got the rest from the clerk downstairs. Came up here, knocked for a while and got no answer. Then I went away."

"Didn't suspect anything, huh?"

"Why should I? I didn't even know what she wanted. How long's she been dead?"

"Helvig says about ten hours. She got it about midnight or one A.M., say. Whoever did it was wise. We noticed everything wiped off—chairs, desk, and so on. She's been living here a month. A guy from *The Herald-Star* says her real name's Mamie Pulofski. She won a beauty contest in Iron City four years ago, got a month on the vaudeville circuit, and then vanished. She was a ham actress. She used the Priscilla Ferne on the stage. This guy says she was in a mess in Buffalo a couple of years ago. At a party in her hotel rooms, a guy fell from a window and killed himself. Nothing criminal, of course—just messy. Then about a year ago, he says, she was beaten up by somebody in Boston. In her hotel room. Nobody knew who. She never told. Kind of a girl, I guess, that drove guys nuts. Maybe she was a teaser. The Buffalo jam was a kind of *antipasto,* the Boston the fish course, and this the *entrée.* Looks as if she ordered it all *à la carte,* but didn't wait for the dessert. The dessert'll be ours—the guy who killed her."

"Any leads?"

"Night clerk said she came in with a fellow last night. He didn't bother looking much. Just a big guy. He doesn't remember when or if they left, or what he looked like. It looks a smooth job to me. It looks like a planned job. If a guy went nuts and killed her, he would have run out without bothering to wipe away his fingerprints. There's nothing—no letter, no marks, nothing. I thought maybe you'd be able to give me a steer."

"I'm dead in the dark, Chauncey."

O'Mara sighed. "Well, I guess we ship her back to Iron City, if she's got relatives there. Bum homecoming, huh? I hate to see 'em go young like this, Cardigan—good or bad, I hate to see 'em go young."

THREE

HARDESTY CALLS HIS BANK

■

She did not get much space in the metropolitan newspapers. A small stick on the third page, and no picture; though back in Iron City she doubtless made the headlines. Cardigan walked into the Medallion at the cocktail hour and knew by the look in McQueston's face that he had come upon the news. McQueston moved his head and Cardigan followed him into a back room and McQueston, with a steely look in his eyes, said, "What the hell kind of horseplay is this?"

"So you call it horseplay."

McQueston looked very elegant in evening clothes, and his thin nose glasses shimmered. "You didn't say anything about murder this morning."

"I didn't know there was murder, Ben."

"I've got an idea you're playing ring-around-a-rosy," the tall man challenged.

"Pack up that idea and put it in mothballs. All you have to do, Ben, is keep your mouth shut, keep Otto's mouth shut, and all the other guys who work for you. And that taxi driver."

"I've talked to him."

"Swell."

McQueston compressed his lips. "But I'm not playing fiddle to any murder. What I did is only temporary, until—"

Cardigan darkened, snapped, "Until what?"

McQueston colored, thinned down his eyes.

And Cardigan went on, deeply. "This guy Hardesty is an old friend of mine. He was tricked, trapped—he was made somebody's fall guy, and he hasn't got a leg to stand on—except mine. Now that jane picked him up in your place. It all started here, and if you start shooting off your mouth to the wrong people, I can make a mountain out of that molehill. Hardesty is up against it and so am I, and this jane was a tramp. How do I know Hardesty didn't get knockout drops here?"

"Damn you—"

"Okay. Damn me. But if you want to keep this joint swanky, if you want to stay on the lee side of the law and keep your name out of the papers—play ball. This is no affair of yours, and it is an affair of mine. You're a nice guy, Ben, but sometimes you start acting like the preacher you look like. Keep your nose out of it. Keep Otto and the rest and the taxi driver dumb. I don't know how this thing will break yet. So far, Hardesty is in the clear—but there were three other guys in it, and I can't figure them or how they'll move."

McQueston, keeping his lips tight, stared at the door. Then he said, "Okay."

"I knew you'd listen to reason, Ben."

"I just hate to get tangled up."

"Come on, I'll buy you a drink."

"I'll buy you one."

Next morning Cardigan was on his way down to breakfast when the ringing of his phone stopped him in the doorway. He went back and grabbed it, spoke for a moment, hung up, and then went out, his brows bent. He did not stop for breakfast, but boarded a cab outside his hotel and drove north, to Central Park. Fifteen minutes later he walked in on McQueston, and McQueston, sitting at the card table and smoking a cigarette, said, "See this morning's paper?"

"No."

"Look at this. Second page."

Cardigan took the newspaper and said, "What?"

"Third column."

"This picture? . . . Oh, I see. Casey Smith. What about it?"

"Read it."

Cardigan sat down and read that at eleven the previous night Casey Smith, the gambler, was found dead in West Forty-eighth Street, with two bullets in him. It had occurred near Fifth Avenue. No one had seen the shooting. Patrolman Kopf had heard the shots, come upon the body five minutes later.

"So what?" Cardigan said.

"Louie called up and said Casey Smith was one of the three guys that came in with the dame the other night." He stood up. "This is getting close, Cardigan! Too damn close for comfort!"

Cardigan's thoughts began spinning. "Hold everything, Ben. Keep your shirt on. This is a hot lead!"

"Hot lead hell! I've got an idea I'm headed for a jam and—"

"Ben," Cardigan said, spreading his arms, "you wouldn't let me down, would you?"

McQueston made an exasperated sound. "You're a damned nuisance, Jack—that's what you are!"

Cardigan tossed the paper to the table, said, "I'll be seeing you, pal," and stretched his legs out of the apartment.

He found Chauncey O'Mara, Knucks Hermann, and two other men in an office at police headquarters. He said, "I didn't think you were busy, Chauncey. I just dropped in to see if you'd picked up anything."

Hermann said, "Didja read about how Casey Smith up and got himself a oneway ticket to parts unknown?"

"Oh, that. Yeah, I saw it in the paper."

"These guys," went on Hermann, "was his pals, as you might say. Wasn't they, Chauncey?"

O'Mara seemed satisfied with his nails. "Cardigan, this is Tom Spinack and Carl Bounds. Boys, this is Cardigan, a private dick."

"Yeah," blurted Hermann, grinning widely. "This is the gazabo that was almost on that Priscilla Ferne job, only she was all choked up by the time he got there."

Mr. Spinack and Mr. Bounds laid blank, ancient eyes on Cardigan, and both nodded politely. They were fairly young men, about forty, but their eyes were ancient—eyes that had no connection whatever with their thoughts. Mr. Spinack was a swart, chubby man, with a moon face, and Mr. Bounds was tall, hatchet-faced, with a ramrod nape and a beaked nose.

"I think I read about that in the paper," said Mr. Bounds, politely.

"You can go, boys," O'Mara said.

Mr. Spinack and Mr. Bounds rose, bowed, and went out.

"Smoothies," commented Hermann, wise-eyed.

O'Mara sighed. "Well, these gamblers get it someday. This case looks open and shut and is on its way to the pigeonhole already. Casey Smith was a big gambler, and for a time I thought maybe these two pals of his had something to do with it. But Casey wasn't as big as Spinack. Last year they cleaned up on the World Series. They hit the prizefighters, too, and the races. Spinack and Bounds were in Gus's, off Madison, when the shooting happened, and Casey Smith was on his way to meet them with a couple of grand they were placing on the Series. The dough wasn't touched. I checked up on all that. It's one of those things. What I'm interested in, is this other case. It's so damned airtight. It gets me—makes me mad."

"I just berl over!" Hermann growled, making a fist.

"Well," Cardigan said, "I'll be getting on. Let me know if you get a break."

Cardigan walked Canal Street, following Spinack and Bounds, and after a while they got in a taxi. Cardigan flagged another and told the driver to follow them. The tail led uptown on the West Side; ended in front of a hotel in a midtown side street. It was a small hotel, crowded on either side, with a flashy lobby, small, noisy, theatrical.

Bounds was buying a newspaper at the stand, and Spinack was waiting. When they turned away from the counter, Cardigan blocked them and said, "I want to talk to you guys."

Bounds, the tall man, looked annoyed.

Spinack lit a cigar and said, "Talk."

Cardigan made a motion and they walked to the rear of the lobby, took seats in a divan behind a flat pillar.

Cardigan said, "You guys afraid to come out in the open about the Ferne dame's killing?"

Spinack looked at his cigar. "What's the connection?" he asked flatly.

"Plenty."

Spinack looked disagreeably at his cigar and Bounds folded his paper and stared at a point on the wall.

"Well?" said Cardigan.

"Well," said Spinack, "nuts."

Cardigan said, "What happened? Did Casey rub out the jane and did you guys have Casey rubbed out for pulling a boner?"

"Listen!" Spinack said, poking Bounds. "Listen to him!"

"Funny. Funny as hell," Cardigan said. "If O'Mara knew the connection, you guys wouldn't be so funny."

"I didn't notice you telling him," Spinack said, holding his cigar in front of his mouth.

"You came in the Medallion night before last with the woman. She left with Hardesty and you joined them later. Do you mix the badger game with gambling?"

Spinack said after a moment, "You know a hell of a lot."

Cardigan nodded.

"Come up to our room," Spinack said.

They went up in an elevator and entered a small two-room apartment, cheaply but flashily furnished. Spinack chewed deliberately on his cigar and Bounds took a seat, unfolded the paper, and pretended to read. Their eyes, Cardigan noticed, never changed.

Spinack said, "You're working for Hardesty."

"That's as good as any."

"I said you're working for Hardesty."

Cardigan smiled. "Okay."

"So what?"

"So what kind of a frame did you guys plant around him?"

"I see. You're not telling O'Mara about us because that would drag in Hardesty." He laughed, drily.

"That's one point," Cardigan said.

"Okay. If O'Mara doesn't suspect a connection, what the hell are you beefing about?"

"I want the check Hardesty wrote out."

"What check?"

"Do you suppose I'm going to believe he was taken to the dame's apartment because she liked him?"

Spinack chewed on his cigar. "My advice to you, Cardigan, would be pack up your troubles and go home. Let things lay."

"You can take your advice and chuck it out the window. This is not just a case to me. Hardesty's a pal of mine and he was taken in by a dame and some lousy grifters. I'm not getting a cent out of this. He was not taken for fun. There's a reason. There's got to be. We can't settle this at headquarters. That's okay by me. Hardesty was doped, and he was doped for a reason. I want to know that reason."

"I'm sorry, Cardigan. You're all wrong. He picked her up and took her home and we joined them. We took her to the club, and we naturally wanted to see she was all right. She said she was and we left her with Hardesty. What happened after that is none of our business."

"Who knocked off Casey Smith?"

"I don't know. I can't imagine."

"Suppose I did tell O'Mara there's a connection?"

Spinack raised his cigar. "Do you want to hang a murder rap on your pal?"

"He didn't kill that dame!"

"Who'll prove he didn't?"

Cardigan bit his lip.

And Spinack said, "I'd hate to get tangled up here, but if you tell O'Mara, I'll have to be. Bounds and I'll have to tell him the last we saw of Priscilla alone, she was with Hardesty, in her apartment, and him blind drunk." He took a leisurely puff. "So if you want to hang your pal, go to it."

Cardigan was coloring. He twisted his mouth, muttered, "You win," and went to the door. He added, "So far—you win," and went out

His neck felt red and hot, his throat dry. He walked into a speakeasy up the street, polished off four beers, and ate a sandwich.

Then he took a cab and drove to the hotel where Hardesty lived. He found Hardesty pacing the floor like a caged animal.

"Jack," he said, "I finally called my bank on long-distance."

"I told you, damn it, to lay off your bank!" Cardigan snapped.

"I know, but—"

"You know! You know a hell of a lot! I told you to lay off the bank because you can't afford to arouse any curiosity. You've got to keep your name out of this. If that check was made out to Priscilla Ferne, and you demanded your bank to stop it, they'll remember the name. Otherwise, it would slide through and they'd hardly notice the name. Suppose your wife does get it? Hell, you've got to make a breast of it. Either that, or get mixed up with John Law—"

"But listen. I long-distanced the bank but I didn't mention any names. I just asked if one of my checks for any large amount had come in. So they looked at my statement, and what do you think? My God, what do you think?"

Cardigan scowled. "I'm sick and tired of bad news. I just had four beers. Give me a shot of rum to take away the taste—and then maybe I can bear up."

"But, Jack, for the love of cripes—"

"The rum first, Sam. Keep your head. Life's a bowl of berries, with a lot of razz in 'em. Do you think I'm going to let you break me down? . . . Calling up the bank! Fathead!"

O'MARA MISSES THE DESSERT

■

Cardigan, learning that Spinack and Bounds were in their apartment, camped in the lobby, far back. It was the predinner hour, and in a little while Spinack and Bounds came down. Both wore tuxedoes. The lobby was crowded, noisy with the tinny voices of second-rate women, thick with the smells of tobacco and cheap perfume. The two gamblers stood for a few minutes lighting cigarettes, and presently Cardigan saw a small man, with long arms, dressed in a baggy suit of dark tweed, rise and go out, mixing with a crowd of half a dozen. Then Spinack and Bounds walked out.

Cardigan tossed a dime, caught it, pursed his lips. He picked the small, tweed-dressed man for a punk or a bodyguard. Going out first that way, on the arrival of Spinack and Bounds, would place him as a bodyguard. This, Cardigan saw, would make things difficult. Walking ahead, the bodyguard would spot trouble, give a signal. Spinack and Bounds would detour. The trouble would start after them, and the bodyguard would fall in behind the trouble and break it up. The baggy tweed suit made good coverage for a couple of big guns.

In a moment Cardigan left the lobby and spotted Bounds and Spinack heading toward Sixth Avenue. They turned north. In the next block there was a shooting gallery, and slot peep machines. The twenty-twos were smacking flatly, and the place was a bit crowded. Bounds and Spinack drifted in, strolled among the slot machines to the rear, where the shooting was taking place. A dozen men, mildly tight and wearing organization ribbons, were cutting loose.

Cardigan got behind one of the slot machines and saw Spinack and Bounds idly enjoying the display of bad shooting. The dozen men were lined up, and they seemed to be playing a game in which all lined up and began shooting at once. Spinack grinned and stepped up to the counter and Bounds joined him; both took up rifles. Onlookers crowded in behind. The little man in tweeds went up to the counter also and took up a .22 automatic pistol. The onlookers, crowding in, obscured Cardigan's view. There was a lull, and the dozen visiting delegates raised their rifles. One shouted "Go!" and the .22s began blazing.

The blast ended and the man in tweeds turned and walked rapidly out of the establishment. The crowd broke up, and Cardigan saw Spinack still leaning against the counter, holding his rifle, his elbows braced on the counter. Someone bumped against him and Spinack turned and fell down. Bounds took one look at him, then spun, made an outcry which Cardigan did not hear, and broke into a run.

Cardigan slipped after him. He caught sight of Bounds walking swiftly up Sixth Avenue, and ahead, a block beyond, he saw the man in tweeds turn west. Bounds followed, and Cardigan followed Bounds. No one ran. It was a walk, a fast, businesslike walk, and the passing pedestrians took no particular notice. Occasionally the man in tweeds looked back, but did not move any faster; he knew, doubtless, that Bounds would not break into a run—not yet, at least, in this crowded district.

The walking chase led westward, past Broadway, past Eighth Avenue and toward the dark, dismal hinterland of Tenth Avenue. Here the bright lights faded away, here the streets grew darker, Here there were drab houses.

Into one of these houses the man in tweeds darted. Bounds followed.

Cardigan reached the vestibule, listened, and then ventured into the hall. Above, he heard climbing footfalls.

He went up slowly as far as the top hallway, and stopped with his ear cocked, his brows bent, and his eyes wary. And then he heard a voice, so close at hand that it startled him. But the voice was behind a door, the door nearest to him. It was Bounds's voice.

"You see I'm unarmed. I followed you to see what it's all about, to make a deal. You put the finger on Casey and you put it on Spinack. No doubt I'm number three. Make a deal. Call your openers."

There was a moment of silence, and then a dry cackle, and, "You can't make a deal with me, fella. I got Casey Smith and I got Spinack and now I'm going to get you. How'd you like the way I got Spinack? Took that .22 and while he was leaning on the counter, I let him have ten shots right through the left side of his chest. How'd you like that, huh?"

"Neat," said Bounds. "Sappy—but neat. Now use your head and make a deal. I've got five thousand dollars that's yours if you take the finger off me."

"Thought you were wise, following me here, huh?"

"I ask for a break. I never saw you before and I don't know what your grudge against me is—"

"I know!"

"I guess you do, but listen to reason."

"To hell with you. You and me are going for a short walk, and then you get what your pals got. Move over!"

Feet scuffled, and then Cardigan heard the doorknob turn. He saw the door open, saw the man in tweeds backing out into the hallway, covering Bounds with two big guns. The little man backed into the muzzle of Cardigan's gun and Cardigan said, "Raise 'em, sweetheart."

The little man hissed through his teeth, crouched, and his guns quivered.

Cardigan jabbed him. "Deaf? Raise 'em!"

The hands rose, holding the guns aloft.

"Get in," Cardigan said. And then, "You, Bounds, back up."

Cardigan entered the room, closed the door, and leaned back

against it. The small man still stood with the guns raised, his back to Cardigan. Bounds's face was very gaunt, very gray—but his eyes were the same: ancient, expressionless.

"I'll call my openers," Cardigan said. "And I'm talking to you, Bounds. You'll listen. Punk, keep the guns up high and keep your back to me. Get fancy and you'll rate a smashed back. Now, Bounds. You're in a tough spot, you'll never be in a tougher one. So what? So you'll tell me the whole story. The story regarding a certain check, a certain dame, and certain mysterious happenings."

"What check?"

"Hardesty called his bank."

Bounds said, "How do I know you're on the level?"

"You don't. But a guy like you, on a hot spot right now, shouldn't worry about a thing like that. I don't feel called upon to make any rash promises. I'm just telling you that if you come across, you walk off the spot. Beyond that, you'll have to take care of yourself. Get started."

The little man sighed, and his fingers moved on the guns; a convulsive shudder shook his body.

Bounds said, "We were laying dough on the World Series. We knew the teams were on par, evenly matched, and big bets were unsafe either way, unless we fixed things." He spoke slowly, with an effort. "We figured that Hardesty would pitch two games and win two, but that the other team could even that. With Hardesty out, the other team would be a certain bet."

The little man was beginning to grunt like a caged animal.

Bounds was beginning to sweat. He went on. "We put the girl on him. She knew what it was all about and she was to get a grand for her part. We spotted Hardesty for a couple of weeks, and finally saw him go out alone and wind up in the Medallion. We picked up the girl and went to the Medallion, and she went after him, telling him what a swell pitcher he was. He asked her to have a drink. She smeared it on, and Hardesty swelled up and drank quite a bit. Then she asked him to take her home, she didn't feel well."

Bounds took a large breath. "We joined them later in her apartment—about half an hour later—after she'd mixed Hardesty a drink and dropped in some powerful medicine. It hit Hardesty like a brick. He got goofy. Then we began asking him for his autograph. The girl asked him first, and then Casey asked him, then Spinack. On sheets of paper. Then I asked him. He could hardly see, but he wrote down his name from habit. The one I asked him for, he wrote on a check. He didn't know it."

"And so?" Cardigan said dully.

"The girl asked him to take it easy, and helped him off with his coat. In his pocket, she found the name of his bank and a couple of deposit slips. We took two slips and made out an original and a duplicate and stuck them with the check into an envelope and addressed the envelope to his bank, airmail. The check was for five grand."

"Who made the check out?"

Bounds bit his lip.

"Who made it out?"

"I did."

"You made out a check for five grand to Hardesty. That's it, isn't it?"

"Yes."

"Why?"

Bounds was running sweat by this time. "Evidence. I was to take it to Hardesty's manager the day the Series opened, showing it had been endorsed and deposited by Hardesty. I was to say that Hardesty had promised to fake illness and stay out of the Series. We knew that with evidence like the check, Carmicheal would not only put Hardesty on the bench, but fire him. We'd have laid a lot of bets on the other team, through various fronts, and would clean up at least a hundred grand."

"And who chucked the wrench in the business?"

Bounds tongued his lips.

"What finally happened to Hardesty that night?" Cardigan asked.

"Well, we took him out of the girl's apartment. Took him as far as his hotel and shoved him in the front door. Then we went home and sat around talking it over. It was open and shut then. But there was no killing on the bill. That wrecked everything."

Cardigan said, "I want the canceled check."

Bounds reached into his pocket, withdrew it and laid it on the table.

"That," said Cardigan, "clears Hardesty. Now who killed the jane?"

Bounds took a deep breath, then kept his lips tightly shut. His eyes shimmered.

The raised guns in the hands of the small man shook. "You know damned well I killed her!" he cried. "And I'm proud of it. Same as I'm proud I killed Casey Smith and Spinack, like I'm going to kill you. I killed her. Why? Because when I went up to stir, I left her ten grand to keep for me till I come out, and ten for herself. And what happens? She spends it all. And not only that. When I come out, I get the go by off her. She's being set up swell by you three guys, and I don't even get a look-in.

"I used to watch her going around to all them swell places, looking like a million dollars. I didn't have the dough to go to them places. I hadda live in a dump like this, and once I was in the dough. It drove me nuts, seeing her looking swell and knowing you guys swiped her off me. So the other night I busted wide open. I choked hell out of her! I couldn't stop! And then I went after you guys, that swiped her!"

He spun on Cardigan. "What right you got to butt in? You ain't got no right, you lousy bum!"

"Punk, learn how to talk to your betters."

"Punk, am I? Damn it, I was a first-rate rod till that woman ruined me! Let me give this guy what's coming to him! I got rights! Damn it, ain't a citizen got rights anymore?"

Bounds said, "I've got to get out of here, Cardigan."

"And I think no more of you," Cardigan growled. "You tried to ruin one of the finest pitchers in the leagues. Not just for this Series, but forever. He can't do anything but play baseball. You didn't think about that. You meant to ruin him, chuck him out of the leagues for good. This little guy is a punk and rat, but so are you, and so were your pals!"

Bounds's voice shook. "You said you'd give me a break!"

"I'd give any rat a break!" He reached up and ripped one of the guns from the little man's hand. "You'll take this rod, Bounds, and go out. You'll both go out. I can't turn him over to the cops without telling the whole story. And I can't afford to tell the whole story. I said, Bounds, I'd get you off this particular spot. Well, I am. Beyond that, look out for yourself. Both you guys, put your guns in your pockets. Walk downstairs with me."

They left the room and marched down the stairs and Cardigan said, "There's no choice between you. You're both rats." They reached the street and Cardigan said, "Bounds, start west. You get a start of a block. Get walking."

Bounds strode off, and Cardigan kept his gun trained on the little man, and he said, "My advice would be to forget it, for he'll forget it. But I'm no judge, and I'm no law. You're dumb and he's smart, but underneath it all you're both rats and a menace to society. Take my advice or leave it. Okay, you can go now."

He stood and watched both men disappear in the darkness, and then he headed east. In his pocket was the check, and that was settled—Hardesty was in the clear. But he was not happy, he did not gloat. He kept walking eastward, and soon the bleat and blare of midtown enveloped him, the lights twinkled, crowds pushed and shoved.

He went into a speakeasy and took up a diet of Scotch, feeling that it would be better to be tight and in the dumps than merely in the dumps.

After a while a couple of men strode in, ordering drinks, and one said, "I hear two guys just shot it out over on Eleventh Avenue. Emptied their guns. Put out each other's lights."

Cardigan mused aloud, "Well, O'Mara missed the dessert."

"Huh?" said the bartender.

"Another Scotch."

SPADES ARE SPADES

■

BY FREDERICK NEBEL

*If there was anything that big dick from
Cosmos hated it was getting thrown in
the jug. And what made it worse—all he'd
been trying to do was hand over a fortune
on a silver platter to a missing heiress.
But the cops would only have laughed
at that one, so there wasn't anything to
do but get tough—then call the Morgue!*

ONE

TWO MANY NOSES

■

The train from New York dragged slowly through the St. Louis yards in the smoky winter dusk. Snow had fallen all the way from Indianapolis. The coaches, the Pullmans were white-blanketed; the hissing locomotive was flecked and spattered with the snow and the bell had a lazy, bonging sound.

Cardigan was standing in the vestibule of the head sleeper, cuddling a cigarette in his palm. His battered fedora was cramped down low on his forehead, his old ulster was wrinkled, its shapeless collar bundled about his neck.

Pat Seaward, small, trim in a three-quarter length raccoon, with a racy antelope beret aslant on her head, came out of the corridor. She said,

"You certainly look as though you slept in those clothes."

"I did, precious, more than once." He took a drag on his cigarette, looked down at her. "So what's it to you?"

The station lights began drifting past the steamed vestibule window and the porter snapped up the metal leaf, opened the door. Snowflakes whipped in.

"Nothing to me, of course," Pat said airily. "Only some night, if you hang around a corner in that outfit, you'll likely be picked up on a vagrancy charge."

He popped his cigarette through the door. "So the candid critic is kibitzing again. Okay, sweetheart, have your fun, have your fun. I can take it."

The train stopped and Cardigan swung down to the platform carrying Pat's patent leather suitcase and his own ramshackle Gladstone. A redcap made for him, but Cardigan shook his head and went swinging his long legs up the platform. Pat followed at a chipper walk. As they passed through the gate into the large, barnlike waiting room, a bright-eyed, eager young man called out,

"Well, if it isn't Cardigan!"

And Cardigan, keeping his chin down, striding onward, ripped out in a low voice, "Lay off the broadcast, Pinkler!"

"But, hey, why the high-hat, Cardigan?" Pinkler cajoled, bobbing along beside the Cosmos man. "After all—"

"After all—scram!" Cardigan rasped, striding on, lengthening his stride and scowling furiously, straight ahead.

A knowing look heightened the brightness in Pinkler's blue eyes, and he said, still bobbing along, "Traveling incog, huh?" He grinned. "Disguising yourself as Cardigan. Look here, Jack; what's in the wind? Promise to keep it under my hat—"

Cardigan snarled, still low-voiced, "Pinkler, you dumb excuse for a reporter, lay off me, lay off me!" He bowled on his way through the crowd, cursing under his breath, with Pinkler still joyously at his elbow.

"Hell, Cardigan, for a guy that used to—"

Cardigan suddenly crowded him into a corner, stared down hotly, and said in his low, angry voice, "Lay off! You hear me, Pinkler; lay off! Leave me alone! Chase rainbows or something— but for cripes' sake stay clear of me!"

The undercurrent of fury in his voice, the dull red growing on his face, frightened the reporter. Pinkler, his grin fading, backed up, shrugged, turned, and drifted off.

Cardigan swung on his way, joined Pat at the door, and they went out into Market Street. He said in his low violent voice, "Of all the prize dumbbells, that potato takes the cake!"

"Who is he?"

"Newshound from *The Times-Express*. I bought him a drink

once, and ever since he's taken advantage of it. . . . Hey, taxi!"
He strode toward the cab, saying to Pat, "Come on; snap on it,
Patsy. We've got to get out of here before—"

"Hey, Cardigan!"

Cardigan dropped one bag, yanked open the cab door. He
looked over his shoulder and saw a man coming toward him
through the windy snow.

"In, Pat," he muttered, his lips compressing.

"Cardigan—"

Cardigan heaved in the Gladstone, then the suitcase. He was on
his way into the cab when the man came up to him and laid a hand
on his arm.

"What's the rush, bo?"

Cardigan backed out, turned and said: "I've got a date with a
minute steak, Scanlon. You know how minute steaks are—"

The snow was blowing into plainclothed Sergeant Scanlon's
face, and he was squinting his eyes against it. "Pinkler back there
said you were disguising yourself as Cardigan—"

"There's a law against having to listen to lousy jokes. I'm in a
hurry and you're standing in my way."

Scanlon had a lazy, sandpapery voice, a mocking twist to his
wide, thin lips. "But what's the rush, what's the rush? I just
wanted to say hello to you."

"So you did, and so now how's to let me get in the cab?"

Pinkler came bobbing up and said, "What's the matter, Dave?"

And Scanlon said, "Oh, nothing, nothing. What I like about
celebrities like Cardigan, they hate the limelight." He chuckled
drily, spitting snow from his lips. "Look at him! Just a shrinking
violet!"

Pinkler laughed. "Yup. Jack always was that way!"

Cardigan growled, thrust Scanlon aside, and pushed on into the
taxicab, slamming the door behind him. Scanlon reopened the
door and said,

"Mind dropping me downtown?"

"Yes I mind!" Cardigan snapped, and slammed the door shut
again; and to the driver: "Come on; get going!"

Scanlon and Pinkler stepped back, with the curtain of falling
snow dimming their faces. The cab shot off. Cardigan looked back
and saw them still standing, Pinkler a small shape, Scanlon a tall
one.

"Where to?" the driver asked.

"Hotel Maxwell."

Chains on the tires kept whanging against the undersides of the mudguards as the cab rolled down Market Street.

Pat was a little worried. "Gee, chief—"

"Muggs, muggs!" Cardigan growled. "By God, you'd think a guy needed a passport to crash this lousy burg! It's times like these I go anarchistic in a big way."

She put a hand on his forearm. "Take it easy, chief."

He slumped in the seat, blowing out a large exasperated breath that was not intended for Pat.

After a moment she said, "Do you think somebody might have heard or seen?"

"Sure, sure," he said, turning seriously on her. "Anybody, anybody . . . the way," he added, scowling, "that half-wit Pinkler song-and-danced me the minute I hit the gate."

Cardigan got a room on the fifth floor of the Maxwell. Pat got one on the fourth. When Cardigan entered the room it was stifling, the steam radiator spluttering. The bellhop opened a window and a blast of cold air came in, bringing snowflakes and coal dust with it.

"Anything else, suh?"

"Uh-uh."

"Maybe some nice gin—"

"I make my own gin, colonel." Cardigan tossed him a dime. "Beat it."

The bellhop grinned, took a bow and left. Cardigan removed his overcoat, draped it over the radiator. Jangling keys, he bent down and unlocked his Gladstone and from it removed a brown paper envelope. He carried this to the small green metal desk, sat down and emptied the envelope of its contents, which he perused for ten minutes. Then he replaced the contents, all except a small photograph and one slip of yellow paper, which he shoved into his inside pocket. The brown paper envelope he replaced in the Gladstone. He locked the Gladstone, and rising, sighed and said, "Well, Genevieve . . ." to the room at large; struck a match on his thumbnail and lit a cigarette.

He telephoned Pat, blew smoke into the mouthpiece as he said, "Stay in out of the wet, Patsy. The old man's going to take a walk. . . . Huh? Nah, I'm not afraid of the big bad cop."

He hung up, whistled a few disjointed bars from "Sleepy Time Gal," and got back into the overcoat, slapped his hat lopsided on his head, and breezed out into the corridor. The elevator plummeted him to the main floor and he sailed into the lobby with his big feet rapping the tiles and the skirt of his overcoat flopping.

He leaned his weight against the front swing door; the door was heavy, of glass and brass, and there was a wind bent hard against it. But Cardigan got it open and the wind pelted his face and drummed the brim of his floppy hat up against the crown. The snow spiraled and twisted down Locust Street, got down his neck, in his ears.

With the wind at his back, he swung on down Locust, turned right into Sixth, crossed Olive and proceeded down Sixth. Here it was darker, the buildings old and secondhand. It became noisier where Sixth crossed Market; farther along, it became tawdrier, the street soaked in slush.

"Keep walking as you are, Cardigan."

The voice was close at hand but garbled a bit by the wind. Cardigan, looking out of the corner of his eye, saw a large, bulky man walking near his right elbow.

The man said, "You're covered. Show me some identification."

As they walked on, Cardigan withdrew his small card case in which was folded his Agency card. "Read it and weep," he said. "But why the identification?"

"I just want to make sure. Keep walking. I thought that guy in the railroad station yelled your name— Here's a light. Stop a minute and keep your hands clean. . . . Okay, now get going again. I'll mind this."

"Out walking for your health?"

"No. Yours."

"Thanks. I like the thought behind that."

"Where you heading?"

"I thought I'd walk down to the river and see if the fish are biting."

"How'd you like to be chucked in the river?"

"You're starting to get personal as hell, fella." Cardigan stopped, turned, and eyed the man. "What's the idea?"

"You look like you could use a thousand bucks."

"I could."

"Take an early train out, then, and make believe this was only a dream."

The man spoke almost laconically, while the stub of a cigar moved in one corner of his mouth. His left hand was sunk in his overcoat pocket, his right held a gun almost concealed in his palm. His eyes were in the deep shadow of his hat brim and his cheeks were full, rather rubicund. He was well-dressed—a man in his forties.

Cardigan threw a half-smoked cigarette on the snowy sidewalk, said,

"You're up the wrong alley."

"I'm up the right alley," the man replied offhand. "I know why you're in St. Louis and the cards read you're not wanted. You're sticking your big nose into three-hundred-thousand-dollars worth of business. Take a tip and lam and buy luxuries with what your heirs will save on funeral expenses."

Cardigan chopped off a brief, caustic laugh. "I know what I'm sticking my nose into, baby. I get paid to stick my nose into things."

"You'd make more keeping it out."

Cardigan pulled a packet of cigarettes from his pocket, slipped a cigarette between his lips, and then dropped the pack. He stooped over, recaptured the packet and, rising again, made a swift pass at the man's gun. He missed as the man jumped backward; but the man lost his footing on the snow and slammed down. The gun went off, almost straight up in the air, and shattered a window in the house nearby. Cardigan ducked toward the corner of the house as a second shot, partially aimed, passed close over his head. The man was struggling to his feet and trying to shoot at the same time.

Cardigan had his gun out now, but he was reluctant to fire. Close at hand a police whistle blew and instantly there was the sound of pounding feet. The man, up now, lunged across the street. Cardigan started after him, but stopped short when he saw several policemen on the run. He backed up, ducked past the corner of the building into the narrow, slushy alley. He ran on, skidding and stumbling and slamming from wall to wall.

Suddenly he met a figure head-on. A man. Obviously the man was waiting for him, for he went into action immediately, using a blackjack that missed Cardigan's head but clubbed his left shoulder. Cardigan struck with his right fist; hit something hard that gave under the impact. Losing his footing, he fell down, lost his hat. A foot hit him in the stomach, but he got up, felt hands clawing at his leg. He kicked backward. There were flashlights coming up the alley, and Cardigan ran on, came to the street beyond, and was able now to break into a long-legged run. In Olive Street, he bought a new, cheap hat.

T W O

CARDIGAN GETS CANNED

■

Near the river, near Commercial Alley, Cardigan saw the blue globe of light, with the snow blowing past it. It was in a dark, a dismal street. The building was two-storied, of brick. Once it had been a stable. There were several cars parked out front, and a taxi. A small wooden shed extended over the door, and beneath the shed stood a man bundled in a great coat. He opened the door and Cardigan went in.

The entrance hall was small, stuffy. There was a bar to the left, a low room to the right in which a five-piece Negro band raved and couples were dancing. The tables had red-and-white-checked cloths on top. A redheaded girl gave Cardigan a check and reached for his hat. He gave her the check back, kept his hat and overcoat on, and went into the bar. A drunk bumped against him and said:

"S' look; you wanna play horseshoes, pal?"

"Uh-uh," Cardigan said, shaking his head.

"Was gonna say if you did we'd be kinda outta luck sorta, because—hic—we ain't got no horseshoes. Too bad. Well, be seein' you, pal."

The drunk's knees kept knocking together as he went out.

"Rye," Cardigan said to the barman; and leaning his elbows on the bar asked, "Where's Mafey?"

"You mean Mafey?"

"Yeah, Mafey."

The barman pointed. Cardigan turned about and saw a man sitting at the only table in the bar. It was in a corner at the rear. Cardigan picked up the drink and took it over to the table, planked it down, and took a chair facing Mafey. Mafey was eating.

"Mafey?"

"Yeah."

"My name's Cardigan. I just got in from New York."

"I ain't been in New York in five years," Mafey said, biting a lamb chop. "Did you want to see me?"

"Yeah." Cardigan lit a cigarette. "I'm looking for a line on Genevieve Stoddard." He blew the match out.

Mafey put down the lamb chop bone and wiped his fat fingers on a napkin. "M'm . . . Genevieve . . ." He looked up with his fat complacent eyes.

"She worked here once," Cardigan went on. "Sang or something, or danced. Sang, I guess."

"Kinda sorry," Mafey said.

"What do you mean, 'sorry'?"

Mafey stared abstractedly at his plate. "Well, Genevieve just upped and walked out and she didn't say where." He raised his complacent eyes to Cardigan's dark curious ones. "Just like that." He spread his palms, then cleared his throat, shoved back his chair, and rose with an unhurried air of finality.

"Maybe you got me wrong," Cardigan said. He stood up and followed Mafey to the bar. "This is no pinch, Mafey. I'm out to do the girl a good turn."

Mafey looked at him. "You smell strictly copper to me."

"I had a talk with one a little while ago, that's why. I'm a private dick. I've got to get hold of Genevieve. It's like this. Her old man is dying; he's got about three or four days left. He wants to see his daughter. He kicked her out of the house three years ago. She had man trouble at the time. He gave her the boot—cut her off completely. Now he wants to see her, before he dies. He's gone soft. There's a couple of hundred grand waiting for her if she turns up." He paused, said in lower voice, "And some guys don't want her to turn up. As the old man's will stands now, his dough goes to his half brother. If Genevieve turns up . . . catch on?"

Mafey's fat lids drooped over his fat grave eyes. "That sounds like a nice story, guy."

"It's on the level. You stalled me about her, so I saw you liked her. Well do something for her. Give her a break. Come on, Mafey, where can I find her?"

Mafey turned to the barman and said, "Give me a beer." He kept his profile toward Cardigan, an unlovely profile, very melancholy. He finished the beer, and after a little while he turned again to Cardigan and eyed him gravely, almost somberly. Then he jerked his head. "This way."

They went into a sitting room beyond the bar. It was a small, a warm room, with a couple of old Morris chairs and a Franklin stove. Mafey closed the door and, with his eyes still gravely on Cardigan, said slowly, in a hoarse whisper,

"See, Genevieve means nothing to me except I liked her like she was my own kid. She ain't here. She ain't been here in months. Too many guys tried to make her, and she couldn't be made. But shadowboxing 'em all the time, it kind of shot her nerves to hell. Me, I don't know anything about her except she was on the deep end. When she first came here, she used to hit the bottle a lot, but I got her off that."

"You act like a white guy, Mafey. With you it should be sentiment; with me, it's a job of work. Where is she?"

Mafey said, "I'll see her first. I'll talk to her first. Come around tomorrow morning about eleven."

"But look," Cardigan argued. "We'll be losing time—"

"Take it, or leave it," Mafey said.

Cardigan spread his palms. "What else can I do in a spot like this?"

Mafey gripped his arm. "And listen, fella—if you're cutting corners on me—"

"I'm on the level like a dance floor, Mafey."

It was going on ten when Cardigan strode from the snowy dark into the lobby of the Maxwell. Here it was warm, cheerful. It was cheerful, Cardigan saw, until Pinkler rose from the depths of a leather chair and called out, "Hi, Cardigan!"

Cardigan did not slow down. He merely changed his course and bore down ominously on Pinkler. Coming face-to-face with him, he ripped out in a very low voice, "If you don't stop yelling my name, Pinkler, by God I'll rearrange that sappy pan of yours!"

Instantly Pinkler wore an abused expression. "Gosh, Cardigan, you don't have to get sore thataway."

"Oh, so I don't have to get sore, don't I?" He began drumming with his index finger on one of Pinkler's lapels. "Just get this, sailor, and get it straight. Leave me alone. Lay off me. You're like flies in August, only worse. And the next time you yell my name out loud you'll be saying 'Uncle' from a position flat on your back. That's all."

He spun on his heel and headed for the elevator bank. Pinkler skipped along at his elbow.

"But listen, Cardigan—"

"Fade, sweetheart—fade."

"But wait. I want—"

Cardigan strode into the elevator and Pinkler hopped in after him, gesticulating. Cardigan spun him about, picked him up by the armpits, and bounced him back into the lobby. The door started closing, but Pinkler stopped it and said,

"What I've been trying to say is Scanlon came over and took that dame of yours to headquarters."

"What!"

"Yowssuh and verily."

Cardigan's lip curled as he stepped back to the lobby. "When?" he clipped.

"About an hour ago. There was a shooting over in—"

"Out of my way. If that tramp Scanlon thinks he can wisecrack around me—"

"Now what was the shooting about?"

Cardigan said, "Come here and I'll tell you." He led Pinkler down a side corridor, suddenly took hold of him, and thrust him violently into a telephone booth. Unpronging the receiver, he wrapped its cord around Pinkler's neck, knotted it. Then he took out a pair of manacles and locked Pinkler's hands behind his back.

He said, "You may mean well, Pinkler, but you're dumb and you've caused me enough headache already. You'll have to put a nickel in the slot to get the operator. You can't reach the slot. In order to open these doors, after I close them, you'd have to reach chest high and pull 'em in toward you. You can't do that. Maybe this 'll keep you on ice a while. Good-bye and good luck."

He stepped out, closed the doors, and went on his way, cursing under his breath. Wind and snow hit him in the street; he strode into the wind, up Locust. At Twelfth he turned left, stretching his long legs, crunching snow beneath his big feet. Every now and then he cut loose with a short, violent oath. Presently he crossed the wide street and entered headquarters. To the man at the central room desk he barked,

"Where's Scanlon?"

"So who wants to see him?"

"I want to see him. Ain't I asking?"

A cop stepped up, said, "Button that trap, wise guy!"

"Stooge, huh? . . . Lay off, copper. Where's Scanlon? I'm Cardigan."

"So you're Cardigan!"

"Don't let the fact get you down."

The man at the desk said, "Show him up, Mike."

When Cardigan walked into Scanlon's office Pat jumped up with a little glad outcry, a vast expression of relief which she could not have equaled in words. She had no time to say anything, for Cardigan, kicking the door shut, said,

"What kind of a rat have you turned out to be, Scanlon?"

Scanlon grinned wickedly from his swivel chair. His long, narrow face cracked into many wrinkles, and raising both hands, he brought them down on his head, drew them downward on his hair as far as the temples, and then clapped them lazily together.

"Kind of get sore, don't you, Cardigan, when you meet a guy a little tougher than you are?"

"Tough?" Cardigan laughed caustically. "Don't make me laugh. You're not tough, Scanlon. You're just a sheep trying to wear wolf's clothing. . . . Pat, did this egg get rough with you?"

"No! Oh, no," she assured him. "He just dragged me over here and asked a lot of questions—"

Scanlon pointed to a battered, sodden hat that lay on the desk. "There was shooting down off Sixth Street and we picked your hat up in an alley. Kelton of the bureau heard the shots and went through that alley and he said some guy hit him with a club. We found Kelton and found your hat in the same place."

"Okay. I was taking the air and suddenly some guy began shooting. I ducked in the alley and halfway down some guy stops me. How the hell should I know who he is? It's dark, I've been shot at, and—well, what can you expect?"

Scanlon leaned forward. "Who fired the shots, Cardigan?"

"I wouldn't know."

Scanlon scowled. "Cut out horsing."

"I tell you I don't know. I didn't stop to ask."

"You've got an idea, though."

"I haven't even got an idea."

Scanlon stood up, jamming his hands against his hips. His brows came together unpleasantly. "When guys begin cutting loose with guns, I want to know." He tapped his chest, said sententiously, "It happens to be my business."

"Yeah?" Cardigan pointed. "When I begin taking potshots at somebody, that's your business maybe. When somebody takes potshots at me, that's mine if I want to make it mine. You thought by snatching Pat Seaward down here you'd be pulling a fast one on me. It didn't get you anywhere. So now what? Do I have to stand here all night and listen to these lousy bromides you get off?"

Pat looked apprehensive. "Chief," she began, making an importunate gesture.

He silenced her with a gesture of his hand, waist high; and he said to Scanlon,

"You mind your business and I'll mind mine. I hate chiselers, Scanlon; I hate 'em like hell. By God Almighty, I can't stick my nose in this town without some crackpot doesn't turn up to stooge on my act!"

"Soft-pedal, Cardigan. You're not in a hired hall."

"I know where I am. I could tell blindfolded, by the smell of guys that work here."

Scanlon's nostrils twitched. He came around the desk, made a stab at Cardigan's arm, gripped the arm hard. His face looked very gray, very narrow. "You go to your head sometimes, don't you? Another crack like that and you'll walk into something."

Pat, behind Scanlon's back, was begging Cardigan to ease up. Her hands, her lips urged, pleaded.

Scanlon said bitterly, "I want to know what happened. I want to know why you came here and why you were shot at."

"Nix, Scanlon. It's on the up-and-up; it's legit; I can't tell you."

"I can be nasty, Cardigan."

"You're telling me?"

Scanlon jerked his arm. "Spring it or take what I can give."

Cardigan shook his head. "You know me, Scanlon."

Scanlon tossed Cardigan's arm free, strode back to his desk, and leaned on it with straightened arms. For a long moment he regarded Cardigan with a hard, mutinous stare. Then he rapped his desk curtly.

"Okay, big boy," he said. "I'm tossing you in the can."

"Listen, you!" Cardigan exploded. He strode to the desk, took a crack at it with his fist. "You can't toss me in the can!"

"Can't I?"

"No!"

Scanlon lit a cigarette. "Sure I can. Attacking an officer. Kelton of the bureau—the guy you socked in that alley."

"That was an accident! I didn't know who he was! How could I, when I didn't even see his face?"

"That's what you say," Scanlon droned. "It's the can for you, Cardigan—with my compliments."

Cardigan's face became red, dull red, and a humid look took possession of his eyes. He clamped his lips shut tightly. He put his fists into his pockets, jamming them way in, to keep them from suddenly going astray. Then he nodded slowly.

And he said in a low-throttled voice, "Your face is going to be redder than mine someday, Scanlon."

"Look how scared I am," Scanlon mocked.

Pat was saying, "Gosh, chief, gosh," in a small, weak voice.

"Forget it, chicken," Cardigan said. "Scanlon thinks he's hit a home run, but it's only a foul ball . . . and plenty foul."

THREE

SIMPLE AS CAKE

■

Locked behind bars, Cardigan was having a few words with Pat before she should leave for the night. He spoke quietly, hardly above a whisper. "You know what to do, Pat. See Aaronson right away. Track him down tonight, no matter where he is. Make him get things fixed so I can get out of here by nine tomorrow morning. Get me, chicken, I've got to get out of here by nine."

"Oh, chief, why don't you tell Scanlon? If you told him, he'd let you go. He'd see there's nothing crooked. After all—"

"After all, we took this job on one condition: there must be no notoriety. That's why old Stoddard's paying us ten times what we're worth. Get it? No publicity. The cops can't know because if they do know the papers grab it."

She was grave, thoughtful. "Who tried to shoot you?"

"I wish I knew. He either came on from New York by plane ahead of us, or he's working under orders from New York."

"Do you think he knows where Genevieve is?"

"I doubt it. It figures that he's afraid I do. If he does know, then Genevieve's not in such a swell spot, either. . . . And listen. Go find Aaronson now. If you can't, get him early in the morning. If all this flops, you'll have to see this guy Mafey yourself."

"Mafey?"

"He's the key to Genevieve. Here's his address."

"Oh, chief, I'm so sorry, so sorry."

"Hey, forget it, Patsy. The only thing I'm sore about is that I've got to pay for a night at a hotel without sleeping there. Scatter. Here comes a guy with his ears hanging out."

She put a warm pressure on his hand, then turned on her heel and clicked off. Cardigan undressed down to his pants and socks and went to sleep.

He was up at seven and had breakfast sent in to his cell. Nothing ever spoiled his appetite, and he ate four eggs, wheat cakes, three rolls, and drank two mugs of coffee. From time to time he asked the keeper if any word had arrived for him. The keeper was on in years, a good-natured fat man, and he told Cardigan he'd keep his ears peeled for any news. By eight there was no word; nor was there any word by eight-thirty. Nine o'clock came and passed and at nine-fifteen Scanlon wandered in and said,

"Thought it over?"

"Thought what over?"

"About springing a little news."

Cardigan looked instantly disgusted. "I don't have to think it over, Scanlon. You heard me last night." He gripped the bars. "For crying out loud, fella, why be a heel? You know damned well you canned me here just to be nasty. Look—I apologize for anything I might have said."

Scanlon grinned. "You'd like to get out, huh?"

"Yeah."

"Ain't that just too bad."

"Listen—"

"I'll listen when you talk my language. Three or four years ago, when you were out here, you used to like to razz hell out of me. I never liked it."

"Can't you forget and forgive?"

"To hell with your soft soap, Cardigan. You're in here for taking a sock at a cop. I can't do anything about it. Sorry. Oh, so, so sorry."

Cardigan snarled, "For two cents I'd reach through these bars and flatten your nose, you bum!"

Scanlon waved with an affected delicacy, saying, "Toodle-oo. And who's the horse on now?" He began drifting away, whistling cheerfully to himself.

At ten o'clock there was some activity in the cell block. The keeper came down, unlocked Cardigan's cell and said, "Okay."

Cardigan barged into the corridor, strode up it to a hollow square where Pat, Attorney Aaronson, and a lieutenant were standing. Aaronson was a small, frail, tired-looking man.

"Where the hell have you been?" Cardigan demanded.

"On a bender. Been out all night. Everything's okay, kid."

"I can go out?"

"You can go out. Why don't you let me know when you blow in town, so I can get set?"

"How the hell did I know the cops were going to play kick-the-wicket with me? . . . Come on; let's go."

"See you later," Aaronson said. "I have to see so-and-so here on a little business."

Cardigan took Pat by the arm and they went upstairs and Cardigan said, "Just wait out front, will you?"

"But why? Aren't you going?"

"I want to find Scanlon and give him a Bronx cheer."

She held on to his arm, said definitely, "Chief, nossir! You darned well know you've got to get Genevieve—Oh, why be a kid all the time. Come on, come on, chief!"

Cardigan looked disappointed, but he said, "Okay, pal," and they went out into Twelfth Boulevard.

The place near Commercial Alley looked down-at-the-heel by daylight. It had not now the darkness to flavor it with mystery, to dab it with a sense of dubious romance. A low, peeling brick building, it stood unadorned by anything but drabness. The snow that was banked against its walls was already sprinkled with soot. The smoke pall hung in the sky, obscuring the winter sun. It was a cold, windless day. Nearby, the river rolled, and a Wabash train thundered.

"That is it," Cardigan said to Pat.

The front door was open and a Negro was sweeping out. Buckets of refuse stood stacked outside. When Cardigan and Pat came into the doorway, the Negro said, "Ain't open till four."

"That's all right," Cardigan said. "Come on, Pat."

Mafey was expecting him. Mafey stood in the center of the barroom, a fat quaint figure with his fat, wet eyes watching Cardigan gravely as the big dick entered the room.

"This," said Cardigan, indicating Pat, "is my assistant Miss Seaward. I brought her along to chaperon Genevieve. Pat, this is Mr. Mafey."

Mafey said "Hello" to Pat while keeping his grave eyes fixed on Cardigan. It was plain the man was still doubtful, still a bit suspicious.

Cardigan was saying, "Well, where's Genevieve?"

Mafey moistened his lips, shifted from one foot to the other. Finally, drawing in a great breath, holding it, he said, "Come on." He led them to the rear of the bar, took out a key, unlocked the door, and swung it open. He entered the room beyond first, stood aside, his big fat hands clenched and a worried shadow on his forehead.

The girl was sitting in one of the Morris chairs. She was tall, with a fine head of russet hair, a poised neck, dark slumbrous eyes that regarded Cardigan quizzically and a little hostilely.

Cardigan, removing his hat, scaling it casually onto the table, said with a grin, "Hello, Genevieve."

"Hello," she said, not smiling.

Mafey closed the door.

Cardigan scooped up a chair, carried it across the room, and planked it down facing Genevieve. Seating himself, he said, "Did Mafey tell you everything?"

"Pops said my father sent you for me." Her voice was low, restrained, not especially cordial. Her dark poollike eyes fixed Cardigan with a constant scrutiny.

"That's it." Cardigan nodded. "He sent me and"—nodding toward Pat—"Miss Seaward."

"Who is Miss Seaward?"

"One of our Agency. Some call her the love interest, but that's just a crack. She's usually on jobs with me where there's a girl concerned. It sometimes simplifies matters."

There was a long pause, and after a while the girl said, "I don't believe my father would send for me."

"Why not?"

"He threw me out pretty definitely."

Cardigan dropped his voice. "You see, he's dying."

Her lips quivered, but she tightened them.

"Why," Cardigan said, "do you doubt me? For what other reason do you think I'd be wanting to take you?"

A low fire began burning in the girl's eyes. She looked away, her breast rising, falling; and then she looked back at Cardigan again. She said,

"I haven't had an easy time since I was thrown out. I—well, I drifted here and there, got in with the wrong people. I didn't know. I didn't know anything about life. Some chaps I knew, they were later involved with the law. I fled from place to place. I haven't done anything, but, you see, I knew these fellows, some women, too. You get to, drifting the way I did. Pops was the only one on the level completely." She smiled at Mafey.

Mafey said in a clogged voice, "That's okay, Genevieve."

"Genevieve," Pat said, "you must believe us. Cardigan took his life in his hands the minute he arrived here. He's been shot at, threatened."

"Why?"

Cardigan's husky voice said, "You see, it looks as if somebody doesn't want the old man to see you. If you turn up before he dies, you get his dough. But he's got to be certain you're alive. If you don't turn up, the dough goes to his half brother."

"Uncle Lafe," she muttered, staring at the floor, coloring. Then she jumped up, clapping her knuckles to her mouth. "Uncle Lafe again!" she cried bitterly.

Pat was at her side, murmuring softly, "Genevieve—"

"That sounds," growled Mafey, "like the guy caused her to be booted out. She never squealed on his name. Only she said it was someone in the family always filling her old man's head—"

"Pops—don't!" Genevieve pleaded.

Now Cardigan took hold of her arm. "Your father's repented. I guess it's kind of getting him, that he chucked you out. He wants to see you. That's on the level. It's God's honest truth, Genevieve—"

"Oh, the money, the money! I don't care about it!"

"Okay. Forget about it. But the old man's cashing in. Give him a break."

"Yes, Genevieve," Pat urged. "Do come with us and—"

Mafey spun at the sound of voices in the bar.

Cardigan muttered, "Scanlon's voice!" Then to those in the room: "Everybody—say nothing. Let me talk." He took hold of Genevieve, said, "Sit down here. Mind, say nothing. If this breaks, they'll smear your name all over the papers." He spun. "Get me, Mafey? Let me talk!"

Mafey muttered, "What the hell is this?"

"Shh!" Cardigan warned.

The door whipped open and Pinkler, grinning idiotically, said, "Hi, Cardigan! Tag, you're it!"

Scanlon thrust Pinkler aside and snapped darkly at Cardigan, "So you pulled a fast one, huh?"

"Fast one? I just took advantage of a point in law."

Scanlon came into the room, jabbed his windy eyes from one occupant to another. Pinkler leaned in the doorway popping mints into his mouth, grinning; he said,

"I just thought I'd keep a tail on you, Jack. The telephone booth idea was a good trick. Gee, it certainly was! I never laughed so much at myself in all my life, no kidding!"

Cardigan, twisting his lip, started for the reporter, but Scanlon got in his way and rasped,

"You're dealing with a guy your size, Cardigan. Leave Pinkler alone or I'll smash you." He poked Cardigan in the chest, snapped, "Get this, smart boy. You've done a hell of a lot of waltzing in this town since you hit it, and I've been on the outside. There's something crooked here. I know it. I'm going to find out if it's the last thing I do." He whirled. "Mafey, how the hell do you figure in this?"

"I don't," Mafey said.

Cardigan said, "Look here, Scanlon, why pick on Mafey? Pick on me. Pick on a guy your size."

Scanlon spun back on him, snarled, "Getting even, huh?"

"Sure."

"Please, please!" Pat implored.

Scanlon whipped at her, "Keep your damned mouth shut!"

Cardigan grabbed his arm, jolted him. "You're talking to a lady, Scanlon. Talk to her right or I'll wrap a chair around your neck." He thumped his own chest. "Pick on me—me!"

Both red-faced, they glared hotly at each other.

"Gee," piped Pinkler, "I like to see Cardigan get mad! Whoops, dearie!"

Cardigan took one step, laid the hard flat of his hand across Pinkler's cheek.

"Chief!" Pat cried.

Pinkler slammed to the floor and Cardigan was spun about roughly by Scanlon, who said, "Now cut that out! Leave him alone!" He shook Cardigan. "I want to know what you're doing here."

Cardigan took a deep breath. "All right," he said, nodding violently. He strode across the room, clapped his hands together, ground palm against palm, turned and said, "It just happens, fathead, that I'm looking for a guy." He took another breath. He was thinking fast, knowing now that Scanlon, chagrined because he had been tricked, was definitely on the warpath. And Cardigan knew that Scanlon was a hard man to shake.

"Get on, get on," Scanlon said angrily.

"This guy," Cardigan proceeded, crossing the room and coming face-to-face with Scanlon, "has been pulling a lot of stunts that our Agency don't like. He's been impersonating a Cosmos man. We didn't mind it until the Agency began to get into a lot of jams. He faked our identification, and since we're known at a flock of hotels in the East and Middle West, he ran up a lot of bills and charged them to the Agency. He also got good jobs on the strength of his bogus identification; he gypped his clients, and of course the comeback came to the Agency. The boss began sending out trailers and we finally got a hot tip that this potato was circulating in this burg. We'd never seen him, but from here and there, from gypped clients, we got a good composite picture of him.

"He's about as tall as I am, maybe fatter—yes, he would be fatter, and apparently in his forties. Red-cheeked—you know, kind of plump red cheeks. We don't know his real name, but he has used names like Phil Taylor, Samuel Gade, and so on. In Buffalo, I ran into a poolhall owner I used to know when I worked in Scranton, and I got to talking about this thing, and he said a guy like that used to hang around his pool hall. The guy said he was heading for St. Louis, and this pal of mine said he gave him the address of a good speak in St. Louis. This is the address he gave. So I lined out, figuring to come right here to Mafey's and see if I could get a line. Then when I arrived at the station, Pinkler began yelling my name. This guy must have been on hand. Everybody in the business knows my name, and this guy must have put two and two together.

"Later, I'm walking down Sixth, when a voice says behind, 'Keep walking, Cardigan, and don't look around. You're covered.' I say, 'Why?' and he says, 'We're going someplace and have a talk.' Well, when I came to that alley I took a chance. I figured this guy was on a big job here and that he figured I would ball up the works. I figured he might give me the works. So I ducked in the alley. He fired, things happened, and there you are. Simple as cake."

Pat Seaward seemed to have a hard time swallowing. She looked stunned.

Scanlon said, "Why the hell didn't you tell me that before?"

"How could I?" Cardigan said reasonably. "We wanted to keep it under the Agency's hat. We wanted to snag this guy, drag him to the smallest, most out-of-the-way town where he'd ever pulled a job, try him and have him convicted there, with a minimum of publicity. In a big city like this, hell, the world would know it, and the Agency doesn't want that. You got me on a spot, Scanlon, where I had to tell you. Ten to one, both Pat and me, even if we catch this bird, will lose our jobs. That right, Pat?"

Pat grimaced. "You're right, chief."

"Gee," said Pinkler. "Gosh. Gee, that's too bad. Gosh, I didn't even have an idea—"

"Our jobs are at stake," Cardigan said. "I don't care about myself, but Miss Seaward here has a mother to support."

Pat hung her head.

Scanlon sighed, made a face, looked at his palms, then at his knuckles. Embarrassed, he growled, "Why the hell didn't you tell me? I would have—"

"I didn't dare," Cardigan said. "Hell, Scanlon, I always thought you hated me and—well—with the misunderstanding and all—"

Scanlon went to the door, stood there, his back to the room. After a moment he muttered, "Okay," and walked out, and Pinkler followed.

Cardigan dragged out a handkerchief, mopped his face. "Do I deserve a membership in the tall-story club!"

"Whew!" blew out Pat, fanning herself. "Please, sir, the smelling salts!"

FOUR

IT'S LIFE

■

Cardigan shoved his handkerchief back into his pocket and, spreading his arms, his hands, said to Genevieve,

"You see, Genevieve, I had to keep you out of the papers."

Rising, she laid a long, white hand on Cardigan's arm. "Cardigan, I believe you and"—she turned, smiled at Pat—"Miss Seaward . . . Pops," she said, revolving, "you won't mind, will you?"

Mafey reddened. "Genevieve, if it's good for you, it's"—he made an awkward gesture—"good for me. I'm just an old guy that had a daughter once and lost her and —ah, well, I mean—" He paused, shrugged, drew a fat hand across his face. "It was like I did everything for my own daughter, only it was you."

She crossed to him, took one of his ungainly hands in her own soft, white hands. "I must hurry then, Pops. Good-bye, good luck, Pops."

A tear came ridiculously to the old man's eye. Pat saw it and her own lip quivered and she turned away.

Cardigan held out his hand. "Okay, then, Genevieve."

She went past him saying, "Poor old Pops!"

Cardigan rubbed his hand on Mafey's shoulder. "So long, Pops. With a name like that, a guy's got to be jake." Then, quickly: "Come on, let's scram."

He turned and opened the door, stepped into the barroom, and the first thing he saw was the Negro lying on the floor. And then he saw a man standing with his back to the bar. The man was holding a gun. Genevieve hurried past Cardigan, but he reached out, stopped her. Then she saw the man with the gun.

"You're not taking her back, Cardigan," the man said.

He was, of course, the same man who had shot at Cardigan in Sixth Street. Tall, stout, well-dressed, with fat red cheeks and small, beady eyes.

Back of Cardigan, Pat gasped.

Cardigan snarled, "Punk, you're out of your class!"

"Am I?" The man stepped forward to the center of the floor, planting himself firmly there, his gun level. He went on: "You're not taking her back, and you know why. I've heard a lot about you, Cardigan, but that doesn't faze me. Leggo the dame. She's coming with me."

Unafraid, Genevieve said over her shoulder to Cardigan, "Who is he?"

"Ask me, he represents your Uncle Lafe. But don't worry, Genevieve, this palooka's not going to take you anywhere."

The man addressed Genevieve. "It's up to you. If you don't want me to cut loose with this rod, walk toward the front door. I mean it. I'd hate like hell to start any fireworks, but the cards read that way. It's up to you. You're staying hidden till the old man dies."

She cried, "Uncle Lafe hired you!"

"There's nothing anyone can prove. Stop spouting and get started."

Cardigan chopped off, "No. Don't."

"I must," she said, and walked slowly toward the door. As she walked, the stout man backed up, keeping pace with her, still holding his gun trained on Cardigan. As they neared the door, the stout man maneuvered so that he was partially protected by the girl, though he would be able still to fire past her side. He backed into the doorway leading to the anteroom. And suddenly, behind him, Mafey appeared. Obviously Mafey had gone around the back of the building, come in another door.

Mafey struck with a quart bottle. He was enraged perhaps, for his aim was not true; the blow grazed the tall, stout man's head, the bottle shattered on his shoulder. The tall, stout man spun violently about, his elbow catching Mafey beneath the chin, sending him wildly to the floor.

Cardigan, his gun drawn, came hurtling across the room, smashed into the big man, clubbed the gun on his head, and crashed with him to the floor. Genevieve gave a little outcry. Pat ran to her, took hold of her arm, said, "Quiet, Genevieve!" in a quick, breathless whisper, and rushed her behind the bar, out of the way.

Mafey was unconscious.

Cardigan and the stout man tumbled into the anteroom. Their bodies—big, heavy—thumped loudly on the floor. Thrashing about, each in the other's grip, they brought down a table; tussled on and fell into the dim dining room, now deserted, chairs stacked on the tables. Here their heels beat a wild tattoo on the floor. Grunting, straining, both powerful men, they heaved violently into another table, toppled it and four chairs, bringing the lot down with a resounding smash.

The stout man buried his teeth in Cardigan's gun hand, and with an agonized groan Cardigan let his gun drop, heaved, twisted, and sank his teeth into the stout man's hand. The stout man howled, kicked; his gun flew away in a low arc, skidded up the floor, spinning round and round.

Fighting each other all the while, they got to their feet. They broke away. Cardigan, seeing his gun, dived for it, and the stout man lashed out with his foot, caught Cardigan on the side of his head, and sent him careening into another table. Cardigan held his balance while the stout man dived headfirst for his own gun. Before he reached it, Cardigan was on him, chopping his fist against the man's ear.

"O-o-o!" the man grunted. "O-o-o!"

They rolled over and over, stopped against the wall. They rose, breaking, and Cardigan drove his fist into the man's face, twisting the fist on contact.

"Ow-w-w!" the man yelled.

"Shut up. You make me sick. You—"

He received a smash in the mouth that uprooted him, but the big dick caught his balance, shifted, and stuck out his foot as the other made another dive for his gun. The stout man did not quite fall. He kept tumbling all the way across the room, but on the way he made a desperate try for the gun, snatched it up, tripped over the one step leading to the anteroom, and slammed down.

Cardigan kicked aside a chair, grabbed his own gun and was raising it when he saw, in the dim light, Pat standing beyond the man. Raising, the man struck at her; hit her a glancing blow. She went down.

Cardigan fired high—he was afraid of hitting Pat—and so he missed the stout man. But the explosion sent the stout man bolting for the front door, and as he whipped it open Scanlon started in.

The stout man slashed with his gun and opened Scanlon's cheek. Scanlon fell to the sidewalk and the stout man hurtled over him and broke into a heavy, bounding run. With his face spouting blood, Scanlon staggered to his feet, lurched about.

"Hey!" he yelled. "Hey, you, stop! It's the law! *Stop!*"

The stout man did not stop.

Scanlon snarled, lifted his gun, and fired. The shot sent the stout man glancing off a house wall but did not stop him. He lunged on, clots of snow flying upward and backward from his heels. Scanlon, pressing a hand to his torn face, ran after him, shouting again, "Stop or you'll get it!"

The stout man looked back, slowed down for a corner, and went reeling and skidding around the corner as Scanlon fired. The slug caught the stout man while he was teetering on one foot. It straightened him, turned him half around. He crashed into a pole, rebounded, spun half around again, and fired wildly. Scanlon fired a third time, hitting the man squarely, sending him bobbing backward, and finally dropping him into a mound of dirty snow where he let his gun fall.

Coming up to him, Scanlon stopped and kept pointing his gun at him. Rage and pain contorted the sergeant's face, but after a moment he realized that the man was dead, there was no longer any need to grip his gun so hard, hold it so level. He let it droop, leaned against the pole, wiping the blood from his torn face.

He heard running footsteps and turned about and saw Cardigan coming toward him.

"What the hell, Scanlon!"

"What the hell yourself!"

Cardigan said, pointing, "Just after you left—well, I was about to leave, and I walk smack into this guy. I don't know who he is and right off the bat he takes a crack at me and then I know—I remember the description—and we go to it. . . . Where'd you come from?"

"Nuts. I was coming back to have a drink and talk things over with you. I was—well, what the hell, I figured we might as well be friends—and so— Aw, nuts!" He turned, reached down, and probed the body on the snow. "Dead as a guy can be." He then began going through the man's pockets. "Not a thing," he said. "One of those guys that carries no identification. Oh-oh, here's something." He rose, looking at a small black card case. He opened it. "Cripes," he said, "it's your own Agency card—your own name on it!"

Cardigan pointed. "See. What did I tell you? Let's see it. Yup— my own name and everything. It's just as if it was my own." He thrust it casually into his pocket, said "Better get the morgue bus, huh?"

"Yeah, I'd better. I'll stay here. Ring in from Mafey's, will you?"

Cardigan said, "Okay, kid."

Scanlon grinned through his torn face. "Okay, kid."

"How's for getting back my old hat?" Cardigan added.

"That's okay, too."

Cardigan strode back to Mafey's. Pat was standing in the doorway and he grinned, said, "Everything's hunky-dory, chicken," and passed on into the anteroom. Mafey was standing on his feet and Genevieve was holding a wet towel to his jaw. Cardigan went into the barroom, entered the telephone booth, and put in Scanlon's call.

Returning to the anteroom, he said, "Pat, you and Genevieve better leave now—just the two of you. Go to the hotel. Get a drawing room for you two and a lower for me on the New York train tonight. I'll have to hang around till this thing's cleared up, then I'll join you."

"But what just happened?" Pat asked, anxious.

"The big guy ran into Scanlon and clouted him and Scanlon went to work on him. The big guy's down the street."

"Dead?" Pat said.

"Well, I just called the morgue."

Genevieve put her face in her hands, began crying quietly. Pat moved over to her, took hold of her arm, said gently, "Come on, Genevieve. It's all over. Everything will be all right."

"Yes, yes. . . . Good-bye, Pops."

Mafey, holding his jaw, mumbled, "Good-bye, Genevieve."

Pat said, "Chief, will Scanlon get nasty?"

"Scanlon?" He laughed. "Hell, no. We're buddies now."

Her eyebrows sprang upward. "Well, of all things!"

"It's life," he said. "Scanlon . . . me . . . Genevieve . . . Pops here . . . and the big mug. Hearts are hearts and spades are spades and bullets are bullets. No matter how you slice it, it's life, precious."

HOT SPOT

■

BY FREDERICK NEBEL

That big dick from Cosmos had opened plenty of branches for his Agency but he'd never found a tougher town than Frisco to get going in. The slickers didn't want him—neither did the cops. And he had a busted arm in a sling to boot. But even with one wing useless Cardigan had plenty of ice left to cool off the hot spot they had him on.

ONE

APPLES AND NUTS

■

The address was down at the fag end of Kearny Street, but Cardigan got out of the taxi half a block away. He tossed a half-dollar in the air, slapped it neatly shut in his palm and then planked it into the driver's palm.

"Play penny ante with the change," he said.

The driver had a cold and said through his nose, "I nedder gabble. Gad afford to gabble."

The cab slewed off and Cardigan stood beneath the streetlight in the wet San Francisco fog. The fog blurred the light, moved sluggishly about it, like wet, oily smoke, and all sounds, near and far away, had a resonant, bell-like clarity. The brim of Cardigan's lop-eared hat stopped the downstream of light, leaving his face mostly in shadow. His left overcoat sleeve dangled; his left arm was in a sling beneath the coat.

He could see the uniformed cop standing in front of the dun-colored brick house. The hall door was open and sufficient light streamed from it to raise a glitter on the cop's buttons whenever he turned about. There were some persons hanging around, and parked at the curb was a car Cardigan recognized as Sergeant McGovern's.

Cardigan moved presently, bulking in the illuminated fog. The cop in front of the house turned. He was big as Cardigan, but fat, with a rubicund face, and the fog had beaded his black visor and now it glittered there.

"Okay if I go up?" Cardigan said.

"Why should it be?"

"Now we get to riddles, huh?" He lit a cigarette. "I'm Cardigan, copper. Do you read the papers?"

"I like the funny pictures. . . . Okay, g' on up."

The stairway was narrow and hugged the wall. The hall was cold, damp, and as Cardigan reached the top of the staircase he saw a door open and a uniformed cop leaning in the doorway. There were voices beyond. The cop looked over his shoulder.

"Hanh?" he said.

Cardigan shook his head. "I didn't say anything. I want to see McGovern?"

"Who wants to see McGovern?" said a foghorn voice within the room.

The cop stepped aside.

"Only little me," said Cardigan, entering, spitting smoke from his lips. He leaned against a radiator. "Thanks for every little thought, Mac. Once a Boy Scout, always a Boy Scout."

"What the hell are you doing out of the hospital?"

"I didn't like the food."

They looked at each other, talking with their eyes only. McGovern was a tall, lean man, tough-built, with grizzled hair, a bony granite-colored face, a jaw like the bow of a tugboat. He had a ferocious glare and used it on Cardigan for a full minute. Then he laughed like a foghorn off-key and took a crack at his thigh. Cardigan grinned.

He said, "Who's the hoss on, Mac?"

"Boy, you're a one, Cardigan; you're a one, all right!" He spun and jabbed a finger at Detective Hunerkopf. "Ain't he a one now, August? Ain't he, now?"

Hunerkopf was sitting on a chair, eating an apple which he pared with a penknife. He was a roly-poly man and, munching a sliver of apple, he chuckled silently, his fat body shaking, his fat head nodding.

Cardigan said, "What's the lay, Mac?"

McGovern looked suddenly very innocent and spread his palms. "Do you see anything?"

"I see an old bedroom with a single bed, a bureau, a chair, a rag rug on the floor, walls that haven't been papered in years; an open Gladstone, a few clothes, some shoes, and two men disguised as detectives."

McGovern tightened his mouth. "Soon as you get on your feet you begin making cracks, huh?"

Cardigan ignored this. He said, "What about Jagoe?"

McGovern shook his head. "Nothing. We been fanning the place for half an hour."

"What's this?" Cardigan said, picking up a sheet of paper.

"A letter," McGovern rasped. "But it don't mean a thing. No name signed."

It was a short note.

> Dear Pete: I'll be back in town on Wednesday. Am verey lonely for you. Will be at the same place and hope verey much you'll come over Wednesday night.
>
> Always yours.

"A jane," muttered Cardigan. "Dated a month ago."

"And signed 'Always Yours,'" said McGovern irritably. "Ain't that a help?"

"Even if it were signed," Cardigan said, tossing the sheet of paper back to the bed, "you'd crab."

"You just wear yourself down being friendly, don't you?"

Cardigan kicked abstractedly at the open Gladstone. "You're a pretty smart cop, Mac—except when you get up against real competition. Hell, I'm not sore. Not much. It was damned smart of you, baby, to try to keep me in the hospital long enough for you to run around town with your nose to the ground. Only it didn't work. The nurse fell for me. Besides, I can use five thousand bucks as well as you."

Hunerkopf lowered his apple and looked very hurt. "Look, Cardigan, we didn't even think of the five-grand reward."

"Of course we didn't!" snapped McGovern, looking very indignant.

Cardigan chuckled deep in his throat. "Just thought of old alma mater, huh?" He chuckled again. "Dry-clean that baloney and pack it away. Listen, you two. I was guarding that bankroll. I was the guy walked down Market with Hamlin, who carried the satchel. We've just opened a branch agency here. I was getting it in shape. And right off the bat this happens. Hamlin's killed and I'm plugged and now I'm getting the razz from the home office. Pete Jagoe pulled a fast one, fast even for me. He's somewhere in this town lugging around thirty grand. As a matter of fact, Mac, I'm looking for no reward. I wouldn't take it. But I hate the razz . . . And then you finagle around and try to talk that crowd into keeping me in the hospital. I can stand a joke, Mac. I've pulled fast ones on you. But lay off the baloney. You slice it too thick to swallow. And stay from under my feet."

Hunerkopf looked very melancholy.

But McGovern could take it. He jammed his hands on his hips and lifted up his jaw. "Okay, Cardigan. It was a fast one. I'll stay from under your feet and you stay from under mine. Monkey around with my parade and you might get the other arm busted."

Cardigan said, "With both arms busted, kid, I'd still have my head, which would still leave you in a jam."

"Have an apple, Cardigan," Hunerkopf said.

"Nuts to you, too."

"I don't like nuts," Hunerkopf said. "They always get stuck between my teeth."

McGovern roared. "Hey, that's a good one, August! That's a pip!"

Cardigan's face got red. He swiveled and went to the door. He turned to say, "Now I remember why that laugh of yours is so familiar, Mac. When I was a kid, I used to breed jackasses."

"Whoops!" exploded Hunerkopf, shaking all over. "That there one was a rich one!"

McGovern glared at him. Hunerkopf shut up and sat looking very guilty.

Cardigan drummed his big feet down the stairway and swung out into the cold fog.

T W O

IN A SLING

∎

Pat Seaward was having a late snack in the coffee shop of the Hotel
Galaty, in Powell Street, when Cardigan pushed past the cashier's
desk and made his way among the glossy black tables. Pat laid
down the corner of a sandwich and looked up round-eyed at him.
Not bothering to remove his overcoat, he sat down, dropped his
battered fedora to a spare chair, and picked up the corner of the
sandwich which Pat had laid down. He ate it, swallowed some
water.

"Well!" said Pat, her eyes still round. "The last I saw of you,
chief, you were in a hospital bed."

A grinning waiter swooped down, bowed and spread a large
menu before Cardigan. Cardigan brushed it aside. "Take it away."

"I beg pardon, sir—"

"You needn't. Just take it away."

The waiter took it away.

Pat reached across the table, said anxiously, "Oh, chief, what
are you doing out in a night like this in your condition? Your poor
arm—"

"To hell with my arm," he muttered under his breath. "Those babies thought they were smart, keeping me in the hospital."

"Oh, but think, chief—"

"That's what I did in the hospital, chicken. I figured it all out. I was being kept there so our mutual friend and pal McGovern could get a running broad jump on me. I kicked that trick in the pants. McGovern's all right. I kind of like him. He kind of likes me. But business is business and I"—he made a fist and pressed it quietly but firmly against the table—"have got to wash the razzberry off my face. Jagoe's in town. All the outbound arteries were blocked ten minutes after he killed Hamlin and wounded me in Market Street. I didn't come to this burg to set up a dime museum. I came here to set up a branch of the Cosmos Agency, and that was a swell recommendation to start on. I'm in a spot, Pat—a hot one. Nobody's going to keep me in a hospital while Jagoe's on the loose."

"You look bad, chief. The blood you lost. Think of it. You look terrible—no color—circles under your eyes—"

"And I feel lousy. So what? So I should stay in bed and do crossword puzzles? Nix." He pounded the table twice, quietly but firmly. "Nix, chicken."

He picked up a newspaper, spread it before him, ran his eyes over the columns. He turned a page, looked at an ad, then frowned and turned back again, bent over the paper and peered hard. He drummed reflectively on the table. His eyes narrowed and his jaw hardened.

"I'll be right back," he said, getting up. "I want to phone."

Leaving his hat, he strode out into the lobby. There was a drawn look on his big face; his complexion was bad. His thick black hair was bunched haphazardly on his head; it curled round his ears and grew far down on his nape. He crushed into a telephone booth, filling it with his bulk, and called the number of the newspaper he held. When he was connected with the proper person, he said,

"I want this put in the Personals column, soon as you can get it in: 'Baby—Meet me corner Grant and Pacific five P.M.' And sign that 'Hon.' . . . Yeah. Charge it to the Cosmos Agency, per Cardigan. . . . What edition will it make? . . . Swell."

He hung up, stepped out into the lobby, and used a pocketknife to cut a small rectangle from the newspaper. He returned to the coffee shop and found Pat finishing a cup of coffee. Sitting down, he said, "Tomorrow at about a quarter to four you go over to Grant and Pacific. Don't plant yourself right on the corner, but hang around near enough so that you get a clean sweep of the place. Watch for a jane. See when she gets there. She'll hang around a while and when her date doesn't show up she'll probably leave. Follow her. See where she goes. Get her located and then ring me. That clear?"

"All except why the hocus-pocus?"

He slid the small rectangle of paper across the desk. "Read that over."

She read aloud: " 'Dear Hon—Verey important you shouldn't see me—Baby.' "

"See anything funny?"

Pat squinted. "Nothing except a misspelled word."

"*Very*, huh?"

"Yes; *very*. She must have stopped in and written it out and the paper forgot to spell it right."

"Maybe she spelled it right and the paper didn't."

He nodded. "Maybe, Patsy. But I was just over at Jagoe's room. McGovern was fanning it. There was a note there, an old one, written by a dame to Jagoe. In that letter, the word *very* was misspelled. . . . Okay. Wipe the coffee off your chin and let's go, sugar. I'd go on this tail myself, but I'm afraid McGovern will pull some more practical jokes. He might put a guy out to watch my moves. You just got in yesterday and you're not known by sight to McGovern."

As they walked from the coffee shop into the broad corridor leading to the lobby, Cardigan put a hand on Pat's arm. He said,

"Fade, Pats. I see McGovern's pal."

Pat ducked out of sight and Cardigan swung on. As he entered the lobby, Hunerkopf, turning, saw him and signaled. Cardigan went toward Hunerkopf. The fat detective was standing solidly back on his heels. He drew an apple from his pocket.

"Have an apple?" he said.

"No," said Cardigan.

"Have a banana?" Hunerkopf said, producing one.

Cardigan shook his head.

"Well, well," Hunerkopf said. "I guess you don't know what's good for you. Fruit keeps me fit as a fiddle."

"And makes you look like a bass drum with swollen glands. What's on your mind?"

"Oh, I just thought I'd kind of drop by. I hate like the Old Nick to see you and Mac all the time riding each other. Thought maybe I could patch things up so you and Mac—well, would kind of—you know—well, two heads is always better than one."

"That depends, August, on whose shoulders the heads are. Did Mac send you around to say this?"

Hunerkopf colored. He laughed. "Mac? Gee, no. If Mac thought I was—"

Cardigan laughed outright. "Great, August! Great! In fact, swell!"

Hunerkopf gaped. "Huh?"

"Take that story out for a walk, copper. It needs exercise." He turned on his heel and went long-legged across the lobby, into a waiting elevator. Pat had stepped into it a moment before. As it rose, Pat said,

"Well?"

"Hunerkopf," Cardigan said.

"Please speak English."

"That's a name, Pat, not a slogan. He's in his second childhood. Likes to tell fairy stories."

It was clear, cold, when Pat walked up Grant Avenue next afternoon. She wore a three-quarter-length lapin coat, lizard-skin oxfords, and a small rimless hat that rode jauntily over one eye. Her bag matched her oxfords and contained a small-calibered Webly automatic. Chinatown's windows shone and Chinese youths, dapper, well-dressed, hurried. She was worried about Cardigan—worried about his wound, his general condition following the shooting. But there was no talking with him when he was determined.

Nearing Pacific, which, coming down from Van Ness, crosses Grant and plunges toward the Embarcadero, she slowed down and stopped at last in front of a shop window. She was a little early and saw no one waiting on the corner, though many persons were in transit, mostly Orientals. But in a little while she turned from the shop window and saw a girl standing on the corner.

The girl was tall, rather well-dressed in dark clothes, a dark narrow-brimmed hat. Pat could see that she was anxious; the girl kept looking constantly about, shifting from foot to foot. Later, she began referring frequently to her wristwatch. Pat looked at her own and saw that it was half past four. Soon it was a quarter to five and then it was five. The girl waited until five-thirty and then started off in the dusk. Pat followed.

A few blocks farther on the girl boarded a taxi and Pat climbed into one a moment later and gave instructions to the driver. The girl alighted at the bottom of Filbert Street and Pat went on for half a block. She got out, paid hurriedly, and walked back. When she reached the corner she could see the girl climbing Filbert. Two men had suddenly appeared on the corner also, and Pat, remembering that Cardigan had said McGovern might shoot out someone to shadow him, wondered if by chance her connection with Cardigan had become known. But she did not hesitate. She walked up the precipitous street, keeping the girl easily in sight. Near the top, the girl turned into a small house. As Pat came abreast of the house, she saw a light spring to life on the street floor, caught a glimpse of the girl pulling down a shade. Pat did not stop but continued on her way up. Looking about, she saw the two men standing diagonally across the way from the house the girl had entered. They did not go in, however. They entered, she saw, a building across the street.

Pat went over the hump of Telegraph Hill. She climbed a wooden stairway, then went along a wooden walk built on stilts; from here she began a long descent by way of old wooden stairways, switchback walks. San Francisco Bay lay spread before her, darkening now, and with tiny lights beginning to wink. Reaching the bottom of the hill, she walked to the Embarcadero, walked on for a while until a cab came along. She took it and stopped at the first telephone pay station. She called Cardigan.

A cab pulled up in front of the drugstore outside which Pat stood and Cardigan stepped out and beckoned with his chin. She walked across the sidewalk and he handed her into the cab, followed and slammed the door shut.

"What's she look like?" he said.

"Tall, good-looking. She wears very smart clothes. She wears the kind of a hat I've been thinking of buying and—"

"How long did she wait on the corner?"

Pat told him.

The cab was speeding along the Embarcadero.

Pat said, "I may be overly suspicious, but two men cropped up on the corner of Filbert—out of the blue, so to speak—and when I reached the top of the hill they were standing looking at the house the woman entered."

"Then what?"

"Then they went in a place across the street. I thought they might be detectives."

"They might . . . Stop here, driver."

They got out, crossed the wide street, and went on toward the base of the hill. Pat started up the wooden stairway first and Cardigan followed, his empty left sleeve dangling.

"Boy," he said, "I remember this neighborhood!"

"You ought. A college football team tossed you down this hill."

"Well," he said, "it took a team, anyhow."

She sighed. "You'll never learn, chief. You'll never learn."

They went up and up in the darkness, reached the top, left the wooden walks and started down the paved street. Here it was so steep that steps had been built into the cement. Lights sparkled in the cold air.

"That's the house," Pat said. "Ground floor. Now what?"

"I don't think she'd open the door for a man. You go in, knock. She may ask who you are. Say—oh, hell, say you're from the Visiting Nurses' Association."

"Gee, chief, I hate to trick people. She didn't look like such a bad person."

"What do you work for, a detective agency or a sob sheet? . . . Where's the other house?"

"Right over there."

"We'll have to take a chance."

Pat entered the hall door of the house the woman had gone in. She left the hall door open and Cardigan, pressing close to the building, listened. He heard Pat's knock, then her voice, then another voice, muffled. In a moment the second voice was not muffled. Cardigan took a long stride into the hall and saw a tall, black-haired woman standing in an inner doorway talking with Pat. The woman stopped talking, started back into the room. Cardigan went past Pat, through the doorway. Pat followed him in and closed the door.

Cardigan snapped, "What's your name?"

"Hazel—" She stopped short, her eyes springing wide. She cried, "Who are you? Get out!"

"Tone it down, Hazel," Cardigan muttered. "This is no public performance."

She groaned, "A trick!"

"Call murder a trick, too."

"Murder—"

"Where's Pete Jagoe?"

Hazel fell back, looking terrified. "Pete—"

"You call him 'Hon,' 'Baby,' don't you?"

"Oh!" she choked.

"In the newspapers."

"Oh, my God, I see it now! Tricked! Trailed!"

Cardigan looked dangerous. He rapped out, "Call it what you want. See this bum arm? That's a trick, too. Or maybe you call it the season's greetings." He took a long step toward her and she crouched against the wall, her lips shaking. His voice was low, deep in his throat somewhere: "Listen to me, Hazel. I want Jagoe. I was guarding that payroll and but for the luck of the Irish I'd be a prospective tenant for a cemetery."

"You're wrong, wrong! I don't know—I haven't—I don't know anything—"

"That's static to me, Hazel. You fell for the wheeze in today's paper like a ton of bricks. Turn the dial to another program."

She started to cry back at him, but suddenly closed her mouth instead. She moved, sat down on a divan, and folded her hands between her knees. It seemed that it was with an effort she kept her mouth closed; her lips were pressed firmly together, her eyes stared fixedly at the floor. She was rather pretty, round about thirty, and the room looked comfortable, it was warm. There was no sound now but Hazel's breathing. Until Cardigan's low voice said, "Why were you so anxious he shouldn't come here?"

She got up and went to a far corner of the room, standing with her back to Cardigan. He went over and stood behind her. She turned and moved to another corner and he followed her. Then she fled across the room and stood behind a large armchair. Her face was white, her lips taut.

Cardigan shrugged. "A guy'd think I meant to slap you down. Why play tag?"

"Get out! Get out!"

He looked bored. "Strong, silent woman, huh?"

"Get out!"

He snapped: "Where's Jagoe?"

"I don't know!" She ran her fingers desperately through her hair. "Leave me alone! Get out!"

His face darkened. "I told you not to yell. Cut out the noise. What I want to know is," he said, coming closer, "why you didn't want your honey bun to come here."

She was panting now, grimacing. She cried, "I—I thought the place was being covered by cops. I—I thought he might try to come here and they'd nab him. I didn't do anything. I don't know where he is. Why are you picking on me?"

"Didn't he phone?"

"No. I haven't got a phone."

"You're pretty soft on this mug, huh?"

She grimaced. "Please, please don't bother me. Just leave me alone—alone. I can't help you. I can't do anything."

Pat said, "Go easy on her, chief. After all—"

He silenced her with a look. Then he turned to Hazel. "Okay, Hazel. I don't believe you do know where he is." He turned and went to the door. "Come on, Pats."

Hazel did not move. She stood behind the chair, her face in her hands. She was crying softly.

Cardigan and Pat passed into the corridor, and Cardigan closed the door.

"Gee, chief, I feel sorry for her."

"Keep it up and you'll make a namby-pamby out of me, too."

"She did what any woman would do. She just tried to warn her man—"

"All right, all right, chicken. You win. Uncle Cardigan is always in the wrong."

He pulled open the hall door and Pat went past him into the street. Closing the door, he followed, took hold of Pat's arm. Two men stepped from the shadows with guns drawn and held close to their bodies.

"Quiet does it, friends," one of them said.

Cardigan looked over his shoulder. Both men were short, the one thin, the other stocky but not fat. They wore dark overcoats, dark hats. It was the stocky man who had spoken. Now he said,

"Walk across the street."

"Getting on the bandwagon, huh?" Cardigan said.

"On you. Get going."

Cardigan kept a firm grip on Pat's arm as they strode across the street and reached the opposite sidewalk.

"Third door," the stocky man said.

They walked down the street a matter of several yards.

"Here," the stocky man said. "In."

"Listen," said Cardigan. "Let my girlfriend go."

The stocky man chided in a low voice, "See any green on me?"

"We wasn't born yestiddy," the thin man croaked.

"In, in," the stocky man said.

Cardigan and Pat were hustled into a dim-lit hallway. The place was damp, cold, and there was about it an air of desertion, as though it had been long unused. Cardigan saw that a candle supplied the light in the hall; the candle stood on the lower banister post. The small thin man removed it and carried it to a door at the side. Here he turned, and holding the candle high, backed into a room. He was well-dressed, and a dark silk muffler billowed between the lapels of his smart overcoat. The stocky man followed Cardigan and Pat, covering them with his gun.

The thin man placed the candle on a bare, scarred table. The blinds had been drawn tight and there was an extra screen rigged up a few feet from the window, obviously to permit not the minutest glimmer of candlelight to be seen from the street. There were a few chairs, a cot with neither mattress nor blanket—nothing but its original spring.

The stocky man said, "We don't usually live like this. We just busted in and took possession for a while. . . . Frisk the big lug, William."

"Stick 'em up," William said.

Cardigan raised one hand.

"The other!" William crackled.

"In a sling. You blind!"

William took away Cardigan's gun.

The stocky man said, "The lady, too."

"Okay, sister," William said. "How's tuh?"

"Why, I have only this little purse." She drew a small change purse from her pocket.

William searched her pockets, found nothing.

"Sit down on the cot," the stocky man said. "You two, I mean."

Pat and Cardigan sat down and Cardigan said, "So this is how you pass the time away, huh?" He looked at the thin man. "Is that a mask you're wearing?"

The thin man looked at the stocky man, and the latter said, "Forget it, William. The boy is bright." He jerked his round hard chin toward the front of the house. "Keep a lookout."

William disappeared behind the improvised screen.

Pat sat white and quiet. She sat very close to Cardigan, close to his bigness, praying in her heart that he would not begin to wisecrack. He leaned back, bracing his shoulders against the wall.

The stocky man moved to the table, picked up a sheet of paper on which there was some writing. Folding this, he tucked it away in his pocket. "I was beginning to write my mother," he said, "when you showed up over there." He nodded toward the street. Then he sat down, removed his hat, and rested his gun and the hand that held it on his knee. His hair was thick, coarse but neatly combed, and his skin white, with rosy cheeks. His eyes looked like pale agates and seemed to have no pupils. His hands were plump, big, well-groomed.

"I suppose," said Cardigan, "your poor old mother is waiting at the end of the lane, keeping a light in the window for dear Sonny Boy."

"My mother's a wonderful woman. I'd die for her."

William croaked from behind the screen. "So'd I for mine, only she died when I was a kid."

Cardigan said, "Both you mugs'll likely die, but not for your mothers." He sat up straight and scowled at the stocky man. His voice rushed out, hard and caustic, "Cut out the comedy. What's the idea of dragging us in?"

"It was my idea," the stocky man said, his pale eyes dancing. "You want something that we want. Catch on?"

"Jagoe," Cardigan said, nodding somberly.

The stocky man grinned, showing a row of tiny teeth. "You mean—thirty grand."

"Same thing."

William said through the screen, "Gee, I hate cops, all kindsa cops, it don't matter."

"They'll be the death of you yet," Cardigan called out.

There was a scuffling sound and William jumped from behind the screen, his face screwed up irritably. "I'm gettin' sick and tired of them cracks. First, am I wearin' a mask and then—"

"William," said the stocky man, raising a hand. "Keep an eye on the dame's house."

William disappeared behind the screen, muttering to himself.

"William," said the stocky man, "is a little headstrong, but under it all, a nice boy."

"Yanh!" mocked William.

Somewhere in the old house there was a distinct thump. The stocky man came to his feet as if spring-driven, and his lips and his eyelids came together at the same time. A sly but tense smile fastened on his lips.

"William," he called softly, almost affectionately.

"Hanh?"

"There is someone in the house."

THREE

THE SATCHEL

William's face screwed up irritably again, his lower lip quivered, and his eyes, big and bulging now, burned on the door. But the big gun he held was steady as a rock in his small, bony hand. His pale, emaciated face looked sinister above the dark silk muffler he wore.

The stocky man raised the fat fingers of his left hand very delicately. "Quiet now, William," he whispered. And to Cardigan and Pat, "Also you, my friends." The sly smile on his tightened lips never for an instant faded.

Silence crowded the old house again. William stood rooted to the floor, leaning backward a bit, his left hand in his overcoat pocket, his right holding the big gun low, with the wrist almost touching his hip. The candle guttered, its wan yellow light smearing the room. The stocky man's eyes were now bright, alert, and his head was slightly on one side, in a listening attitude. His bright eyes danced from William to Cardigan, back and forth, continually.

He seemed amused when he whispered, "Doubtless some very intimate friends of mine have chosen to muscle in."

"What of it?" Cardigan said. "You're muscling in on Jagoe."

"I happened to plan Jagoe's job for him," said the stocky man. "Jagoe is a very thankless man. His instincts are not those of a gentleman."

"'S what I allus sez!" hissed William. "He ain't had no upbrungin'."

"Shh!"

Three minutes went by.

"Maybe it was a rat," whispered William.

"Seeking its kind," observed Cardigan.

Pat nudged him anxiously.

The stocky man smiled sweetly but sinisterly at Cardigan.

After a few minutes William, at a sign from the stocky man, slithered to the door. He opened it quietly a matter of a foot, stood with his gun leveled at the dark opening. Then he opened it a little more. He stood there for two minutes, then shoved his head out. Instantly he was yanked through the doorway.

The stocky man struck the candle out. A low voice snarled in the hallway; feet rasped on the floor. Cardigan jumped up, pulling Pat with him, and dived with her toward the rear of the room, where he had spotted another door. He yanked this door open and rushed with Pat into a pitch-black room. From his vest pocket he drew a small, flat flashlight, kicked the door shut behind him. The small beam of light probed the darkness and Cardigan heaved against a heavy old bureau, shoved it against the door.

The sounds of fighting grew in the hallway.

"Oh, chief!" Pat cried in a whisper.

"Shh!" He listened, then muttered, "They're in the room now."

He pulled her toward another door, opened it as he switched off the flashlight.

"It's the hall," he whispered. And then, "If I only had a gun!"

She said rapidly, "When we came into the hall before—you remember it was pretty dim. My handbag was under my arm. They didn't see me do it, but I laid it on the radiator near the hall door and—"

"Come on."

Close together, they pressed up the hallway. The fighting was going on in the front room. Wood was splintering. There were short, low cries, snarls, oaths. Cardigan stretched his legs, making Pat hurry on her toes. He found the wall, followed it to the front, passing the open door of the room where the men struggled. He found the radiator. Groping, he found Pat's bag. He opened it and thrust his hand inside; his hand closed on the small Webley automatic. Next moment they were in the street.

"Whew!" breathed Pat, with relief.

Cardigan's low voice snapped, "You go down the hill—go home to the hotel."

"But chief—"

"Papa's talking to you, precious."

"Chief, I'm not going to leave you here alone!"

"Pat, for two cents I'd fan you!"

"I won't go! Your poor arm and all—"

"You hear me? Scram!"

"No!"

"Yes!"

"No!"

He sighed. "You're like all dames. You make me sick."

"Am I? Do I? Very well. I resign. I'll take the first train out in the morning!"

She turned and started off. He moved to stop her, but held himself in check. He thought he would rather have her resign than get tangled up in what he expected to happen tonight. He watched her small, trim figure go down the hill, saw it fade away in the darkness. It made him feel kind of low, for Pat had been his aide a long time. But he didn't want her to get hurt tonight. He knew William and the stocky man were dangerous birds.

He crept back to the house, listened at the hall door. The sounds of fighting were still going on, but he did not go in. He looked at the house across the way and knew that there lay one of his main objectives. These men were watching for Jagoe to come to the woman. He himself felt that Jagoe might come—that Jagoe might have seen the fake item in the newspaper and that that alone might prompt him, even against his better judgment, to come to the woman. He went up the hill, keeping close to the house walls. Then he crossed the street and came down on the other sidewalk; reached the front of Hazel's house, and crept into the hallway.

Here, he thought, he could hide, lay in wait for Jagoe if Jagoe should come tonight. The stairwell was roomy, dark, and he crouched there. His arm began to pain him now. It was all this activity, he supposed.

After a little while he heard voices; they were muffled and indistinct, and at first he thought they were overhead, then somewhere behind him. He stepped from the well and listened intently. When he moved toward the rear of the hall, the sound of the voices faded. He went forward along the wall, and the sound grew. He came at last to Hazel's door and knew they were here. Hazel—and a man.

He pressed his ear to the panel. He could catch only broken bits of conversation:

". . . did the other day . . . went down . . ."

". . . and how could they know . . . the coppers don't . . . been laying low and . . ."

"Why did you? I asked, begged . . . you said . . . how many times . . . and you promised. . . ." That was Hazel. ". . . so a plane to Tijuana . . . for four hundred . . ."

There was silence then and Cardigan forgot the pain in his arm, the nausea that was swelling about him.

And then Hazel, "Go . . . go now! I tell you they're hanging around! . . ."

There was a low male muttering, and then a long silence. Then suddenly a lock clicked, the door was opened by Hazel. Cardigan jammed the Webley against her and barked, "Out of the way! Up, Jagoe!"

Jagoe was a big, dark, and handsome man. His left arm encircled Hazel's throat suddenly, he pressed her back against him and whipped backward across the room, drawing his gun.

"As you are, Cardigan!"

Cardigan, with one foot across the threshold, jammed to a halt. Jagoe, using the woman as a shield, had his back against the opposite wall. Cardigan's big face became very sullen, his shaggy brows came darkly together, and his lip curled wolfishly.

He snarled in a low voice, "Jagoe the petticoat heel, huh? If I drilled her I could drill you, too."

"I'll drill you first."

"Listen, you sweet son of a punk; there's a gang of heels across the street having a free-for-all right now. Cut loose with a gun and they'll forget petty squabbles and come down on this place like a flock of bricks.''

Jagoe's eyes glittered. "Stay back, Cardigan! I crashed one of your arms and this time I'll bust open your belly. I mean it!"

There was a small satchel on the table. Cardigan smiled ruefully. He said, "I see you lugged the poke over here, huh? You are dumb all right. Don't you ever read the Personals?"

"I missed it. I didn't see it. Never mind talking. Back out of that door. Scram. Beat it. You hear me!"

Hazel stood drawn up to her full height, her face white with shock, her eyes wide with terror.

Cardigan was sarcastic. "Hell, Jagoe, you look funny hiding behind a woman. Boy, you sure look a joke!"

"Get out!" rasped Jagoe, his voice straining. "Get out or I'll open you wide!"

"I can fire as you fire, Jagoe. I can drill the woman clean as you drill me. I can fire three shots before yours would take effect. Go ahead, let her rip, honeybunch."

Hazel said nothing. Her chin went up and she closed her eyes, as though waiting, ready for the death blow.

Suddenly there was a snapping crash of glass and the window shade billowed. Cardigan ducked instinctively and then Jagoe hurled the woman across the room. Crying out, she crashed into Cardigan and both went down. Jagoe grabbed the satchel and plunged through a doorway toward the rear of the house. Cardigan heaved the woman off, jumped up, crashed into a chair, and went down again. The pain in his arm drained the color from his face, made him sink his teeth into his lip, but he got up and, his battered hat crushed low over his eyes, he lunged through the doorway.

A door slammed. He found it and whipped it open and saw he was in the hallway again. And he saw the tail of Jagoe's coat as Jagoe went out through the hall doorway.

He skidded out into the street and heard a window crash across the street, saw a dark shape fall halfway out.

"Chief!"

He turned.

Pat was crouched against the house wall. She said, "I—I crashed the window, to break up that tension. He would have killed you! So I—I threw a rock through the window."

"Thanks, Pats. Beat it now. For God's sake, beat it!"

He turned and climbed the steep grade. Ahead, quite a distance ahead now, Jagoe was lugging the satchel. Cardigan fought the upgrade grimly, and then Jagoe was at the top, making for the beginning of the wooden stairways and treacherous walks. As Cardigan reached the crest, he could hear Jagoe's feet pounding on the wooden boards.

FOUR

THE BERRIES

■

There was the crack of a gun and the nearer disturbance of lead splintering the wooden handrail. Cardigan bounded sidewise from the splinters, dropped to one knee as a second shot banged, and made the wooden rail jump. Then the rapping of heels began again, and Cardigan followed.

He could not clearly see Jagoe; sometimes he saw his fleeting image, more like a shadow, and so he held his fire, knowing that Jagoe had fired wildly, and close to him only by chance. House lights winked on the hill. Windows were flung open. And then back of him, above him, Cardigan heard other racing footsteps. That meant that the fighting at the stocky man's hide-out had broken up, and that some of them or all of them were now in on the chase.

By this time Cardigan was halfway down the long series of treacherous steps. The Bay was black beyond, with small lights moving across it. The wind was fresh, cold, and down below the long pier sheds bulked at the Bay's rim. The wind cleared up

Cardigan's head a bit, made him feel less nauseated. But behind him footsteps were pounding. Reckless, he gained on Jagoe.

And again Jagoe tried a shot. And then instantly from up and behind Cardigan another gun cracked twice. The wooden step directly to the rear of Cardigan's flying heels was splintered. He cursed and ducked as he ran. Jagoe fired and Cardigan felt a tug at his flying, empty sleeve.

Jagoe reached the bottom and was away, fleet-footed, and Cardigan landed fifty yards behind him and a bullet from above smacked the ground alongside him. Jagoe made for Embarcadero. He was stretching his legs, his coattails flying. The approach was dark. To shoot with even the smallest degree of accuracy was impossible. But then suddenly a truck swung round the corner and for a brief instant its headlights shone on Jagoe. He realized it and flung wildly to one side, but Cardigan fired. The truck speeded up, whanged out of sight.

Then it was dark again and Jagoe was running on, but not swiftly; his gait was something between a hop and skip and when Cardigan, pounding on, yelled, "Stop, Jagoe!" the man turned and desperately fired into the darkness. The shots were pretty wild; and then Cardigan, firing at the flash, heard Jagoe cry out, heard his body hit the pavement.

Cardigan ran up to him.

"I—I'm wounded, Cardigan," Jagoe panted.

"No! Are you?"

Cardigan reached down, yanked up the satchel. Footsteps were rapping toward him and a shot crashed out, and then Cardigan, gripping the satchel and the gun in his right hand, ran out. He came to an alley and ducked into it, plunged along in the darkness, hoping his pursuers would pass it up and go. But soon he came to a dead end—a high board fence, twice as tall as himself. He bumped against a large covered can and stepped up on it, but still the fence was too high and he had but one able arm.

A passing car momentarily illuminated the mouth of the alley, and he saw the silhouettes of two men there. He jumped from the top of the can, then turned on it, yanked off the cover. It was half full of old papers. Snapping open the satchel, he felt packet on packet of crisp bills. He drew a handful of papers from the can, then dumped into it the contents of the satchel. Into the satchel he shoved the papers, adding a few rocks which he found on the ground. He replaced the cover on the can.

Then he made his way up the alley and did not stop until he reached the mouth of it.

"I thought you went in there," said the stocky man politely. "You see, I know this neighborhood. Please hand over the bag."

Cardigan said, "You guys'll sweat for this."

"Him that laughs last laughs first," observed William. "You boin me up like I'd got nuts. You heard! Hand it over!"

Both William and the stocky man looked as though a cyclone had struck them. Their collars were torn, their clothing ripped, and there were welts and cuts on their faces.

Cardigan argued, "This is bloody money, muggs. It'll be the end of you. Use your heads. You can't get away with this—"

William hissed, "Here they come!"

The stocky man struck Cardigan on the head, ripped the bag free of Cardigan's hand. Stunned, a little groggy, Cardigan staggered backward. There was no wall to stop him and he wobbled into the alley, shook his head, cleared it a bit, and then went forward again. Two men went racing past the mouth of the alley.

"Get him—now!" one shouted.

"Right!"

A gun cracked.

Cardigan walked out into the street, looking after the running men, and called, "Hey!"

But they did not stop; they ran on, firing. Cardigan picked up his feet and followed.

"Mac!" he yelled.

One of them looked back.

"It's me—Cardigan!" Cardigan yelled. "Wait—"

"Hoss on you. Cardigan!"

"But I want to tell you—"

"Hire a hall, pal!"

Cardigan shouted, "You big dope, you!"

At this instant there was a spattering of shots and Cardigan flattened himself against a house wall. He saw what had happened. William and the stocky man had run into uniformed policemen and now they were cutting back and trying to cross the street. McGovern and Hunerkopf were heading them off.

From three points the guns spoke—loud, harsh. The echoes ripped and tore down the street, clattered among the buildings. William went down headfirst, his legs flying, and the stocky man, cornered, came to a dead stop, dropped his bag, and held up his hands.

Cardigan walked out in time to hear McGovern say, "Well, wiseguy," to the stocky man.

"I assure you," said the stocky man, "that I am beaten."

"Oh, yeah? Not yet, mister—not yet you ain't beaten."

"I'm afraid William is hurt very badly."

"You don't have to be afraid. Let him be."

The cops came up and sprayed their flashlights about, and one snapped, "Hey, you—who are you?"

"Me?" said Cardigan.

"I said you, didn't I?"

"Oh, him." McGovern laughed, picking up the satchel. "Why, he's my old friendly enemy Cardigan. Just came to town and started a branch for a detective agency. Nice guy, Cardigan. Him and me spat around a lot, but he's a good egg, ain't he, August?"

"He is a egg—I mean a good egg," said Hunerkopf.

McGovern was tickled. "Only he thinks he's a hard-boiled egg. He's really a fried egg, though, with a lot of ham thrown in. Boy, there's a good one for you! Hey, August?"

Hunerkopf was shaking with silent laughter. "You're a one, Mac. You are a one, all right, yes."

Cardigan said, "Tell me, Mac. How'd you get in on this?"

McGovern was in the best of humor now. "Well, I'll tell you, Cardigan. I had a tail on you, see? I seen you meet that little dame, and then drive along the Embarcadero. Me and Hunerkopf followed you, but kind of lost you on Telegraph Hill. But we were poking about when we seen you and the dame and two other guys in the street. We seen you go in the house with the guys.

"Well, we figured maybe you were tying up with some hoodlums in order to get a line on Jagoe. So we go around back and I get in with a passkey. Then William here pokes his head out of the room and I nab him. Before I know it there's a fight on my hands." He showed signs of the fight, with swollen jaw, a torn coat, and a dent in his derby. "In the dark we lay into each other, and because these muggs know their ground, they got the best of it. I was afraid to shoot account of I figured the little dame was in that room, too, keeping quiet. Then these guys get away and we tail 'em, and we find they're tailing somebody else, and up the street we find Jagoe on the sidewalk, who can't talk. But when I ask him about the dough he points, and I know these guys have it. And," he added, tapping the bag, "I got it. Sorry, Cardigan, old kid, old pal, old sock, but you're just too smalltime to put one over on Mr. McGovern. See? I get the dough, and I also get Jagoe. . . . August, go back there and take care of Jagoe and you"—to one of the cops—"call an ambulance."

Cardigan lit a cigarette. "Well, Mac, congratulations."

"Thanks, Cardigan. I always did like you, always will, and after this I guess you'll realize kind of that I'm a pretty good copper, up on my stuff."

"You're a lulu, Mac," Cardigan said, and walked off.

He entered the alley, went to the can in the rear, and using his small flashlight, emptied the can of the bills he had placed there. Then he pulled out a newspaper, laid it on the ground, stacked the bills evenly, and wrapped them in the newspaper. Around this bundle he strapped his tie, knotted it, and went to the mouth of the alley. He heard heavy footsteps, running, and placed the bundle just inside the alley. Looking out, he saw Hunerkopf coming down the sidewalk.

Cardigan stepped out and pretended to be idling along.

"What's the rush, August?"

"Jagoe! Jagoe ain't there anymore! Mac'll lose the pinch!"

"That's tough," Cardigan said.

He was puzzled. Doubtless Jagoe had regained sufficient strength to get up and stagger off. Hunerkopf ran on.

Cardigan recovered his bundle and walked down the Embarcadero until a cab came along. He boarded and said, "Hotel Galaty." He felt very tired. His arm pained him again, and his legs, his whole body ached. But when he thought of McGovern—good old friendly enemy McGovern—he laughed.

Walking into the lobby of the Hotel Galaty, he saw Pat sitting in one of the big leather chairs. She saw him at the same instant and rose, and there was a thankful light in her eyes; he saw rather than heard a long breath of relief flow from her lips.

His low voice was tired. "Well, Pats, I guess we've got the bacon and Mac is holding the bag."

"Oh, I'm just so glad you're back safe," she said. "You'll never learn—the way you go running about getting smashed up all the time." And then: "But I'm glad for your sake, chief, that you got the money back."

"When do you resign?" he said.

She flushed. "Oh—gosh—well, I guess I was just mad at the time. I didn't mean it."

"It was lucky you went home when I told you to, precious. It was a circus. Those guys were regular spendthrifts with their lead."

The red color on her face grew a little deeper. "B-but I didn't go home. I—well, I followed you up the hill. I saw all those men after you, and so I went, too. I was the last one and of course I couldn't make as good time, what with my high heels. But I went over and down Telegraph Hill, and then I found a man lying on the sidewalk, wounded—and then I recognized him as Jagoe. So I got a cab and took him to a hospital, and then I called up the police station *and* the newspapers and said that the Cosmos Agency had brought in Jagoe. D-did I do right, chief?"

"Did you do right!" he exclaimed.

He dropped into a chair, let the bundle drop, let his arm dangle to the floor.

"Patsy," he said, "you're the nuts."

Then he began laughing. He laughed so hard that veins stood out on his forehead.

"Now what?" Pat said.

"McGovern! I'm just thinking of McGovern!"

"Oh, you're a big silly. Both you and he are big sillies."

"Yeah, I know," Cardigan said, getting up, his laughter ebbing away. "But look at the fun we get . . . Just wait a minute, Pat."

He went to a house telephone and called the headwaiter. He said, "Have you any fresh razzberries? . . . Good. I'd appreciate it if you would send a box of fresh razzberries to Sergeant McGovern, police headquarters. And charge it to Cardigan."

KICK BACK

■

BY FREDERICK NEBEL

*When those chiseling insurance racketeers
crossed that big dick from Cosmos they
should have known better than to mix
murder with their game. A get-rich-quick
scheme is all right but a killing in cold
blood is something else again—and can
only end in a lead kick back!*

ONE

"SHOES"

∎

Cardigan, his suspenders looping down from his waist, his shirt off, came out of the improvised pantry of his California Street apartment crackling celery between his teeth and carrying a brace of Scotch highballs. He planked one of the drinks down on the table, still littered with a haphazard assortment of used dishes, and took a long, noisy swig at the other. Halfway through the pull, he lowered the drink, looked down at "Shoes" O'Riley, and shook his big head.

"Nix, Shoes," he said. "Uh-uh."

Shoes O'Riley looked melancholy. "Geez," his wistful voice said, as he reached absently for the drink.

"And lay off," Cardigan pursued, pointing with his glass, "this crap about the Irish should stick together, and this palsy-walsy stuff, and all this slop about my old lady knew your old lady when."

Shoes O'Riley took a drink, gulped, wagged his turnip head. "I guess I'm just a sort of a kind of failure. I'm just like whatcha might call the Forgotten Man."

"Forgotten, hell! There's not a cop in this town or ten other towns that'd ever forget that pan of yours. . . . Listen, you hopeless jailbird. I had one bad slam in this burg when Jagoe knocked off practically the first client the San Fran branch of the Cosmos had. I cleaned that up—but what the hell"—he hunched his shoulders—"the guy got knocked off and certain wiseacres I don't need to mention have since been calling us the Cosmetic Detective Agency. And then you pop up fresh from a two-year stretch for petty and want to become a private detective. You must think I'm nuts or something."

"What's that?" Shoes said, twisting his head around.

"What?"

"Scratchin' like."

Cardigan drank, said, "Rats. Cold weather drives them in."

Shoes took another drink, looking very sorrowful. "It's just like I want to turn over a new leaf kinda. I got a good heart, Jack. I don't mean no harm. Geez, this time I was wanderin' around in a joolry store and kind of absentminded like I pick up some jools to look at 'em just. I'm thinking about some gal give me the boudoir eye outside and then absentminded, like I said, I waltz out with the jools—not meanin' to, y'understand."

"Yeah. And about the stretch you did in Ohio State for slamming that night watchman on the conk with a hunk of lead pipe?"

"Geez, why'n't you set traps for them rats?"

"I'm talking about the Ohio State stretch."

"Oh, that. Well, it's me hard luck again. I go into this warehouse to get outta the rain and the cold, me on me uppers, and suddenly some strange guy I never seen before piles into me. Well, I think it's just an old hunk o' rubber hose I pick up, but it turns out to be a hunk o' lead pipe and—"

"It wasn't lead pipe, either, monkey. It was a blackjack."

"Oh," said Shoes, slightly surprised. "It was? Huh, I wonder how come I got hold of that. Now—let—me—think. . . ."

Cardigan walked across the room, rapped on the wall, as if to frighten away the rat, and said, pivoting, shaking his palms toward Shoes, "Nothing doing, kid. I split a T-bone with you tonight, gave you a couple of drinks, and I'll give you ten bucks as a pick-me-up. That's personal. But the Agency's something else. We'd have the cops and the press on our necks if we hired Shoes O'Riley. It's tough, baby, but that"—he spread his palms—"is the lay of the land."

"Ah," sighed Shoes, getting up. "I'm just a failure. I ain't no credit to me mother or nobody. I'm just a port without a ship—I mean a ship without—"

"Take this," Cardigan said, tossing a ten-spot to the table. "Buy yourself some flops with it. I'd hang around here with you tonight, but Bert Kine's on a job and I got to meet him at Powell and Bush in half an hour. I'm not Santa Claus, Shoes, but if you ever need a meal, buzz me and I'll stand you. Here's the office card."

"Thanks, Jack. Only back up there in the pen I was lookin' forward to bein' a private dick for a change. Me old woman always wanted me to go on the cops like me old man, and thinkin' about her and all— Well, that's life; there today, here tomorrer. Thanks for the chow, Jack. And I'd do somethin' about them rats. They're right by this door."

He put on his overcoat, a lumpy, misshapen figure, forty-odd, and opened the door. He jumped back with a short, hoarse outcry as a man's body, which evidently had been propped kneeling against the door, flopped at his feet, the head making a loud thump against the floor.

"M'gawd!" groaned Shoes.

"Look out," clipped Cardigan, thrusting him aside, dropping to his knees. He started to heave the body around, but stopped midway, and his jaw sagged. "Bert . . ." he muttered. His dark eyes flashed as he glared up at Shoes. "It's Bert Kine!"

"Hanh?"

"Bert—"

"It musta been him clawin' at the door and us thinkin' it was rats."

Cardigan, still kneeling, held the young blond man in his big arms. The blond head lay backward, the eyes wide open. Cardigan felt one of the wrists, then pushed his hand beneath the overcoat. Then he put his ear to the chest, listened. He laid Bert down, got up and went into the bathroom, returning with a mirror. He tried the mirror test. Then he shrugged, his big frame sagging, his eyebrows coming together sullenly, a humid wrath growing in his eyes. He was looking at Shoes, but not seeing him; though Shoes, gulping, retreated apprehensively.

Cardigan turned and scuffed his big feet to the telephone, stabbed sullenly at the instrument, and scooped it up. He called police headquarters, spoke in a thick, chopped voice, hung up. Shoes still eyed him apprehensively, as a man might eye some strange, dark piece of magic, uncertain as to what course it would take next.

But Cardigan no longer paid any attention to Shoes. He returned to the body, dropped to one knee. He mumbled thickly, "Hell, Bert, old sox," and his mouth was twisted in a half-angry, half-sickly grimace. Bert was so young—hardly more than a kid—and had come on fresh from New York only two weeks before. A guy Cardigan felt he could have trusted anywhere. "Hell, Bert. . . ."

Shoes ventured: "He was a kind of a sort of a pal?"

"Yeah," Cardigan muttered, "a kind of a sort of a."

"Geez," sympathized Shoes, genuinely, removing his hat and holding it piously in front of his chest.

There was a small, artificial rose in Bert's lapel, and Cardigan unpinned it and turned it round and round in his fingers. Just beneath the rose was a small strip of yellow paper with the words LA ROSA MEMORIAL HOME stamped on it.

Shoes pointed. "Looka, Jack. One of his hands is open and the other's kinda shut hard. I been noticin' that, but not wantin' to butt in. . . ."

Cardigan shoved the artificial rose into his pocket, leaned over and pried open Bert's hand. Tiny beads, the size of small peas, fell to the floor; and one by one Cardigan picked them up. They were made of glass. Nine of them. Some were dark red, some green, some blue. Cheap beads. He felt his heart pounding more slowly now within his chest. He rose, went to his desk, took out an envelope, and placed the nine beads and the artificial rose inside. There was a dark, sly, and thoughtful look in his eyes, and his thick wiry eyebrows were locked above his nose.

Then he started, said, "You, Shoes—you get the hell out of here! Go on, scram!"

"Hully gee, Jack—I ain't done nothin'!"

"Did I say you did anything? But breeze. The cops are coming. I can't afford to have you here and what's more you, just out of stir, can't afford to be here. Is that plain, Shoes, or do I have to draw a diagram?"

Shoes blinked. "I get you," he panted, nodding. "Them guys, you mean, might think—"

Cardigan took hold of Shoes's arm and marched him to the door. "Exactly."

Shoes was suddenly scared. He had no particular ill feeling for coppers, but the coppers usually did not like him. He reeled away from Cardigan and his lumpy, comical figure went hiking down the corridor. He took the stairway down, almost tripping twice, and rushed to the hall door. Opening it, he barged out into the misty winter rain, went down the stone stoop and, slipping, careened into a uniformed patrolman.

"Hey!" growled the policeman.

"Oh, excuse it please, mister."

The glow of a streetlight dripped through the rain, shining on the patrolman's black rubber coat, on the black visor of his cap. And Shoes, looking up, frightened stiff by the sight of buttons, a shield, gibbered, "I—I was just—so to speak kinda—"

"Hey, wait a minute—"

"So to speak—"

"Hanh?" drawled the copper, holding on fast. "I seen that mugg o' yours somewhere."

"In the movies, maybe. I was an actor oncet."

"Says you. Take it easy, bud—take it easy. I'm tryin' to think where I seen you—"

A black sedan drew up to the curb. Its rear door opened and Sergeant McGovern, plainclothed, stepped to the wet pavement and spat neatly at a fire plug, hitting it. Detective Hunerkopf, a roly-poly man with a rubicund face, stepped out next.

McGovern said in a tough, forghorn voice, "What's this?"

"I'm Sleary," said the copper.

"Yeah? And who's this potato?"

"I'm tryin' to think. He came bustin' out o' that house there, piled into me, and began talkin' like he had marbles in his mouth."

McGovern, a bony, lean man with a jaw like the bow of a tugboat, bent a ferocious glare on Shoes. "You got marbles?"

"No. Honest, Officer—"

"Cram it. Hold up your kisser . . . M'm." He jammed his hands on his hips. "Shoes O'Riley, huh?"

Shoes tried to get off a friendly laugh. "Well, well, Sarge. I—uh—that is—well, how's things?"

"I'll take care of him," McGovern said to the patrolman, and he grabbed hold of Shoes's arm.

The man from the medical office arrived in a flivver coupe and stepped out with his little black bag. "Hello, Mac," he said. "Looks like rain, eh?"

"What I was thinking."

Hunerkopf held out his hand, said placidly, "Yup, it's raining out all right."

"Up here," McGovern said, and, hauling Shoes with him, led the way into the bow-windowed house.

Cardigan had not closed the door. He stood in the center of the room, his trousers hung low on his hips, the cuffs doubling on his shoes. He was taking a drink, his chin down and his dark eyes looking up from beneath his brows at the doorway. McGovern came hustling Shoes in through the doorway, took one look at the body on the floor, one look at Cardigan, and then sent Shoes spinning into the nearest armchair. The man from the medical office strode in briskly, brightly, dropped a smile of clinical delight toward the body on the floor, and promptly knelt to his business. Hunerkopf wandered in placidly humming "Ach, Du Lieber Augustin," and, looking dolefully at the corpse, made his way to the kitchenette, still humming.

"So it's you," McGovern said to Cardigan.

"Yeah, me."

"And the stiff?"

"Bert Kine—a new operative of mine."

"Was," said the man from the medical office, brightly.

"Split hairs; go ahead, split hairs," Cardigan said.

"So," said McGovern, grinning his hard tight grin, expanding his chest, "the Cosmetic Agency is in the limelight again, and good old McGovern lands smack into it. Well, what happened?"

"I was sitting here and I heard a scratching at the door, and when I opened the door Bert fell in. He was dead when I opened the door. Must have tried to get here and tell me something."

"What do you guess?"

"I can't guess anything."

McGovern laughed. His eyes gleamed and he jerked his chin

toward Shoes, who sat crouched in the chair, his face gray-white, his eyes round with suspense. "Take a good look at Little Boy Blue here. I tell you, Cardigan, I'm always on the job. I pick him up outside. Shoes O'Riley's his name. He's just done a stretch. A dead guy up here, and Shoes O'Riley cramming out of the hall door into a copper's gentle arms. Ain't it beautiful?"

"It sounds swell. Now what?"

McGovern stopped smiling and turned a ferocious dark look at Shoes. He snapped, "Well, so what?"

"Ugh—hanh?"

"What were you doing in here?"

Shoes gulped, flicked a half-look at Cardigan, stammered on. "Well, you see, me shoelace got undid, and I was walkin' along, trippin' over it. I stop outside and try to tie it, but me paws is too cold. So I see the hall downstairs, with a light and all, and I slip in and warm me hands on a radiator, and then I can tie me shoelace. Then I fall down the steps goin' out and—"

McGovern held his ears, made a face. "My God, how you think 'em up, I don't know!"

Hunerkopf appeared in the pantry doorway. "Hello, Cardigan. You got any apples?"

Cardigan scowled at him. "No."

"Any grapes?"

"No."

"Bananas?"

"No!"

Hunerkopf looked crestfallen. "I could go a fig, if you got a fig around."

Cardigan's face seemed to bloat redly with repressed anger, and he quickly took a swig of Scotch.

"Knifed," said the man from the medical office. "He hasn't been dead long."

McGovern spun, knelt, and rifled Bert's pockets. "Don't this guy carry any dough?"

"I advanced him fifteen this afternoon."

"Well, he's got none now."

McGovern shot upright, pivoted, made a beeline across the room, and yanked Shoes out of the chair. From one of Shoes's pockets he withdrew a ten-dollar bill. It was folded. McGovern unfolded the bill and a Cosmos Agency card slipped into his other hand. His eyes suddenly blazed.

"You dirty, lousy piker!" he snarled at Shoes. He laid the hard knuckles of his hand across Shoes's face and Shoes smashed backward into the armchair, fright stark on his face.

Cardigan licked his lips. Shoes had tried to use his head when he fabricated that story about the shoelace; Shoes had not wanted to tell McGovern that he'd been in Cardigan's rooms. Cardigan's hands closed tightly in his pockets.

McGovern was still red with rage. He snarled again at Shoes, "Where's the knife you cut him up with?"

"I d-didn't cut nobody—"

"Shut up! What the hell were you doing in the hall?"

"Like I said—"

"Like you said!" grated McGovern. "Listen, you mutt-faced punk. If you spring that bughouse fable again about shoelaces, I'll go out of my mind. Like that time you were found in a guy's car, driving it through the Presidio. Telling us it was a new make of car you wanted to see how it run, so maybe you could buy one for your sister-in-law back East. Listen—" He hauled Shoes out of the chair again, pointed to the body on the floor. "You killed that guy."

"Me? N-no, Sarge. Honest—"

McGovern smashed him back into the chair again.

"You see?" McGovern flung at Cardigan. And then his chest swelled up again. "Guess it kind of makes you feel low, huh? I mean, me walking right in and copping a suspect right under your nose. Why'n't you laugh it off, huh?"

Cardigan was brave, thoughtful. "I don't feel like laughing, Mac. I'm looking at Bert."

"Well," McGovern went on, "this is open and shut anyhow. I'll take Shoes over and maybe we'll have to slam him up all night, but he'll come through. Get up, punk."

Shoes stood up, looking very desolate, very resigned.

Cardigan lips tightened. "Hold on, Mac."

"Go ahead. I can listen."

"As usual, you're screw-loose. Shoes didn't do it."

"Trying to pull a fast one?"

"I don't have to—on you. The slow ones work plenty." He

shook his head. "Shoes didn't do it. Shoes had dinner here with me tonight. He was in here for two hours before Bert fell through the door. Shoes got the ten-spot and the Agency card from me."

McGovern scowled, his eyes narrowing, becoming very bright, hard, and suspicious.

Cardigan said, "You gave me the horselaugh too soon, Mac. Too soon."

"You're lying!" McGovern snapped.

"Why the hell should I be lying when an operative of mine is dead on the floor there?"

McGovern reddened, looked cornered, stung with chagrin. His eyes danced, but not happily. He shot out, "One of your big jokes again, huh?"

"No. I just happened to know Shoes when he was a kid and I don't want to see you guys play kick-the-wicket with him. He was here—for two hours. I'll swear to that, so don't make a monkey out of yourself by making a collar here."

"Who did kill him then?"

Cardigan smiled ruefully. "You go your way, Mac, and I'll go mine."

McGovern gnawed on his lip. His eyes glittered. "Wiseguy now, huh?" He leveled an arm at Cardigan. "Cardigan, the big shot of the Agency, consorting with criminals like Shoes O'Riley! Okay, big boy. Go your way. Go it. But this is going to finish you in this city, fella. Wash you up! Okay!"

Hunerkopf yawned, took a polite but not very intense interest in the goings-on.

"Call the morgue bus, August," McGovern growled.

Hunerkopf did; adding, "And listen, Mike. Tell Louie to pick up a couple of apples on the way. . . . Yeah, apples. No oranges, account of I always swallow the pits."

TWO

BLOOD ON THE ROSE

■

The Hotel Citadel stood in the shadow of the St. Francis, around the corner from Union Square. The Citadel was small, decent, with a decorous gray front and a rectangular lobby hung with pictures of the redwood forests, Yosemite, and Half Moon Bay. Cardigan's noisy entry broke up the quietude of the lobby. He bore down on the desk, his big feet smacking the tiles, his battered hat crushed low on his forehead, and all the buttons of his shabby ulster fastened in the wrong buttonholes.

The ancient, parchment-faced clerk was adding a column of figures and the boisterous arrival of Cardigan did not rouse him. He merely looked up, counting to himself, then looked down again and ran his pencil up and down the column. Cardigan shifted impatiently from foot to foot, started to speak several times. Finally he reached over, took paper and pencil from the clerk, bent, and calculated rapidly, dashing off the total in large numbers.

"One hundred sixteen dollars and ninety-nine cents," he said, reversing the sheet of paper, tucking the pencil in the astounded man's breast pocket. "And now," he said, "please ring Miss Seaward and tell her Mr. Cardigan is down here."

The man fled to the small switchboard and, with an astounded glance still dwelling on Cardigan, telephoned Pat's room. Taking out the plug, he said, "Miss Seaward will be down directly."

"Thanks," said Cardigan, and swiveled away.

Pat came out of the elevator a couple of minutes later. She looked small, neat, trim in a brown suit and a short fur coat, high-collared, open now in front. A small round hat, Russian in manner, seemed to ride capriciously on one smartly penciled eyebrow. She saw Cardigan standing in the lobby as if he owned it. There was a worried look on her face.

"Hello, Pats," he said, turning. "Bert got knocked off."

She almost stumbled, the news hit her so hard. Her fingers flew to her lips and through them she said, wide-eyed, "Oh, chief! Oh . . ." She was suddenly at a loss for words, her pretty lips parted and her round eyes searching Cardigan's face anxiously.

"Yeah," Cardigan muttered. "Yeah." He stood tapping one foot and shooting squint-eyed, vindictive glances about the higher regions of the lobby, as though Bert's killer might be hiding up there somewhere. "Knifed. He tried to make my place. Maybe he didn't think he was hurt as bad as he was. Probably figured on coming there, telling me something, and then getting a doctor there."

Pat touched his arm, grimaced. "I know you thought so much of him, chief. Oh, it's awful, miserable, terrible."

He slapped his big hand on hers, gripped it, and led her over to one of the divans. Tears in her eyes, she unbuttoned his overcoat and then rebuttoned it properly.

"You never do it right," she squeaked.

He muttered, "Don't let it get you down, Pat. You go on bawling here and for all I know I may, too. So cut it out. . . . You had dinner with Bert, didn't you?"

She nodded, sniffling behind her handkerchief. "Then I came right back."

"What time'd you leave him?"

"Seven-thirty—at Powell and Market. He said he was going to drop by the office a minute and then meet you later. He'd left his office key at the hotel, so I lent him mine."

Cardigan had his eyes fixed on space. "He turned up—dead—at

my place at eight-forty. He was stuck between seven-thirty and eight-forty. He was working on the Detronius case—Lou Detronius. We were to go over data tonight at my place. He went to the office to pick up those briefs. Poor Bert!"

He stood up. "Come on; let's chase over to the office."

They got in a cab outside and it was only a ride of five minutes through the rain to the Agency office in Market Street. The building was a walk-up, and the office was on the third floor. Cardigan unlocked the door, reached in and turned on the lights.

"Pike this," he said. "Pike it."

"Goodness!"

Steel filing cabinets had been rifled and sheafs of paper lay on the floor of the outer office. Desk drawers were open. In the back office—Cardigan's—the drawers of his desk stood open also.

Pat said in a hushed voice, "They must have fought here."

"Uh-uh," Cardigan said, shaking his head. "No signs of a struggle here, chicken. Chairs in order, nothing knocked over or even off the desks. They didn't fight here. That took place elsewhere. Look at this," he said. "Telephone wires cut." He strode back to the outer office, knelt, and began running through the scattered files. "The Detronius papers are gone," he said, and stood up.

"Let's see," Pat spoke up. "The Detronius case is the one—"

"Fake insurance, we think. Anyhow, the Underwriters' Committee thinks so. Like this. The Laborers' Welfare Guild, so-called, was organized by this Greek, Lou Detronius. Not a labor union or anything like that. It was, as a matter of fact, a labor union that finally brought it to the attention of the Underwriters' Committee. The line went this way: a laborer was approached, shown a lot of fancy literature, and told that for five bucks a year he'd get a tin button, addresses of correspondents, and that if he died by accident his family would get five hundred bucks. Well, the gag goes on like this. A number of families have got the five hundred bucks, see? But it was worked this way. The Guild took out a number of accident policies on these guys, some of the policies totaling as much as five thousand bucks each. But the family still got only five hundred. Well, that was okay. If the Guild took out the policies payable to itself and paid the premiums, which it did, you can't kick back at them. But here's the rub. Quite a number of these insured laborers have accidentally died during the past year. Some here, some in Los Angeles, Denver, San Diego, Seattle, and so on. The one two weeks ago—a guy named Rico—took place here. Drowned, ostensibly, after a fall from Fisherman's Wharf one dark and stormy night. Had a bump on his head. Verdict was that in falling over he struck his head on the side of one of the boats. He was drunk. Thing is, chicken, did he—and the other guys—die accidentally, or were they pushed?

"We had a lot of data on the Guild, picked up here and there from relatives of some of the guys that died. Pike it. It's gone. It wasn't worth a hell of a lot anyhow, since what's needed is the goods on these guys—red-handed. Not data or ideas—but the goods. That's how and why we're in it. The mugs must have figured we knew more than we actually did—and crashed the office."

"But Bert—"

Cardigan wagged his shaggy head, scowled. "I don't know. He must have followed them and got jammed up."

"And to think," she cried, "poor Bert had to die for nothing. The ones that killed him—well, it would be like finding, or trying to find, the needle in a haystack."

"I like," said Cardigan, looking angrily about the littered floor, "to look for needles in haystacks."

She pointed. "They even wiped up their wet footsteps. You can see where the floor's been wiped. Which means they wiped away fingerprints, too."

"You've got eyes in your head, honeybun."

He idly reached across the desk, among the papers, and closed an inked rubber-stamp pad, while Pat said, "Should I call the police?"

"Uh-uh," he muttered, shaking his head. "I'll have enough trouble dodging Mac as it is, without inviting him in."

"Oh, chief, I wish you and McGovern would stop it. Fighting all the time. One always trying to cut the other's throat."

"It's only in fun, kitten. Mac's a good egg—a little on the fried side, or maybe the scrambled—but still a good egg. . . . We'll clean the office up tomorrow. Come on."

"Where?"

* * *

Market Street is the broadest thoroughfare in the world. Pat and Cardigan crossed it in the drizzle—crossed the four lanes of trolley tracks, dodging traffic. The traffic was thick, noisy, and fast, and lights blazed up and down the street, crowds jammed in front of theaters; one crowd was pushing into a small store where jewelry was being auctioned off.

Shouldering his way through this jam—it bulged out to the curb—and making a path for Pat, Cardigan ran smack into Shoes O'Riley, and Shoes said, "If it ain't Cardigan again—Jack, old boy, old boy!"

"You're mistaken. My name is Smith."

"Yeah." Shoes grinned, falling in step beside him. "I'm the Prince o' Wales, too—Oh, excuse it; I didn't see the lady right off." He lifted his hat, revealing his turnip head.

"This," said Cardigan to Pat, "is an old college chum by the name of Shoes O'Riley. He got that name because he always would rather spend dough on new shoes than a square meal."

"Yup," said Shoes. "A man's character is told by the shoes he wears. Look, Jack: with them ten bucks you give me I bought me a new pair. Like 'em?"

"Try getting another ten sometime, baby. Go on, scram, Shoes. Beat it. I told you not to be hanging around me."

Shoes grinned. "Geez, I forgot again." He stopped, saluted. "So long, Jack. Be seein' you."

In the next block, Cardigan stopped before a plain-looking young woman who was selling paper roses in front of a movie house. He gave her a quarter, received the rose, and looked at it. It bore a small ribbon on which was inscribed LA ROSA MEMORIAL HOME.

"How many of you are working on this tonight?"

"Six of us."

"When did you six come on?"

"At four this afternoon."

Cardigan dropped his voice. "Mind telling me where the other five are stationed. Do you know?"

"Yes, because each night we rotate."

He took out a pencil, used the back of an old envelope. As she told him the points where the others were stationed, he wrote them down. Then he and Pat walked on and stopped beneath a streetlight, where he peered down at the addresses. Pat got up on her toes, peered past his arm.

He crossed the first address off, saying, "That's another theater. I don't think that'd do it. Nor the next. This is in front of the Mark Hopkins. Now this one—this is in front of the Casa Domingo. That might do. And this one—the Golden Boot—is a Russian restaurant. I don't think so. This one's at the railway station, of course. Nix on that."

"What do you mean?"

"Come on. See if I mean anything. We'll try the Casa Domingo. Grab a Powell Street cable car."

The cable car hauled them slowly up Powell Street past the St. Francis. Beyond, the hill became steeper, with Union Square far below. The car went over the hump, then headed for a dark, outlying district. Cardigan and Pat got off at a dimly lighted plaza. Dark buildings rose in the cold drizzle. On the other side of the plaza, an electric sign winked—CASA DOMINGO. It was the only electric sign on the plaza. They crossed toward it, reached the sidewalk, and walked along beside a high board fence. A couple of cabs were parked outside the Domingo. A young woman, plainly dressed, was walking up and down. She carried a small basket of paper roses. A liveried doorman stood beneath the red canvas marquee.

Cardigan said to the young woman, "Sell many of those tonight?"

"Oh, a few."

"What do you do, get the taxis as they arrive?"

She smiled good-naturedly. "I try to."

"Remember selling one to a guy a little shorter than me. He had yellow hair and a small yellow mustache and wore a big tan trench coat and a derby. He probably smiled. Had a swell smile, lot of teeth. Young guy. Maybe it was about eight o'clock."

"I seem to remember— Let me think . . . Do you know if he had a trick of tossing a coin in the air and catching it behind his back? Because I seem to—"

"That's him," Cardigan chopped in. "Did he go in here?"

"Yes."

"Did you see him come out?"

"I—don't think so. Of course, he may have."

"Thanks."

Cardigan and Pat went into the Casa Domingo. The foyer was hung with dark red drapes touched up with gold brocade. The girl who took Cardigan's hat and coat was small, plump, dark, and wore a Spanish comb in her hair, a Spanish shawl. The man who met Pat and Cardigan at the entrance to the dining-and-dancing room wore black velvet trousers, high-heeled boots, and a short red jacket with gold cuffs. There was a rhumba orchestra, small shaded table lamps, more red-and-gold drapes. The place was pretty noisy though only half full. Pat and Cardigan sat down at a table alongside the wall and Cardigan ordered a couple of highballs.

"And the boss," he added.

"Who?"

"The guy runs this place."

"Mr. Delbanca?"

"If he's the boss."

A few minutes later a large, elegantly dressed dark man bore down on the table, bowed stiffly from the waist. Cardigan, lighting a cigarette, squinted up at him.

"Sit down, Mr. Delbanca."

Delbanca, looking politely curious, sat down. His hands were plump, pale, and there were rings on them. His hair was thick, black; it began low on his forehead and went over the top of his head in beautiful waves.

Cardigan said, "A man came in here about eight tonight and turned up later, elsewhere, at eight forty-five."

Delbanca put his hands gently together, nodded, but curiously. "And so meester?"

"So he turned up, I mean, dead."

The liquid-black eyes of Delbanca steadied on Cardigan. "Say, meester," he said slowly, liquidly, "is this a zhoke?"

"What do you think?"

"I think she's a zhoke, meester."

"Dead guys are jokes, huh?"

"No, meester. Just the way you tell her, meester."

Cardigan went on. "This fellow followed somebody else here— maybe two guys."

Delbanca laughed unhurriedly, good-naturedly. "Meester, what you think for kind of hombre I am? Look around. I got wan big place here, hey? Lots of over'ead, hey? What you think, meester, this she's a clip joint?'' He shook his head slowly. ''See, I'm sorry your frand he turns up d'ad, but''—he shrugged—''your frand he do not get d'ad in Casa Domingo. Tha's on the op-and-op, meester, for sure, meester. You want, go gat the police. I'm no' 'fraid. Me, I'm on the op-and-op, meester.'' He rose, bowed, smiled. ''So sorry, meester.''

Cardigan did not try to detain him, and Delbanca walked off calmly, slowly.

''So what?'' Pat asked.

''The guy looks okay to me, chicken. Somebody's goofy and maybe it's me. But Bert wouldn't have come here for the show.'' He rose. ''You stay here a while.''

He made a casual tour of the entire place, but did not enter the door leading to the talent's dressing rooms. When he came back, he sat down and spoke with Pat quietly for five minutes. And ten minutes later Pat rose, circulated, went to the rear and, while the orchestra was playing loudly, opened the door Cardigan had not opened and found herself in a short corridor which opened into a large, gaudy room alive with the chatter of a dozen-odd girls in tights.

Pat assumed a fatigued attitude, a slightly, casually hard-boiled manner. ''Hello, girlfriends. I'm looking around. I'm from the press . . . human interest stuff.''

''Sister,'' said a redhead, ''we're both human and interesting. What do you want to know? I've got a past that would put Pompadour to shame.''

''Who's Francesca Durango?''

''See?'' said the redhead to the others, ''By human interest she means the star. We're just the goils in the street. Francesca?'' She pointed rearward. ''Down at the end of that passage, lady. Door on the left. She goes on in a minute. In fact—''

At this moment a tall, jet-eyed girl swept out of the corridor. She carried her chin high and her long Spanish skirt corkscrewed effectively about her legs. She noticed no one, but went on out.

''That's her,'' the redhead said.

''I'll wait,'' said Pat.

In a little while the other girls filed out, and Pat slipped down the corridor, into Francesca's room. In a moment she reappeared and made her way back to Cardigan's table.

She nodded gravely. "Yes," she said.

"That's all I want to know. Which one?"

"The star—Francesca Durango."

"I could go for her myself. And not in a small way."

Pat said, "There's a window in her room overlooking a yard or court, I could not tell which. Except that it's easy to get to, or from. I—I unlatched the window, thinking you might—"

"Pats, you always think of things. Come on."

They went out to the foyer, where Cardigan put on his hat and overcoat. Then they went out into the cold drizzle and walked till they came up alongside the high board fence.

He said, "From now the evening's yours, kid. Grab a cable car and go home."

"But, chief—"

"Mind your uncle now. Scram. The night air's bad for little girls. Besides"—he nodded upward—"you couldn't hop this fence anyhow. Git along, little dogie, git along, git along. Shoo."

When she had gone, Cardigan reached up, jumped, and caught hold of the top of the fence, hauled himself up and then swung over, landing in short, wet grass. Through the drizzle and the dark he could see several lighted windows of the Casa Domingo, and he heard the muffled beat of the orchestra.

T H R E E

GLASS BEADS

■

Weeds grew along the way he went, and there were the ruins of an old foundation into which he almost fell. Mounds of rocky earth rose from the weeds. There were little puddles and his big feet splashed in them. He came at last to a low window in the rear of the building. The windowsill was level with his chest, and inside the room he saw Francesca, in black tights. He thought she looked pretty swell. He stood there, waiting, for twenty minutes—until Francesca, wearing another costume now, left the room. Then he opened the window, stood on his toes to push it all the way up. He had little difficulty getting in, and closing the window, he stood listening. The rhythm of the rhumba band pulsed in the walls, the floor.

Across the room was a large alcove, lighted, with a highboy in it. Hanging across the alcove doorway was a bead curtain—long strings of beads of many colors; glass beads, quite small, suspended from a rod, almost touched the floor. Cardigan crossed to this bead curtain. Something crackled beneath his feet. He looked down. His feet had crushed several beads on the floor. He looked up and saw that one of the strings was broken. When he took the beads from the envelope he carried, he saw they were of a size identical with those hanging before him.

The room was rich with the smells of perfume and powder, and there were photographs of Francesca, many photographs, many poses. Cardigan unbuttoned his overcoat, shoved his hat back on his head. He lit a cigarette and leaned back against a steam radiator, his ankles crossed.

When Francesca burst in, flushed from her dance, Cardigan said offhand, "Hello, Francesca."

She had slammed the door before she was aware of his presence, and now she was brought up short, a handsome figure of a girl, her breath stifled in her throat.

"Who are you?" she demanded.

"Clark Gable."

"*Pfft!* You are not Clark Gable!"

"All right, I'm not Clark Gable. And *pfft* back at you, good-looking."

"I weel call a policeman!"

He growled scowling, "Take your hand off that door, Francesca. Take it off!" He went toward her, lowering. "Nobody's going to hurt you, girlie. And don't yip. Keep quiet. Low voice, see?"

"This," she complained. "is an embarrassment, *señor.*"

"It shouldn't be—if you act nice. Look here, Francesca. There was a guy in this room at about eight or so tonight. A young guy. Blonde. Pal of mine. He got a knife in his guts, *sabe*?"

The color on her tawny cheeks was very high. Her lovely dark eyes were very round, and from her body drifted a faint perfume. Cardigan saw her full red lips tighten. Black fire flashed from her eyes.

"What is this you talk?" she demanded in her thick liquid accent.

There was a knock on the door, and spinning, Francesca opened it and Delbanca strolled in saying, in Spanish, "Francesca, the new dance is a thing of rare beauty—" And then seeing Cardigan, he stopped. He smiled, almost affectionately, and his heavy eyelids drooped.

"Meester, you have what you call magic, hey? First here, then there." And to Francesca, "This wan a frand of yours?"

Tight-lipped, she shook her head violently; then snapped, "He is certainly most not, *señor.*"

Delbanca's face seemed to become very drowsy, and his soft voice drawled, "You no want him in here, hey?"

She shook her head, again violently.

"Meester," said Delbanca, "this is no zhoke, meester. You weel please to take the air."

Cardigan took two long strides; they brought him face-to-face with Delbanca.

"You look like a nice egg, Delbanca, and maybe you are. If you think I take the air when every Tom, Dick, and Harry tells me to, you're behind in your lessons. Understand this, *amigos,* a pal of mine tailed somebody here. I know he came in your place. He was knifed. When I found him, he was gripping some beads in his hand." He pointed toward the alcove. "See that? One of those strings was broken recently. I even crushed some beads on the floor. Well, the beads my pal had in his hand were the same as those over there. He grabbed at that curtain, either ducking out of the way or when he was knifed, and broke one of the strings!"

Francesca put hands to her cheeks. "No!" she cried in a low terrified voice.

Delbanca went across, fingered the bead curtain. A couple of beads crackled beneath his foot. He looked down. Then he looked at the curtain again. Then he turned and looked at Francesca; from Francesca to Cardigan.

"No! No!" Francesca cried. "I swear I did no' see any man keeled in here. Oh, I swear it!"

Delbanca looked at her a long time. She shrank from his drowsy speculative gaze. She whimpered. Presently he went to her, took hold of her hand, patted it. Then turned to Cardigan.

"Meester, you come with me, hey? This becomes now no zhoke. We talk, eh?"

"After you, Delbanca."

Cardigan went with Delbanca to the latter's office. Delbanca put on a white silk scarf, a blue chesterfield, and a derby. He took a stick and gloves.

"Come, meester. We go what you call places."

Cardigan stepped in front of him. "What kind of a runaround are you trying to hand me?"

"Meester, this is no runabout; she is serious business. We take a taxi."

They rode away from the front of the Casa Domingo, and Delbanca, producing two fat cigars, gave Cardigan one, slipped one in his own mouth, and held up a light. It was an excellent cigar, Cardigan found. But he kept his hand near the lapel of his coat, primed to dive for the gun in his spring holster. He watched Delbanca out of the corners of his eyes.

On the slope of Russian Hill, Delbanca told the driver to stop. He paid the fare, spun his stick, leveled it off, saying, "We go this way, meester."

He looked up into the cold, dripping drizzle. "She is not a good night out, hey. We will drop by and see this frands." He motioned to a doorway and led Cardigan into the broad foyer of an apartment house. He told the elevator operator to take them to the fourth floor, and at the fourth floor they got out and Delbanca, benign, gently smiling, led the way down a warm, rich corridor.

He knocked on a door and presently the door was opened by a short, squat man in black tie and black alpaca coat.

Delbanca spun his stick. "Meester Delbanca and a frand calling on Meester Detronius."

The houseman blinked stolidly. "Sure. I'll tell him."

A moment later a voice called, "Come in, Delbanca!" and then the houseman appeared to take their coats, but Delbanca, smiling politely, shook his head.

Cardigan, startled, confounded, followed Delbanca through the doorway. They came out on a balcony overlooking a long living room where mellow pools of light lay, where cigars glowed, and several men sat.

"Yes, yes, Delbanca, my good friend, come right in. It's jolly good to see you!"

Detronius stood now in one of the pools of light, beckoning Delbanca down. He was a very small man, with a white baby face and a tiny, pointed mustache; dancing, happy eyes. He wore a tuxedo. Delbanca, going comfortably down the stairs, smiled in his slow, benign way.

Cardigan, a couple of steps behind, was again startled when he saw McGovern stroll into one of the pools of light. And then he saw Hunerkopf sitting in the largest armchair, with his feet toward the fireplace and a huge basket of fruit in his lap. When Cardigan came into the light, McGovern recognized him and looked blank for a moment.

"This, meester," said Delbanca to Detronius, "is Meester Cardigan."

Detronius's merry eyes danced; his chubby, babylike cheeks bunched up as his mouth widened in a bright, cheery grin. "So glad to know you, Mr. Cardigan. Over here . . . Sergeant McGovern and Detective Hunerkopf, of the police."

Delbanca's eyes strayed, though he still smiled; but he was a little puzzled. He said, "I be happy to meet you, yes."

McGovern held a notebook in his hand.

"You see," said Detronius, "Sergeant McGovern just dropped in for my contribution pledge to the fund for Patrolman Schmidt's family. Poor Schmidt was, you know, killed in line of duty. Pity, pity. Will you gentlemen have a drink?"

"Please, for me, no," said Delbanca. "You are busy with business now and so, meester, sometime again I see you. She is no great hurry." He lifted his head, smiled. "Very glad seeing you, gentlemens," he said to McGovern and Hunerkopf.

And Hunerkopf said affably, "Take an apple along."

"Please, for me, no."

Detronius shook Cardigan's hand zestfully. "So mighty glad to have met you, sir. I do hope we'll meet again."

Cardigan did not smile. His face was heavy, his eyes dull. "Yeah," he muttered. "Yeah." He was puzzled, and he could see by the look on McGovern's face that he also was puzzled.

Then McGovern snapped his notebook shut. "Well, I got to get along, anyhow," he said. "Thanks for the pledge, Mr. Detronius. August, come on."

"But don't hurry," urged Detronius.

"Thanks, but I got to." McGovern had fixed a sidelong, suspicious stare on Cardigan.

Hunerkopf filled his pockets with fruit, and passing Cardigan, he said sorrowfully, "Someday you'll prob'ly regret you didn't eat more fruit. Mark my word, old fellow. Well, well, I guess we all live and learn. Thanks very much for the refreshments," he said to Detronius.

The two detectives went out.

"Maybe now," said Delbanca, "we do not have to make so

much hurry." He smiled wistfully, leaned on his walking stick, laid his soft, sad eyes on Detronius. "There has been maybe wan big zhoke, but me, meester, I guess I have no' the sense of humor."

"Ah, yes you have!" Detronius laughed gayly. "Do remove your coats, gentlemen. Do! Perhaps I can offer you some wine——"

The buzzer sounded and in a moment Francesca rushed into the room, her face flushed, her breath coming in quick gasps. Her black eyes were bright with anguish and fear, and seeing Delbanca and Cardigan, she was momentarily stunned. Detronius bit into his lip.

"Francesca!" he said, starting toward her.

Delbanca stopped him with a hand. "Meester, this zhoke I speak of is no zhoke, not so much."

Francesca broke into tears.

"Do not cry, *muchacha*," said Delbanca; and to Detronius, "Me, meester, I have been very hospitable with you at Casa Domingo, and I do not like much the big zhoke. Tonight you were in Francesca's room at Casa Domingo. For dinner you came to Casa Domingo. The show she was not start yet, and only Francesca was there. So you go to her room. By and by, soon, two frands from you come in and I say you are with Francesca, you are her frand, and they go back to the room. Francesca comes out and sings wan song, but you and these frands are back in the room. Meester Cardigan says a frand from him goes to Casa Domingo, too, but I do not see him. It appears this frand also was in Francesca's room, but she does not see him because then she is sing the song. This frand, meester, is now d'ad, I am told. Therefore it is no' the big zhoke."

Detronius laughed. "Ridiculous! Preposterous!" He turned on his heel and started away.

"Pull up," Cardigan snapped, and his gun came out in his big hand, he looked now very dark and sinister. "Pull up, Detronius, and watch your step."

Detronius turned, smiled lightly. "Lovely guests, I must say."

"Who the hell said I was a guest? . . . Delbanca, Francesca, you'd better bail out of this. Go on, beat it. I'm dragging the Greek over to headquarters."

Francesca was gripping Delbanca's arm desperately. "Emilio, I am so much afraid! I am——"

"Do not be, Francesca."

Detronius's eyes were dancing, but not happily. "My dear fellow—"

"I'm not a dear fellow," Cardigan rasped. "And never mind getting your hat or overcoat. If you catch cold and die, that'll be swell. Come on, lift your dogs, sweetheart. We're scramming."

Detronius still chose to hesitate. Cardigan bore down on him, grabbed him by the arm, and whipped him toward the stairway. Delbanca and Francesca were already on the balcony. The four of them went toward the doorway. The houseman looked scared. He cleared out of the way.

"This is an indignity," Detronius complained.

"Swell," said Cardigan. "I'm glad it is."

Francesca was crying in her handkerchief as they went down in the elevator and Delbanca held her hand, patted it gently, murmured soothing words in Spanish.

Cardigan marched Detronius across the lobby—so fast that the Greek almost skipped.

It was still raining in the street, and as they went out, Cardigan saw McGovern and Hunerkopf, with Shoes O'Riley between them. Shoes looked very uncomfortable.

"Yeah," McGovern brayed, "I come down and find your pal waiting in the lobby. Imagine! You, the big cheese in the Cosmos Agency, consorting with criminals!"

"See," said Shoes. "A poor guy can't ever live down his past. Me, that never had a evil thought—"

"Stow it!" McGovern rasped.

"I wouldn't yell so loud," Hunerkopf suggested, "account of it's late and you might wake up the neighbors."

"You shut up, too, August!"

Four men came walking across the street from a parked sedan, and one, a tall man in a gray belted raincoat, clipped, "First guy moves, things happen to him. Okay, put 'em up and hold 'em there."

F O U R

BANANA OIL

■

McGovern spun, bumping against Cardigan's gun. Hunerkopf, about to eat a banana he had just peeled, dropped it. Delbanca pushed Francesca behind him, and Shoes O'Riley's mouth gaped in surprise. All of them stood out in clear relief beneath the lighted marquee of the apartment house. The four men reaching the curb, were still in darkness, but their guns gave off liquid glints.

"What is it, Lou?" the gray-coated young man said.

"A pinch," said Detronius.

"You?"

"Yes."

"Okay, Lou. Go over and sit in the car."

"Thanks."

McGovern brayed, "You lousy clucks, I'm McGovern!"

"What are you bragging about?" asked the gray-coated man.

"Don't irritate them, Mac," Hunerkopf suggested.

The gray-coated man pointed. "You, Delbanca—and the jane, you two get over in the car, too."

"Say," McGovern bawled, "what the hell is this? Who is on whose side and why?"

"You heard me!" the gray-coated man snarled at Delbanca.

Delbanca kept Francesca behind him. He said, "Meester, I am no' deaf. I hear' you. You do no' see me move, hey? You take Francesca, meester, first you got to take me."

The gray-coated man ripped out, "Why, you dirty spig, you!" and strode across the sidewalk. Suddenly his feet shot from under him—the banana which Hunerkopf had dropped—and the gray-coated man slammed violently to the sidewalk. Shoes O'Riley stepped on his face, pinned him down, and wrenched the gun from his hand. A gun blazed in the drizzle and Shoes teetered a bit and said, "Ouch, geez," and then loudly, "Who the hell done that?"

"Look out, Shoes!" Cardigan barked. Cardigan shoved Shoes out of the way with his left hand, fired with the gun in his right. Detronius stumbled and fell against the car opposite, but he did not go completely down.

McGovern dragged his gun out and his foghorn voice boomed: "You muggs out there in the street—drop those rods!"

"Says you!"

"Says me, by God, says me!"

McGovern fired and lead whanged in the body of the car on the other side of the street.

"Oh, Emilio!" cried Francesca.

"Just you stay behind me, Francesca."

McGovern and Cardigan fired at the same time. Glass shattered. There was a low, choppy outcry. Detronius was trying to start the car, but one of the other men apparently had the ignition key. Detronius swore desperately. He yelled, "Where's the key?"

Hunerkopf slipped on the banana and took McGovern down with him, and the gray-coated man jumped up and down and made a frantic dive for the wet darkness. Cardigan swung to fire at him, but Hunerkopf heaved up, in the way.

"Where's the key?" Detronius yelled frantically.

"In the lock, in the lock!"

"It's not!"

"I tell you it is. I was driving. I oughta know."

"It's—"

A cab drove up, its horn blowing, its headlights flooding the men in the street. Somebody shot the headlights out and the cab stopped, its driver leaped out and holding his hands behind his neck, galloped away. Detronius, while his men blazed away at the apartment house facade, stumbled from the sedan and jumped into the cab, whose motor was still running.

"In here!" he yelled.

Backing up, still firing, the four men piled into the cab, and it lurched away. Hunerkopf, shot in the thigh, was sitting on the sidewalk moodily. Shoes O'Riley was going round in circles while Cardigan was trying to grab him and throw him out of the line of fire. McGovern was running after the cab. He swerved and then made a beeline for the sedan, and Cardigan reached it at the same time.

Pat turned up and said, "Here's the key. I was watching from that doorway, and when they went over I reached in and took the key out."

Cardigan snapped, "I thought I told you to go home!"

"But I couldn't! I felt I had to cover you and—"

"Stop crabbing, Cardigan," McGovern growled. "Drive it."

The sedan swung away from the curb, leaving Pat on the sidewalk. Cardigan clicked into high gear and McGovern rolled down the door window on his side and leaned out.

"Douse your lights," he said.

"Idea." Cardigan nodded, and doused them.

"Now step on it, sweetheart. This baby feels like she could step."

"With twelve cylinders, why not?"

The cab shot out on a wide, dark square, and beyond, the lights of Casa Domingo blinked. It was doing about fifty. Striking the streetcar rails, it slewed, seemed for a brief instant to straighten out. But it did not. It reeled, heaved, spun round, and smashed head-on into the high board fence, going clean through with the sounds of cracked boards and torn metal screaming through the darkness. The top of the cab was ripped off, and steam, escaping from the broken radiator, hissed and spouted.

Cardigan braked and let the sedan slide over the curbstone, and he was out of it before the car quite came to a stop. McGovern was at his heels, and as they went through the hole in the fence, three figures were seen hopping through the weeds.

McGovern fired, and one of the figures began to stumble ahead faster. Then suddenly all three vanished. Short, startled outcries rose, and Cardigan snapped, "They fell down into an old foundation. Watch it, Mac! . . . Here it is!"

"Okay. Let's jump."

"Right."

Without pause, they leaped down into the gloom and Cardigan landed on a head that was just rising. He bore a man down with him into a slough of mud and water. Close beside his cheek a gun blazed, deafening him. Then another gun exploded, and McGovern yelled, "Take that, you sweet so-and-so!"

Cardigan got a grip on the back of an unseen neck and pressed downward. He shoved the man's face into the mud. Someone else fell into him and he struck out wildly, connecting.

"By cripes—"

"You, Mac? I didn't know!"

"Glug-glug," said the man whose face he was holding in the mud.

Cardigan stood up, hauling the man with him, jamming his gun in his back.

"I got one," McGovern yelled. "I think I killed the other egg."

"I've got one, too," Cardigan called back. "There's one in the car yet, I guess."

"Come on; let's get these guys out of here."

"You hurt, Mac?"

"Well, either there's mud in my eye or it's the eye you just closed on me."

By the time they headed toward the cab there were flashlights sweeping about it. People had gathered in the street and there were half-a-dozen uniformed cops grouped round the car. They had hauled out Detronius, who was now sitting on the sidewalk, bruised and bloody and with his shirt half torn off. The cops swiveled about, and McGovern barked, "McGovern, boys. Got a squad car?"

"Yeah."

"Okay. Take these two potatoes and toss 'em in it and sit on 'em—I don't care how hard. Two of you guys take flashlights and go back to that old foundation. There's a dead heel laying in it. Fish him out. Somebody call the morgue bus. Look at me eye, closed tight."

"Who did that?" one of the cops asked.

"Big beautiful here," McGovern said, nodding toward Cardigan.

The cop took a swing at Cardigan with his nightstick.

"Hey," shouted Cardigan, "I'm the home team, you fathead!"

McGovern brayed, "Stop that, Homer! Who the hell told you to slug him?"

The nightstick had been aimed with perfect precision, and Cardigan took a few broken-kneed steps, then collapsed.

"Now look what you done, Homer," McGovern rasped.

A lieutenant walked up and said, "Hello, Mac. What's this all about?"

McGovern scowled irritably. "Now you're asking me something. There's been a fight. There's been a guy or two killed. A cab stolen. I've been slugged. Hunerkopf's wounded. That little guy there looks like he's outward bound and—well, you'll have to ask some other guy what it's all about, Lieutenant. I'm damned if I know anything about it!"

Cardigan came to in Delbanca's office in the Casa Domingo, looked drowsily about the room, saw Delbanca, Francesca, McGovern, Pat. He licked his lips.

"Gee, chief," Pat said. "How—how do you feel now?"

"Lousy, thanks." Then he laughed. "Hey, Mac—boy, what a shiner you've got!"

"Something to remember you by, kid."

"Where's everybody?"

"Well, August and this mugg O'Riley are in the hospital, not serious. Detronius died out in the street, but not before he talked. A pal of his, Bughouse Delaney, is dead, too. The other eggs are in the can. And to think that me— There I was sitting with Detronius only tonight getting a big pledge from him— It burns me up!"

"Who killed Bert Kine?"

"Him."

"Detronius?"

"Yeah. In a back room of this place. This girl's room. The Greek said Bert Kine walked in on him and two other guys. These other two guys had looted your office and Kine followed 'em. Tailed 'em right to that room and tried to collar 'em. Well, Detronius used a knife. Then they didn't want this girl here to see the job. They heard the music stop and knew she'd be on her way in. They thought Kine was dead and they just dumped him out the back window and got the window closed just as the girl came in. She never knew anything about it. Detronius used to call on her a lot and she kind of liked him, she said, but not in a big way. They figured on going out a little later and getting rid of the body, but when they did go out, well, Kine was gone. Detronius got a little scared about this and told these two mugs to get two other pals and keep his apartment house covered from the outside. Told 'em that if they seen any dicks walking him out, they should butt in. Well, they did. But the kick back was too much for 'em.

"We got back those papers they swiped from your office. And that laborer, by the way—that guy that drowned—he was pushed over. Other guys before him were pushed, too. It was a sweet game, and Detronius cleaned up a couple a hundred grand. But this girl here—she knew nothing about the killing—"

"Please," cried Francesca anxiously, running over to sit on the arm of Cardigan's chair, "you do believe so it is, no?"

He put his arm around her waist. "Francesca, from your lips, hell, anything sounds like the truth. Can I come up some time?" He patted her hip, then said, "Oh-oh, Uncle Delbanca is looking daggers this way. Shoo, little firefly."

Delbanca smiled joyously as Francesca returned to him, and he said, "Please, meesters, for to have a drink on me."

Instantly everyone looked very cheerful, and Cardigan, rubbing his hands together, cocked an eye at McGovern. "Well, Mac, I guess the Cosmos Agency came through again, eh?"

"Came through!" exploded McGovern. "Why if it wasn't for me, you big mugg—"

"Baloney. If it wasn't for Pat there, these babies would have got away. She swiped the switch key."

McGovern gritted his teeth. "Okay. Give her her due. I'm a gentleman. But if it wasn't for August dropping that banana—"

"Phooey on you, Mac!"

"And I'm beginning to believe," said McGovern darkly, "that you gave me this shiner on purpose."

"Yeah? Maybe I don't think you put that cop up to sock me on the head, so you could take all the credit and—"

Pat stamped her foot, cried, "Please—stop it, stop it! You should both thank your stars you're alive! Bickering—bickering all the time; like a couple of school kids."

Both Cardigan and McGovern bit their lips and looked down at the floor.

A cop poked his head through the doorway and said, "Excuse me, Sarge, but Merkel just stopped by on his way from the hospital and told me to tell you Hunerkopf said will you please bring him a bag of fruit—apples and bananas mostly, but no oranges on account of he swallows the pits all the time. That guy Shoes O'Riley asked Hunerkopf how he could be a good cop, and Hunerkopf told him he should eat plenty of fruit, so Shoes is now trying to trade five gold teeth for a barrel of apples."

McGovern groaned and said, "Quick, Delbanca—give me a drink before I go gaga! . . . Imagine! That mugg wants to become a cop!"

"That's an idea, Mac," Cardigan said cheerfully. "Why don't you try becoming one?"

"Chief!" cried Pat. "Stop it! Stop it! Stop it!"

HELL COULDN'T STOP HIM

■

BY FREDERICK NEBEL

*It started out to be a simple, routine dis-
appearance set-up, but in one short afternoon that big dick from Cosmos saw the
angles shift into a murder pattern. That
wasn't what bothered Cardigan, however.
It was just the hot weather, an army of
granite-jawed private police, and a whole
amusement park full of chiseling hot-shots
that kept getting in his hair.*

ONE

MANHUNT

■

Cardigan loomed in the doorway of the Cosmos Agency at 11:00 A.M., banged through the wooden gate, sailed past the secretary, the office boy, the two file clerks, and wound up in the private office of George Hammerhorn, who was studying a set of fingerprints.

Patricia Seaward sat in one of the leather chairs, a patent-leather traveling bag beside her. Cardigan grunted "Hello" to both, went on to an alcove back of a screen, mixed baking soda with water, downed the concoction. As he rinsed the glass, he burped, muttered, "Excuse me," but to no one in particular. Then he said, "Ah," but this to himself, the ravages of indigestion having been put to sleep.

He wore a baggy blue serge suit, no vest; a soft white shirt with collar attached, and a badly arranged black bow tie. His bashed and battered fedora had once been steel-gray, but now it resembled something that might have been kicked around the street and then left hanging in a tree during the rainy season. He took it as he reappeared from behind the screen and sailed it into a chair.

George Hammerhorn, stocky, well-pressed, said without looking up, "Does it take you two hours to get from Thirty-seventh street to Fifty-third?"

"Did it take me two hours?"

"Exactly."

"Then it must take two hours, George."

Hammerhorn made a small impatient gesture. "It's damn funny that Pat can get down from Sixty-fifth Street, dressed and all, in forty minutes, whereas you—"

"Her old man was a fireman. It's in her blood."

Pat said, "All the time I've wasted waiting here, I could have got a manicure. I wish you'd think of someone besides yourself, for a change."

"Sorry, Patsy."

"All you think of is yourself and—"

"I said I was sorry, didn't I? What do you want me to do, set it to music?"

She turned her back on him.

Hammerhorn said, "Now, now, cut that stuff out. There's no use getting personal about it. Jack, you and Pat are going up to Stanfort. I've reserved two rooms at the Blackman Hotel, radio and running ice water in each room."

"Why the Blackman?"

"They give us a rate."

"They ought to, with the house dick they've got working there. A moron by the name of Hubbel. It's the hotel where they have the solarium on the roof. Hubbel thought solarium was a kind of major operation. He's always got an earache from getting in drafts that come through keyholes and—"

"Okay. I don't want a lecture on Hubbel." Hammerhorn pushed a photograph across the desk. "That's a picture of Kenneth Drew. Take it and don't lose it, because Kenneth Drew is the fellow you're looking for. He's thirty-two years of age, looks younger. He's five feet nine, weighs a hundred and fifty-five. There's good money in this job, and because of the nature of it, the police are not to know about it. It's absolutely on the level, but if the police catch on, that means the press catch on, and our client is engaging us primarily to avoid publicity, not so much for his own sake as for Kenneth Drew's. You see, we begin on an angle of uncertainty.

"Our client is James T. Lorrison, vice president of the Surety Bank and Trust Company, this city; he not only handles Drew's accounts, he's a very close friend. Drew left the city twelve days ago, as near as Lorrison can figure it out. Where he went, no one knows. He took his car. There's a description of the car, and its license number," he said, passing a slip of paper to Cardigan.

"Now here's the gag. Checks made out to cash by Drew have been coming into the Surety. Here are five canceled checks, each made out to cash. The signature is authentic. The lot amounts to seven thousand dollars. These checks have been endorsed by a woman named Clara Rubio and deposited in the Stanfort State Bank. To date, all of that money has been withdrawn with the exception of five hundred dollars. Lorrison found that out by calling the State Bank.

"Drew still has about fifteen thousand in his checking account. I understand he goes in for binges now and then; he's a gay blade, comes of a very good family and at heart is a swell guy, though a little on the reckless side. Lorrison's got a hunch something is wrong. You're to go to Stanfort and find out. Pat's going with you, because there's a woman in the case. Lorrison spoke with the manager of the Stanfort bank and said you were coming up to look into the matter. He pledged the bank to secrecy. See if by a great effort of willpower you can make the eleven-forty."

Pat stood up, said in an injured tone, "I'm sure *I'm* ready."

Cardigan was picking up the memoranda. "I like her, George," he said. "I like her a lot. If I send her back to you wrapped in cellophane, don't be surprised. . . . Give me that suitcase, kid, and don't act like Garbo denying herself. You're a grand girl, you're tops, but lay off a guy with a hangover."

Her face softened, she murmured, "I didn't know you had a hangover. I'm sorry. I just thought—"

"Now, now," broke in Hammerhorn, "don't go into a song and dance, Pat. You've got a train to make."

Cardigan said, "Pipe down. Stop yelling at her."

George Hammerhorn groaned, covered his face with his hands.

The afternoon sun blazed white above Stanfort. Heat danced on the streetcar rails. The shop awnings were down and pedestrians kept to the shadows of them in the busier streets. The hum of electric fans could be heard through open shop doors. The traffic cops had discarded their coats, wore light blue shirts. Many men carried their coats over their arms, mopped their faces as they walked. Cool waves flowed out of the screened doorways of butcher shops. The smash of the sunlight in Penfield Square was terrific.

The State Bank was in a street off the square. It was a narrow building, two-storied. Cardigan went through the swing door into a small, cool interior at ten to three. There were four brass wickets, each with an identifying sign above it. Opposite, a fenced enclosure containing two desks. A small bank.

Cardigan said to the uniformed guard, "Where's the manager?"

The guard pointed to the fenced enclosure, squinted curiously at Cardigan. Doubtless with reason, for the hot train ride had wrinkled the big op's suit and criticism could have been leveled at his shirt, his half-undone tie. A rectangular brass sign said MR. FLOOM on the flattopped desk behind the mottled marble fence.

"I'm Cardigan, Mr. Floom, Cosmos Agency. Mr. Lorrison phoned you about me."

"Yes, of course. Come in," Floom said, opening the gate. He was a thin, slight man, middle-aged, dressed in lightweight dark clothes, crisp linen, cool nose glasses. He had the prim, small mouth of a cautious man. "Sit down, please. Rather curious, this business. Now what can I do for you?" He clasped thin, dry hands together, not tightly.

Cardigan had slapped his disreputable hat down upon the desk. Now he was drying his forehead. "I won't bother you a hell of a lot, Mr. Floom. I'll want, naturally, that address of this woman, this depositor of yours, Clara Rubio."

Floom spoke to his secretary, who departed.

"And how long she's been a depositor here," Cardigan added. "I'd also like to know what she looks like, approximate age."

"I don't believe I ever saw her," Floom replied with his small, cautious lips. "We have, however, only two tellers. I daresay they'll know."

The secretary returned with a card which she placed upon the desk. Floom glanced at the card, leaned over, and laid it down before Cardigan. Cardigan read it, took an old envelope from his pocket, wrote down the address and the date on which Clara Rubio had become a depositor.

"Were her monthly statements mailed, or did she call for them?" Cardigan asked.

"There were instructions left to hold them. She called for them."

Cardigan said, "Now let's see if the tellers know her."

Floom pressed one in a row of electric buttons and in a minute a short, bushy-haired man appeared. Floom said to him, "Do you remember a Miss Clara Rubio, one of our depositors?"

"No, sir, I don't. I think she always went to Mr. Cable's window."

"That's all," Floom said, dismissing him with a gesture, pressing another button.

Cable was younger, a fair-haired man of about twenty-five with very bright blue eyes.

Floom said precisely, "This is Mr. Cardigan, representing the Surety Bank and Trust of New York. Describe to him one of our depositors, a Miss Clara Rubio."

Cable bent his brows in thought, placed a finger on the point of his chin. "Let me see," he said presently. "Rather short, rather stout. In her forties, I'd say. Fat face, with red cheeks and, I believe, a gold eyetooth. Yes, I'm sure. Whether it's on the left or right, I can't remember. Quite a deep voice, almost like a man's." He shook his head, adding, "Not very good-looking. Oh, yes—a distinct mole on the side of her chin; I think the left side, though I can't remember." He put his bright blond face on one side, asked, "Anything else?"

"That's enough, thanks," Cardigan said.

Floom sent Cable away. To Cardigan: "If there is any way in which I can help you—"

"I'll let you know, you bet. Thanks a million, Mr. Floom. If I ever get in your hair, say so."

Mr. Floom, who was bald, bowed.

Cardigan left the bank, crossed Penfield Square in the welter of sunlight, his hat poked down to his eyebrows. It was five blocks to the Hotel Blackman and as he swung his big feet into the cool, air-conditioned lobby he took off his hat, blew out a breath of relief. As he cut sharply around a pillar he collided with a man who had begun to move from behind it. The man grabbed for his dislodged straw hat, smacked it instead of catching hold of it, and sent it spinning through the air. The hat landed definitely on the silvery hair of a dignified old gentleman who was snoozing in one of the high-backed lobby chairs. The old man popped awake, panic-stricken, while the hat rolled away across the floor, its owner in clumsy pursuit.

Cardigan, slightly annoyed by the whole business, leaned against the pillar and stuck a rumpled cigarette between his lips, exploded a match on his thumbnail, and immersed the end of his cigarette in the flame.

The lumpy man recovered his hat, went over to bow before the aged gentleman and spout apologies; then, red-faced, harried, he looked about. His face fell back into place as his eyes narrowed in a squint. He had a streamlined face, his nose being most prominent, like that of a rat's, his chin and forehead the least prominent features of his clay-colored face. Recognition then sprouted in his small knothole eyes. He went toward Cardigan breaking his pulpy lips in a buck-toothed grin.

"I thought, yes, I thought I recognized you, Cardigan!"

Cardigan said simply, "Hello, Hubbel. Still at the old post, eh?"

"Yes, sir. Yes, sir!" Hubbel beamed, thrusting out a hand.

Cardigan pressed it, dropped it.

Hubbel's eyes glittered with an insinuative quality which his voice aptly matched when he said, "Well, well, well! So here you are in Stanfort, and at the Blackman! Well, now, isn't that interesting!" He revolved one of his hands round the other, daylight gleaming on his buck teeth. "I know the town, Cardigan. The town knows me. The right people know me. So"—he dropped one muddy-colored eyelid—"if you need a hand—"

Cardigan's rough voice said good-naturedly, "Thanks, Hubbel. I just came up for a little sun on the beach. A man needs a vacation once in a while."

"Sure, sure, sure." Hubbel grinned but his small eyes danced with wicked, unbelieving mirth. "Only, just in case . . ." He laughed, shook Cardigan's arm, winked, and walked off: a chubby, knockkneed man with fat narrow shoulders and a bulging neck.

Cardigan went up to his room. Directly he closed the door he stopped, his wiry brows coming together. He remembered that when he had left the room his Gladstone lay on its side, with an express label on top. It was not on top now. He turned the bag over, saw it on the underside, and opened the bag. He hadn't locked it, there was nothing in it of any importance. He observed that its contents had been disturbed.

He went down to Pat's room, at the end of the hall, and she let him in. She had bathed and was wrapped in a lemon-colored silk dressing gown.

Cardigan said, "Do you know Hubbel the house dick by sight?"

"No. Why?"

"He's a dumpy little guy with a balloon-tire neck, pipe-organ teeth and an airflow nose. He's twice as nosey as he looks. If he pumps you—waltz. The cluck just tried to put on that he was surprised to see me. I go in my room and find somebody's been through my bag."

"Hubbel?"

"You don't have to guess. He offers me a hand downstairs, but what he means is he's looking for a handout. The guy's a grifter and a two-timer, a stool for the cops. Stay out of his way as much as possible."

She nodded. "What did you find out at the bank?"

"One thing, anyhow. I had half an idea, Pats, that this guy Drew was just tangled up with some gorgeous gold digger who was taking him over the money hurdles." He shook his head. "But no. There's a kind of mean-looking angle to it. The dame that deposited those checks is in her forties; she's short, fat, and hell to look at, according to the bank. . . . I'll see you for dinner. Wear the green dress they forgot to put the back in, and give the local boys a break."

"Where are you going now?"

"To see an address about a dame."

T W O

BEACH PARTY

■

Ellingston Street began five blocks west of Penfield Square and made a beeline south. It began in a cluster of provision markets, radio stores, secondhand stores, with a sprinkling of dingy flats. Farther south, there were garages, frame dwellings, many of them rooming houses. Beyond that, a lumberyard, an ice plant, a tool factory, empty lots.

The taxi driver said over his shoulder, "You say 1400 South Ellingston?"

"That's right."

The driver nodded to an auto-repair factory. "Well, that's 1320."

They drove on past a storage warehouse. "That's 1364," the driver said.

Now there were fields again, with a river beyond. Then a wood-and-coal yard with a battered frame building in front. The driver pulled up and peered for a number. Finding none, he got out and entered the office at the right side of the building. He reappeared, coming back toward the taxi and shaking his head.

"That's 1426. There ain't no 1400 along here." He waved a hand. "Them empty lots is where it'd be, if it was there, which it ain't. Maybe you got the wrong number."

Cardigan, frowning, made no reply. He looked toward the empty lots, dropped his eyes to the slip of paper in his hand. His lips pursed, then tightened. He leaned back in the cab.

"Drive me back to the Blackman," he said.

He went up to his room, skated his hat across the bed, and sat down at the telephone. The bank's doors would be closed, but he reasoned that someone would still be in the office. There was. Mr. Floom was there.

Cardigan said, "I'd like to check up on that address." He waited, and in a few minutes Floom's voice returned to the wire, saying, "It is 1400 South Ellingston Street."

"An empty lot," said Cardigan, "with a river view."

"But how strange! What do you suppose you will do?"

"Oh, I'll find her," said Cardigan, "but it'll take time."

He hung up, took the telephone directory from beneath the table, and turned to the classified section, to the hotel section. There were eight hotels listed. He began at the beginning, phoned the Hotel Ardmore and asked, "Is a Mr. Kenneth Drew registered there?"

There was not a Mr. Kenneth Drew registered there.

Cardigan went through the list, unsuccessfully.

He took time out for a drink and a smoke, sitting with the chair tipped back, his feet on the edge of the bed. Then, suddenly, he swung his feet off the bed, set down his drink, and picked up the telephone directory, this time turning to *Garages* in the classified section. He checked those nearest the center of town, especially those which specialized in twenty-four-hour parking service.

Drew was a gay blade; doubtless he would have chosen a garage that never closed its doors. Cardigan whittled the list down to nine garages and phoned the first. He gave the make of the car, the license number, and asked "Is it parked there now, or has it been parked there within the past twelve days?" He asked this of five garages. The fifth came through.

Cardigan hung up, punched a hole in the air, downed his drink, and whipped out of his shirt. He kicked off his pants and took a shower. Shaved. Dressed. He ran a comb through his hair, which was a waste of effort, for his hair looked just the same; partless and bushy and thick around his ears, on his nape. The bath, however, had refreshed him immensely. He took a particularly long drink and went down the hall to see Pat, the flask on his hip.

"I thought you might like a drink," he said.

"It's much too warm for liquor," she told him.

"You'll be sorry someday, always drinking water."

She was doing something to her eyebrows. "What about that address?"

"A gag. There's no such address. But I had some luck, kid. When I couldn't find Drew registered at any of the hotels, I began calling garages. He drove into the Central Garage twelve days ago. The guy there knows him, because Drew used to drive up quite frequently and he always parked his car there. He stopped at the Athletic Club for the night and left next morning at about ten, with the car, of course. Now get this, Pats. The man at the garage told me that when Drew left he told this guy he was going down to the beach for a swim and then he was driving on up the coast that afternoon, for Boston."

Pat had finished with her eyebrows. "Of course, he never got to Boston."

"He never got out of this vicinity. The checks prove that. He went down to the beach for a swim. . . . You've got a swell back, Patsy. Let's go down and grab some dinner."

They spent an hour over dinner. As they left the dining room and headed into the lobby, Pat giving the local boys a break, Hubbel appeared from behind a pillar, pretending it was accidental.

"Oh. Oh, Cardigan!" He bowed toward Pat. "And Miss Seaward, I believe." His unwholesome smile crawled all over his face. Then suddenly he was grave, saying, "Cardigan, could I have about a minute of your time?"

Cardigan dropped his eyes shrewdly across Hubbel's face, said to Pat, "Wait here, Patsy, will you?"

Hubbel again bowed to Pat, turned to Cardigan, said, "I got a little office back here." He led the way, his fat knees swishing against each other, his fat hands held lightly against his thighs. His office was a cubbyhole next to the checkroom. He indicated the only chair. "Sit down, Cardigan."

"You take it," Cardigan said.

Both remained standing, Hubbel revolving one hand round the

other and smiling reflectively, almost absentmindedly. He said, "This Kenneth Drew . . ." He pursed his lips and grinned up at Cardigan. He pawed his receding chin. His long heavy nose cast a shadow across his mouth. "Vanished, eh, Cardigan?"

Cardigan's face was stony. He said, slowly, "So you listened in on the switchboard, huh?"

"Oh, I wouldn't say that, Cardigan."

"I would."

Hubbel shrugged. "Have it your own way. I just asked you a question and—"

"Go ahead; ask me some more."

Hubbel looked pained. "Now don't act that way, Jack, old kid. It's just that I like to lend a friend a hand. I knew you were kidding me when you said you were up here just for a vacation. So I thought it'd be a joke to listen in and—"

"You slice it thick, Hubbel, and you spread it on thicker. What's on your mind? Nuts with the bushwha. What's on your mind?"

Hubbel grinned jerkily and looked pained at the same time. "Now please, Jack, old pal—"

"You heard me."

Hubbel got very red. His tongue flicked at his upper lip. "Honest. You know I know the town up, down, and across. I'm on the inside track here, I know the cops, they know me. I know my way around. I thought I'd be doing the right thing by offering you a hand."

Cardigan said, "Thanks, Hubbel. Thanks a lot. But I don't need any help." He turned toward the door.

Hubbel took hold of his arm. "This Drew comes of a very wealthy family, Cardigan. I can put two and two together. He vanished and you're looking for him." He had dropped his smiling mask now and his eyes were very small. "There's no law against me looking for Drew, is there?"

Cardigan regarded him somberly. "What are you doing, Hubbel, rehearsing for an accident?"

"No. I'm cutting in."

"The rat after the cheese, huh?"

Hubbel's pulpy lips broke over his buck teeth. "Calling me names ain't going to get you anywhere, Cardigan."

"Who wants to get anywhere with you, Hubbel? Listen, you

tramp!'' he snarled suddenly, grabbing Hubbel by the throat and slamming him back against the wall, holding him there. "The last time I was in this burg, two years ago, you pulled a fast one on me. You didn't know I knew that, did you? I was smack on the heels of Danny McHugh, the bank robber, the last of the Patch Gang that stuck up that armored truck in the Bronx and got away with two hundred grand. All but Danny were killed during the next two weeks. Danny was the last, the only guy that knew where the money was hidden. I was out to get him alive and I was all set, I'd waited two weeks, day and night, to get him right. Then the cops sailed in with half-a-dozen machine guns, shot the building to hell, and Danny with it. Nobody ever found the money. I found out later from one of the cops—I met him in a New York bar one night—that you'd tipped them off. So now you think I want to get somewhere with you!''

"Leggo! You're—choking—me—"

Cardigan slapped his face three times, hard. Hubbel's lips jigged, he pressed his eyelids shut.

"Smart, you are," Cardigan growled. He tossed him to the floor and said, "I recognize you now. You were the backward boy at the Century of Progress.''

Hubbel was panting, holding his hand against his cheek.

Cardigan went to the door, turned to level a finger and to say, "Get underfoot again, you crackpot, and I'll take you apart and see what was left out when you were born." He went out, slamming the door.

"Oh—oh," said Pat, seeing Cardigan's dark scowl as he rejoined her. "So what?"

"That was Hubbel."

"So I judged." She nodded.

"He's the kind of a guy you can't forget—like a bad dream. Someday I'm going to step on that baby and leave only a wet spot."

"If I were you, chief—"

"Shh!"

She looked curiously at him.

He turned suddenly away from her and strode long-legged to the door, disappeared. In a few minutes he reappeared, unhurried this time, and Pat, wide-eyed, said, "What happened to you that time?"

"Do you see that window over there?"

"That one? Yes, of course."

"There was a guy looking at me. I saw just his eyes and his hat and there was something funny in his eyes. The minute our looks met, he ducked."

"I wonder who it could be," she whispered, breathless.

"I've seen those eyes before, somewhere, but I can't place them." He went over to the checkroom and got his hat; returned to Pat and said, "Now you stay here. No, sit over there by those phone booths. They're on outside wires." He entered one of the booths, jotted down the number. Coming out, he said, "If I need you, I'll ring this booth. If I rang your room, Hubbel'd listen in."

"Where are you going?"

"The beach."

Seafront Park covered about a square mile. It was two miles by bus from Stanfort. It was noted for its fine bathing facilities, its roller coaster, nine-tenths of which ran over water, and its tremendous Ferris wheel. The park was a complete unit and employed its own police.

Cardigan arrived as the sun smashed into the sea and spread red color over the water and the sky. The bus terminal was hard by the boardwalk. Cardigan stood upon the boardwalk and shuttered his eyes against the red fire of the sun. It was a warm evening and quite a few bathers were still on the beach. Many strollers followed the route of the boardwalk. Cardigan heard the Tin Pan sound of the merry-go-round, the echoless racket of .22s in the shooting gallery, the clang of a gong as a man swung a sledgehammer and sent an iron weight upward, the screech of the roller coaster plunging down a grade, the various whistles and bells and horns of the vendors, and the shouting of the hawkers.

Cardigan headed for the huge parking lot, following the signs. He turned into an alleyway that ran between two large frame buildings and was hardly wider than the spread of his shoulders. Before he quite reached the end a man entered, dawdling along toward him.

He was a very tall, gangling, thin man, with a straw hat set ridiculously upon the top of a backwoods haircut; a suit of brown-and-reddish plaid, too short of arm and leg; white socks and yellow shoes. As he drew near, he raised large melancholy eyes and turned sidewise in order to squeeze past. But then he stopped, his eyes grew wider, his mouth opened.

"Sam the Mope." Cardigan chuckled.

"Geez, if it ain't Jack Cardigan—now if it ain't Jack Cardigan! Palm me hand, palm me hand!"

They shook hands and Cardigan said, "When'd you get east?"

"Just about a mont' ago. Dem guys at de state fairs was gettin' hep to me an', t' tell you de trut', Jack, me life was not me own. One o' dem foxy johndarms out in Ioway got de line on me an' it was on'y by me superior intelligence dat I hooked a milk train out one mornin', de local bastille bein', as you might say, too confinin' for a citizen burnin' wit' a love for de wide, open spaces. Lemme see. I ain't saw you since dat time in St. Louis when I got meself crocked on bourbon an' accidental pulled dem loaded dice on you in dat bar in Sixt' Street. Dat was a mistake, Jack. So help me, I was mindin' dem dice for a friend. I never blamed you for gettin' mad Jack. I knew you was goin' to slap me down, but I always appreciate de way you did it. 'Member? When I seen it comin', I says, 'Jack, don't hit me in de teeth. I just bought dem.' So when you hit me between de eyes, as I'm passin' out I says to meself, 'Sam, dere's a gentleman.'" He took hold of Cardigan's arm. "Let's I an' you go around to a bar an' froth at de mouth over a beer."

"Can't, Sam."

"Busy, hahn?"

"Sort of."

"Well, look pal. Dese private park cops around here are de muck."

"Thanks. You still rolling the bones."

"Nope. It's poker now, Jack. I pertend I'm a yokel, see? Dere's a couple guys been tryin' to egg me into a game for de past t'ree days. I pertend I'm cautious an' hold off. I t'ink dat tonight I'm gonna let dese babes take me in." He winked. "If you get what I mean, pal."

"I catch on. Good luck, bozo."

"Maybe I'll be seein' you."

Cardigan went on his way; left the wooden walk and headed across sand toward the parking lot. He slowed down, drifted through the gate, and began meandering up and down the rows of parked autos. Quite a few persons were preparing to leave and the attendants were kept busy and Cardigan found himself unmolested. He took his time, going up one aisle, down another. It took time, for there were many cars parked there. There was a small, white-stucco building, of one room, with two gas pumps out front. Cardigan passed this twice. Suddenly he came upon a Packard phaeton bearing the license plate he sought. The car was covered with a film of dust. He ran his finger over the leather of the front seat, found it, too, was covered with dust. Obviously the car had not been used in many days.

"Looking for something?" a voice said behind him.

Cardigan turned around. "Yeah. This buggy."

The man was dressed in brown khaki coveralls which had the words, *Beach Parking,* sewn across the chest. He was an angular man with a hooked nose bent over a heavy mouth and a jaw like a doorknob.

The man said, "Okay. Let's have your ticket." He pulled a ticket from the windshield wiper.

Cardigan shook his head. "You've got me wrong. I've got no ticket. The car belongs to a friend of mine."

The attendant slipped his ticket back beneath the windshield wiper and said, "Sorry, bud. You got to have the other half o' this ticket to take the car."

"You've still got me wrong. I don't want the car. I'm looking for the man that owns it."

"Well, hang around. He's probably on the beach."

Cardigan pulled the ticket from beneath the windshield wiper and looked at the date stamped on it. He said, "I suppose he's been on the beach eleven days, huh?"

"What d' you mean?"

"I mean this ticket was issued eleven days ago."

"Well, I can't help that."

Cardigan looked up at him, smiled dryly. "Did you report to the police?"

The man was scowling. He growled, "Why should I?"

"Didn't it occur to you that with a car parked here eleven days, the owner of it might have drowned?"

"That's no business of mine."

"That's what you think. There's a state police post a mile or two up the line. Come on over to your station and we'll phone 'em."

Cardigan turned and strode off across the cinders. He reached the small stucco building and ducked in through the door.

"Now, hold on," the attendant said, clattering in behind him. "Not so fast. I don't want to have them state cops down here crawlin' all over my neck. We got police here. There's one stationed regular at my north gate."

"Private police, mister."

The man shouted, "Okay, suppose they are? Anything like that, you report to the park police and they take it up with the state police." He put himself between Cardigan and the telephone. "I got a business here and a family to support and I ain't goin' to have it crimped by a guy that busts in here like he owned the place." He called out the door, "Joe, go get Brady!"

Cardigan regarded him somberly. He was still regarding him when there was a step in the doorway. Cardigan turned. A man in a white shirt, white breeches, thin leather boots, and a white-topped cap came in and stood spread-legged. He was lean, hard-boned, and deeply tanned.

"What's up, Gus?" he grunted.

Gus said, "This guy's actin' like he owns the place."

Brady looked daggers at Cardigan. "What are you—drunk or just funny?"

Cardigan was lounging easily on the desk. "I want to make a phone call to the state police and Gus here thinks it's kind of bad etiquette."

"If you got a bone to pick," Brady said sullenly, "let me hear about it. The state cops don't want to be pestered with crank calls. We can handle Seafront Park."

Cardigan said, "Okay. I'm looking for a lad named Kenneth Drew. He parked his car here eleven days ago and hasn't been heard from since."

Brady was still sullen. "We'll look into it. Our headquarters is down on Surf Street. Come around in the morning and we'll give you a report."

"Swell," Cardigan said. "Meantime, I'll phone the state police." He stood up and reached for the phone.

Brady snapped, "I told you, lardhead, that we'll do any reporting to the state cops." He put his bronzed hand down on the phone, added, "Go roll your hoop and come around headquarters in the morning."

Cardigan smiled thinly at him. "Are you tough, or do you just get those lines out of your book of rules?"

Brady narrowed his eyes. "You trying to start something?"

Cardigan put his hands on his hips and stared at Brady with hard amusement. Brady's hand closed around his white nightstick. Gus moved over to stand beside him, fingering a wrench. Brady said threateningly, "Pick up your feet, monkey, and climb out of here before I wrap this club around your thick head."

Cardigan's hands shot forward and downward; one gripped the club in Brady's hand, the other gripped the wrench in Gus's hand. At the same time he shifted on his feet, planting them. Both his arms moved in a complete, a violent circle. He tore the club free, tore the wrench free. Brady fell against the desk and Gus wheeled through the open doorway, off balance, and crashed into the cinders.

Cardigan flung the wrench and the club into a corner, where they clattered among empty tin cans. He brushed his hands together, said contemptuously to Brady, "Child's play. You're not tough, fella; you're only a tough piece of ham that gets in a guy's teeth."

Brady's face was dull-red, sullen. He muttered dully, "Stick around the park, stranger, and you might turn into a major hospital case."

Cardigan laughed harshly, contemptuously. "You worry the pants off me, you do." He ducked out through the door as Gus was getting up. Gus decided to lie down again. Cardigan stepped over him, but gave him no more notice than he would have given to a log. His big feet crunched away on the cinders.

Hubbel stepped from behind the stucco building and watched him go. In Hubbel's small eyes was a crafty look, on his pulpy lips a small, treacherous smile.

THREE

BLONDE TROUBLE

■

Cardigan telephoned Pat from a booth in the Sundown Café, a beer parlor on the boardwalk. "Listen, Pats," he said. "Put on some plain clothes and grab a bus and come down here to the beach. I'm a bloodhound. . . . Well, there's a bad smell somewhere. I just want to be covered. I'll be sitting at a table in the Sundown Café. You can't miss it. It's smack on the boardwalk. . . . No, don't join me. Take a table by yourself and just cover me."

As he stepped from the booth, he heard a familiar voice say, "Now don't look around, Jack. I'm talkin' to you from de other boot'. One o' dem fancy coppers in white pants tailed you up to de door an' den he talked to two other coppers an' kinda pointed you out. You ask me, Jack, dose boids ain't up to no good. Any copper dat wears white pants, I suspicion him; an' I would not t'ink high of dat boid dat tailed you in any kind of pants. He wears, was you to ask me, a potickly unkind puss."

Cardigan was looking toward the door. "Thanks, Sam."

"Mention it not, pal-o. I would sit an' have a beer wit' you, except I have an apperntment wit' dose two angels dat t'ink I am a

Ioway hog-raiser. Dey are waitin' just inside de door, an' bein' as I am supposed to be a total stranger here, I don't know you."

"I get you, Sam," Cardigan said, and strolled away. He took a brief glance at the two men standing just inside the doorway. They were dressed in white flannels, and one wore a blue coat, one a coffee-colored Norfolk jacket. They looked hard, suave; men about the beach. Cardigan grinned faintly to himself. They did not know Sam the Mope, whose specialty was trimming trimmers; except when he got tight, when he had a foolish habit of trying to trim policemen.

Cardigan sat down and ordered a beer. He saw the two sharps take Sam by the arm, lead him off into the dusk. Rifles were cracking in the shooting gallery. The roller coaster screeched. Cardigan could see the lighted Ferris wheel revolving slowly. He could smell hot frankfurters, roasted peanuts. A stein of beer was shoved before him. The café was filling up.

Some Negroes appeared with instruments, sat down, and began to play. A girl in white tights appeared on the floor doing a fast cartwheel, then half a dozen fast somersaults. She was tenth-rate, but the crowd applauded. She bowed and then the orchestra softened and she began to sing, going from table to table, rolling her eyes at the men. Some came through with contributions, dropping them in the small gilded bucket which she carried in one hand.

Presently she came to Cardigan's table, rolled her eyes, flashed her teeth, hitched up her hips. Cardigan looked her over lazily, from head to foot, while she held the bucket out. He took a drink of beer.

Between verses she said under her breath, "Baby needs shoes," and gestured with the bucket.

"So do I," said Cardigan.

"You don't look like a piker."

"I'll give you a buck to stop singing."

"Wiseguy, eh?"

"I've just got an ear for music."

"Nuts to you, brother."

"Okay. Roll along, sister, and wash your lingerie."

"I got a mind to bust this bucket over your head."

"Roll along, roll along, and don't start anything you can't finish."

She set her bucket down on the floor, stopped singing. Her face and shoulders were red. Straightening, she struck him across the face with the flat of her hand.

His lips tightened. "Beat it, will you, before you draw a crowd?"

She kicked him in the shins. He rose, towering, and said under his breath, "Sister, you look old enough to know better, but if you make another pass at me I'll turn you upside down and paddle you."

Magically, four park policemen appeared, Brady among them, and grabbed hold of Cardigan.

Brady said, "What's the matter, miss?"

"This drunk," she cried, "insulted me!"

The four cops rushed Cardigan out of the café, got him into an alleyway, and clubbed him through it. He tussled, but two of them held him by either arm, whacked him across the legs, the arms, and on the head. Blind with anger, Cardigan kept on heaving and kicking out at them; he fought the whole route, but the men were big, there were four of them, and they hit where it hurt.

Cardigan was slammed through a doorway in a small clapboard bungalow. He fell over a footstool and hit the floor so hard that the building shook violently. He spun on his back on the floor, scooped up the footstool, and flung it from where he lay. It cracked into the jaw of the nearest cop and knocked him stone-cold. The other three ganged on Cardigan, hauled him to his feet, and walloped him down into an armchair. They stood above him with their clubs raised.

Brady said, "Easy now, Cardigan."

Cardigan wondered instantly how Brady had come to know his name.

He said, "That was smart, guys—putting the dame up to starting something."

"Nobody put her up to anything," Brady shot back in his hard, sullen voice. "You asked for trouble and you got it."

"Okay. Okay. Take me to your headquarters and let me talk to the guy that brass-hat's this ice-cream-pants outfit."

Brady said, "You're in headquarters now, sweetheart, and you're talking to the boss."

Cardigan noticed for the first time that Brady was more

elegantly dressed than the others. Cardigan said, "Swell. Now turn me over to the state police."

"Don't jump so far ahead."

"You can't arrest me, Brady. You can hold me for the cops, but you can't arrest me."

Brady said, "I guess we do as we please around here. You'll spend the night in the cooler, Cardigan."

The doorway opened and Hubbel stood there, a pudgy man beneath a brown fedora. His fat lips were pursed in a smile. Brady and the other cops looked at him. Brady, puzzled, said, "Yeah?"

Hubbel flourished a cigar, placed it between his lips, took a puff, removed the cigar, and let the smoke flow from his long heavy nose.

"My name's Abe Hubbel," he said. "I'm the house officer at the Blackman Hotel."

Brady was scowling. "Well, why ain't you there?"

"Oh, night off," Hubbel said, enjoying himself. "I saw you fellows giving Cardigan the works. I know Cardigan, you know. What do you intend to do with him?"

"What's it to you?" snapped Brady.

"I just asked."

"Chuck him in the can."

Hubbel showed his buck teeth in a vast grin. "You got no right to do that, you know. If you want to prefer charges against him, you got to turn him over to a law officer, right away."

Brady looked very dark. "You telling me my business? I know what to do here."

"Good." Hubbel grinned. "You see, besides being house officer at the Blackman, I'm a deputy sheriff." He took his hand from his pocket, showed a badge lying in his palm. "So you can turn Cardigan over to me."

Cardigan rasped, "Go hang your head out the window, Hubbel! I'll stay here."

Hubbel shook his head. "Oh, no, Jack. Oh, no. The law is the law. I got to take you over."

"I won't go! I wouldn't be seen walking down the street with you!" Cardigan was glowering. "I know what's in your mind, Hubbel. It stinks."

Hubbel was dangling handcuffs. "Nevertheless, Jack, you got

to come along. What is it?" he asked Brady. "Disorderly conduct?"

Brady took a casual sidewise step, swung his club. Hubbel went down without a sound. Brady's face was very dark, very sinister; there was a desperate, tight warp in his mouth. One of the other cops gasped, "Geez, boss!"

Brady silenced him with a hard look.

Hubbel lay in the shadows.

Cardigan snapped out, "Look out, guys! Hubbel's going for his gun!"

The three men fell upon Hubbel.

Cardigan was on his feet, his own gun drawn. "Gag," he said.

They turned their heads. They straightened slowly.

Cardigan's dark eyes were glittering malignantly. He nodded toward the door at the rear of the room; the door was made of steel grating.

"Open it, Brady."

Brady licked his lips.

"Open it," Cardigan said somberly. "You other two guys go with him."

They crossed the room and Brady, taking a ring of keys from his pocket, unlocked the door, pulled it open.

"Now," said Cardigan, "carry Hubbel in."

They picked up Hubbel. "Put him just inside the door," Cardigan directed. "Then do the same with this pal of yours I knocked out."

When they had removed both unconscious men to the cell, Cardigan said, "Okay, Brady. Chuck me the keys."

Brady tossed them and Cardigan caught them in his left hand, said, "Now you guys back in and close the door behind you."

Brady growled, "Now look here—"

"I am. Right at you. Get in before I start a crime wave."

When they were all in the cell, Cardigan locked the door. He said, "I want to see all your hands gripping these bars till I get out. Come on, snap into it! Grip the bars!"

He backed across the room, ducked out of the bungalow, and strode long-legged through the darkness. Across the rooftops he could see the top of the Ferris wheel, its lights turning slowly. The harsh clangor of the merry-go-round came across the flats. He heard the rumble of the roller coaster.

* * *

Gus, the filling-station attendant, was sitting in his little stucco building eating a ham sandwich and drinking a bottle of beer. Cardigan came through the doorway, kicked the door shut. He strode across the room, pulled his gun, and held it casually in front of him, low, the heel of his hand against the pit of his stomach.

"I'm not going to waste a hell of a lot of time with you, Gus," he said.

Gus's left cheek bulged with food. His eyes grew very round, a yellow, ghastly color seemed to spread over his gaunt face.

Cardigan said, "Now what about that Packard?"

Gus began to look very ill.

"Either spit that grub out," Cardigan said, "or swallow it."

Gus swallowed it, gulping. He looked transfixed at the muzzle of the gun.

Cardigan muttered, "How did Brady find out my name's Cardigan, Gus?"

Gus shook his head. "I—I don't know. I didn't know what your name was."

"Why the hell did you make such a fuss when I wanted to call the state police? Why'd you throw a fit and send that guy after Brady?"

Gus was like a man in a trance.

"Talk, damn it!" Cardigan ripped out. "I've been kicked around enough here! I'm going to start some kicking around myself!" He leaned forward. "Get this. Brady and some of his rats landed on me and whaled hell out of me and dragged me over to their headquarters. I got out of that. I not only got out of it, but I locked Brady and the others up in their own cell. Now you'll talk, Gus, or God help you!"

Gus's jaw shook, he moved his head stupidly from side to side. "Geez, I don't know nothin'. I ain't done nothin'."

"Why didn't you report that Packard to the police?"

"I did."

"When?"

"It was, honest, the second day. I told Brady—"

"Now we're getting somewhere."

Gus gulped again and seemed very miserable. "Well, I told him, that's all. And he said, well, that was all right."

"What else did he say?"

Gus got very red. "Well, he just said if anybody come after the car, I should call him. Geez, I got to do what he tells me. I got to stay in good with the park cops or else."

"What else did he say?"

"Well, that's all. He just told me I shouldn't worry about the car, that's all."

"Did you think there was anything funny about that?"

Gus grimaced. "Hell, mister, I got to stay in good with them guys. If Brady says it's all right, I got to think it's all right. I got a wife an' two kids to support. I can't go gettin' curious with them cops."

Cardigan put his gun back into his pocket. "Okay, Gus," he said. "That's all I want to know from you. Now take a tip and stay right here and keep your mouth shut. I'm a nice guy, except when people get under my feet."

He banged out, crossed the parking lot, took the narrow alleyway to the boardwalk, and went up to the Sundown Café. He sailed into the café, returned to the table where he had sat, and looked around for his hat. The headwaiter came over.

"Looking for something, mister?" he said.

Cardigan turned on him. "My hat."

The headwaiter shrugged. "Maybe you lost it somewhere else."

"I lost it here," Cardigan snapped back at him. He looked around some more but failed to find it. Cursing under his breath, he headed for the door, turned on his heel, and came back to the headwaiter. "Where's the chemical blonde who put on the act?"

"Beg pardon?"

"The blonde! The floosie that kicked up her heels!"

"She's through for the time being. She'll do her act again at eleven."

"Where is she now?"

The man shrugged. "Probably walking on the beach."

Cardigan strode out of the café. He was heading for the passageway that led to the headquarters bungalow, when Pat fell in step beside him, said, "Here's your hat, chief."

He looked down at her, but did not stop. "Where'd you get it? Keep walking, keep walking—and not too close to me."

"I found it in that café, under the table where I sat down. It was all bashed in. I felt something was wrong. At the next table I heard some people talking about a fight. I heard one of them say, 'Looked to me as if the blonde started it, deliberately. The big guy was minding his own business. I saw the cops standing outside that door when she first appeared. They were standing there as if they expected something. Then when she began to pick on the big guy, why, the cops began to come nearer the door. It sure looked like a frame-up of some kind. Look, there she comes now.' So I turned and saw a girl come out of a door back of the bandstand. Seeing your hat there, and hearing those men, I knew something had gone wrong and I reasoned, from their talk, that the girl had had something to do with it. So I followed her out of the café."

"Swell!"

"And then a peculiar thing happened, chief. I followed her to the Old Mill, down near the end of the boardwalk. She got in one of the boats all by herself. It was number Thirteen, I remember that. Well, when number Thirteen came out of the tunnel again, five minutes later, she was not in it!"

"You sure of that, Pats?"

"Positive!" she said.

"Give me my hat."

She gave it to him.

He said, "Now where's the Old Mill?"

"Not far."

FOUR

HELL COULDN'T STOP HIM

■

The Old Mill had a gaudy interior. The flat-bottomed boats came out of a tunnel on the left, stopped long enough to take on passengers, and disappeared in a tunnel on the right. Between the two tunnels a huge, wooden waterwheel threshed slowly. There were many boats, and some had to be sent on empty to permit room for those that followed. Cardigan bought two tickets and he and Pat entered one of the boats and were shoved off into the black mouth of the tunnel.

Cardigan said, "I used to do this when I was a kid. It was always a great chance to neck."

"Well, don't suddenly go boyish."

"Did I ever make a pass at you yet?"

"I was only kidding." She laughed softly.

They moved slowly through the black tunnel, the boat propelled in places by cogs just beneath the surface of the shallow canal. Ahead, there was an amber glow. Presently the tunnel widened into a broad, greenish cave. Trick lighting made weird designs on the walls. The boat moved slowly between two wooden platforms.

Cardigan stepped out, muttering, "Hold the boat here a minute. Hang on to the platform."

He crossed the platform to the wall of the cave, felt around with his fingers. He used a pocket flashlight the size and shape of a fountain pen; sprayed its light on the platform. He shook his head and climbed back into the boat. The cogs moved the boat along.

They entered another tunnel, the boat rubbing against the wooden sides of the canal. The air was cool, damp. In a little while they came out into a cave where there was a waterfall with a floodlight centered on it. Cardigan again stopped the boat and told Pat to hold it. He stepped to the wooden platform, crossed swiftly to the cave wall, which from the boat had appeared to be solid, with no breaks. But now he saw a fissure, taller than he was, and wider. He poked into a passageway lighted by a blue light. At the end of the passageway was a door. He turned and went back to the boat.

"Something here, Patsy," he whispered. "Shove off. Wait for me outside."

But she had sprung from the boat, letting it move off. "And let you have all the fun by yourself?"

"Listen, when I tell you to do a thing, chicken—"

"Duck! Here comes another boat!"

They fled into the shadows. Cardigan pointed to the fissure in the cave wall. He pressed through it and made his way down the blue-lit corridor, with Pat tiptoeing at his heels.

There was no knob on the door. He felt around the edges for a button, found none. On the varnished door panel he saw no wear and tear left by knuckles. He looked at the corridor walls, then up at the blue light, three inches above his head. A light cord dangled. He pulled it. The light did not go out, but somewhere behind the door he heard the sound of an electric buzzer.

A small Oriental opened the door, bowed, said, "Yiss," and stepped aside.

Cardigan and Pat entered a small anteroom. The Oriental closed the door and reached for Cardigan's hat. Cardigan shook his head. The Oriental bowed, said, "Yiss," and held aside drapes, revealing part of another room. Cardigan went in first.

A black-haired woman was half reclining on a velvet-covered divan. She was tall, sumptuously built, with carved red lips. She wore deep-blue, velvet lounging pajamas, the jacket full, with a Russian collar. Her skin was tawny, her cheekbones high, her eyes wide and meditative. She wore her hair in bangs. She seemed unmoved, unimpressed, by the entrance of Cardigan and Pat.

She said, "You wish to see someone specially?"

"The blond song-and-dance gal from the Sundown Café," Cardigan replied.

"I'm afraid I do not understand."

"I think you do."

She asked languidly, "What reference have you?"

"None."

"Fu," she said languidly, "bring wine."

"Yiss," said Fu.

Cardigan slapped his hand down on Fu's wrist, said, "I didn't come here to drink wine. Pat, keep her covered."

Pat drew her small automatic and trained it on the woman. Cardigan ripped loose a portiere rope, bound Fu's hands behind his back. He made the Oriental lie on the floor, bound his feet.

The woman's languid voice said, "A man of few words."

"How quick you catch on," Cardigan growled. He spun on his heel and strode across the room, climbed three steps, pulled aside a portiere, and stepped into another room, smaller, dimly lit, and furnished with Oriental pieces. He heard the low, uneven drone of voices. On a table was a bowl containing fruit, nuts. In a corner was a small roulette wheel.

He crossed to a doorway, drew nearer the sound of voices as he moved down a narrow corridor. A closed door drew his attention. He put his ear to it. The voices were behind the door.

He put his hand on the knob, turned the knob slowly until it would turn no more. He felt the door give. It was not locked. He thrust against it.

It jammed at the first six inches and he realized instantly there was a chain on the other side. He heard the scuffle of feet, of chairs. A voice said, "Who's there?"

Cardigan heard the rattle of poker chips.

He said, "Sorry, I thought there was a game going on."

There was a movement of feet toward the door. Cardigan put his gun back into his pocket. A face appeared at the opening.

Cardigan nodded up the hall, said, "She told me there was a good game going on."

The door was opened by a man Cardigan had seen before, somewhere.

"Well, if she said so, pal, that's okay by us. Come in."

Cardigan entered. It was a plain room with a round table in the center. At the table sat another man Cardigan had seen before. And then instantly he knew. Sam the Mope was also at the table. Sam the Mope stood up, his face beaming.

"Why, Jack, old kid, old kid!"

Cardigan felt like flooring him. At the same instant Sam the Mope must have realized his mistake, for his jaw fell, his eyes hung stupidly in their sockets. The other two men were the sharps who had walked out of the café with Sam. There was a fourth chair at the table, unoccupied; but there were chips before it on the table, and a drink.

The man who had opened the door brought his eyelids shrewdly together. He looked from Sam to Cardigan, swiftly. Then he addressed Sam in a deadly voice. "I thought you didn't know anybody around here!"

Practically all the chips were in front of Sam. Sam said, "Well, you see, Jack, dis pal o' mine he useter raise hogs right next t' me out in Ioway. Doggone, you know I ain't seen Jack since it musta been t'ree years ago, at de Ioway State Fair. We was both showin' prize hogs, I an' Jack, an' bless me soul if he didn't cop de blue ribbon from right out under me nose! An' den he gave up hog raisin' an' sold out his farm an' left for de East." Sam felt proud of his story and hooked his thumbs in his suspenders, beamed, shook his head. "No, sir. I allus said dat when Jack Cardigan left Ioway—"

The man beside him jumped up, lashed out, "You hear that, Jake? He said *Cardigan*!"

Cardigan pulled his gun. "Okay, fellows. Upsy-wuppsy."

Jake staggered backward across the room, muttered, "By cripes, Steve!" in a gagged voice.

Sam looked bewildered. In fact, he was so bewildered that he raised his hands also.

The part down the middle of Steve's black glossy hair was like a thin white stripe. Beneath it, his pale hard face was rigid. "It's a trap, Jake. This yokel took us in."

Sam said, "I would like to resent them woids, Steve. Woids of that kind do make me most resentful."

"Sam," said Cardigan, "pick up your winnings and get out of here. There's going to be trouble. Come on, drop your hands, Sam. Take what you won, and blow."

"Jack, dat is most consid'rat' of you. I won so far four hunnert an' sixty-eight bucks." He began taking the money out of a cigar box. "Pretty poor pickin's, Jack, but what can a guy do when he's playin' against stacked cards? Tsk, tsk. An' guys wit' guns under dere arms. Okay—dere's me winnin's—a paltry sum."

Cardigan, tight-mouthed, said, "Now beat it. Fast."

"Jack, I ain't a guy dat forgets a good turn. I'm gonna—"

"Get out, Sam!" Cardigan barked.

Sam shrugged, picked up his straw hat, and ambled toward the door. As he passed Cardigan, he said softly, out of the corner of his mouth, "Watch it. Dere's someone in de back room." Then he went out, shaking his head regretfully.

Cardigan said, "Tell the other guy to come out of that back room."

"There's nobody in there," rasped Steve.

"Tell him to come out."

"Who?"

Cardigan smiled grimly. "Would it be Kenneth Drew?"

The two men looked steadily at him. Steve moistened his lips, moved his head. The white stripe down the middle of his hair gleamed. The pulse at Jake's temple was beating.

Cardigan raised his voice. "Come out of that back room!" He approached the table. On the edge of the table a cigarette was smoldering. There was lipstick on the end of it. Cardigan looked up at the men, tightened on his gun. "Don't try it, Jake. Is Clara Rubio a good poker player?"

They were regarding him darkly.

He yelled again. "Come out of the room before I shoot into it!"

The door opened and the blonde from the café leaned there, her eyes sultry, her full lips sullen. She strolled into the room, leaving the door open. "Well, here I am. What about it?"

"Join the waiting line, sister. I know a frame when I see one, and that was a frame at the café. Now I don't want to blow you guys apart. I want Kenneth Drew and I want Clara Rubio. It figures as plain as simple addition. Brady's mixed up in it because he told the guy at the parking lot not to worry about Drew's car being parked there. It was Brady put you, sister, up to starting that brawl at the café, so's he could gang on me for disorderly conduct. You, sister, were tailed here. You're in it, too. You're all in it: you and you and you and the good-looking dame with the bangs. Now come clean. Where's Drew? And where's this old fat dame Rubio? I want something like seven grand back from her."

Tho two men and the girl remained motionless, like images. Finally Steve, the white stripe down his hair glistening, said, "Why didn't you bring a flock of cops along?"

"This is private. If I don't get what I want, if I don't get Kenneth Drew—then I'll go to the cops."

They smiled sinisterly at him.

The blast of a gun shook the room. It was not Cardigan's gun. It was not the gun of anyone else in that room. But Cardigan knew he was hit: there was the sensation of a jolt somewhere in his body. He fired through the open door into the darkness of the room beyond. He turned on Steve.

"Don't," he gritted.

But Steve had ideas.

Cardigan shot him in the middle of the chest. The blonde screamed and tore at her hair and Steve drew himself up to his toes, his mouth straining. He put a hand against the table, turned half around to lean on his arm. He fell face forward across the table.

Jake did not get his gun clear. A second shot exploded in the darkness beyond the doorway. Cardigan felt the hat on his head twitch. He jumped to one side as a third shot blazed out of the darkness. Wood splintered somewhere behind him. The blonde pressed her body against the wall, her eyes wild with horror, her mouth open and out of shape and sucking her breath.

Steve's body fell off the table. The blonde screamed. Jake made another try for his gun, clawing at his left armpit. Cardigan fired and smashed Jake's arm.

"Ask for it, Jake, and you get it."

Jake looked stupidly at his bloody hand and the blonde made a mad, frenzied rush for the corridor door. Cardigan tripped her and she slammed down to the floor.

"You too," he muttered.

Pain was beginning to pump through his body. It seemed

centered in his right side, high, up beneath his arm. He slapped at the light switch, put out the lights. He heard Jake sit down on the floor and swear. Cardigan crept along the wall, felt his way around to the edges of the open doorway. From his pocket he drew his small cylindrical flashlight. Snapping it on, he rolled it into the doorway, its beam spraying into the other room.

Inside there was an outcry of fear. Cardigan backed across the room. Now he could see into the other room. Explosions banged in his ears. He saw a man trying to shoot out the flashlight that lay on the floor. The bullets tore into the floor. The blonde screamed again. The gun in the other room clicked. It clicked again. Cardigan saw the man stare horrified at the empty weapon.

Cardigan called out, "Okay. Chuck it and stick your hands up, brother." He rose, turned on the lights. He went across the room, picked up the flashlight, and stepped with it through the doorway. He played its beam on the man's face. Instantly he remembered the eyes he had seen regarding him through a window in the Blackman lobby. Blue. Wide and very blue now.

"Sweet cripes," muttered Cardigan.

It was Cable, the local bank clerk, the youth who had given him so detailed a description of Clara Rubio. He was shaking, his teeth were chattering. With an agonized cry in his throat he rushed forward, tried to fight his way past Cardigan.

"Let me go!" he screamed. "Let me go!"

Cardigan said, "Don't be funny," and locked Cable's arms behind his back, clipped on the manacles. "Where's Drew?"

Cable choked, "You damn well know he's dead!"

"I had a stinking suspicion of that."

"I didn't do it!" Cable panted. "Brady—with his nightstick! He was so damn free with his nightstick!"

Cardigan marched him across the room, out into the corridor, down the corridor, through the small room, and down the three steps into the room where Pat was still covering the woman on the divan.

Pat let out a cry of relief. "Oh, chief—thank God!"

The woman with the bangs stood up, placed her palms against her cheeks. Terror crawled across her face.

Cable choked, "I tried my best, Clara—"

"Clara!" Cardigan grunted. "You told me she was a fat old dame with an ugly puss!" The woman slumped to the divan.

Cable muttered, "Sure. I gave you a bum steer."

There was a sudden splintering of wood, then a crash. Cardigan whirled toward the anteroom. The drapes whipped back and two state troopers came in, their guns drawn. Cardigan lowered his gun and said, "Okay, boys. Take it away."

"Who are you?" the first trooper said.

"I'm a private dick from New York. Cardigan."

The trooper grinned. "Glad to know you. We got a phone call that there was something hot here and the guy explained just how to get here."

"What guy?"

"He wouldn't give his name. He said like this: 'I beg to surprise you of de fact dat a very swell guy by de name o' Cardigan is in very much of a jam—'"

Cardigan nodded. "I get it, I get it."

"You don't look like you're in much of a jam." The trooper grinned.

"Well, the guy that called you is an awful pessimist."

The trooper said, "What's the matter with the private police in this park? They fall asleep?"

"You don't know the half of it, trooper." Cardigan chuckled. He stopped chuckling, staggered a step, braced himself against the wall. "I forgot," he muttered, his face growing pale.

Pat ran to him. He closed his eyes, smiling ruefully to himself, and slid down the wall.

"Hell, I must be a sissy," he muttered.

He was lying in bed in his room at the Blackman next morning, his head propped up against two pillows. It was a quarter past ten. Sam the Mope, in a green-striped shirt and lavender sleeve garters, has just removed a breakfast tray from the bed. Now he placed a cigarette between Cardigan's lips, struck a match, and held the flame against the cigarette's end. Cardigan inhaled; exhaled.

"Thanks a million, Sam."

"Well, as me tailor says, 'Hoy-kay, keed.'"

There was a knock on the door. Sam crossed to it, opened it. George Hammerhorn, who had flown up at midnight, came in with

Pat Seaward. George went right to the bed, put a hand over Cardigan's, pressed it.

"How's it, boy?" he said, looking very proud.

"Nothing to it. I'll be up for the six-ten."

Hammerhorn sat down, said, "Of course, they got Brady. Those guys were still locked up when the troopers got there. I know the whole story as well as if I'd played a part myself. Pat and I have just come from the police barracks. Brady and his pals got in an argument with Hubbel while they were all cooped up where you locked them, and they beat the tar out of him. The troopers took him along, think he was implicated.

"They found Drew's body about two hours ago. You see, Brady'd killed Drew only the day before yesterday and they hadn't yet decided on a way of disposing of the body. It was hidden in an old trunk in that hideout you crashed."

Cardigan said, "If we'd been on the job a day sooner, we'd have saved his life."

Hammerhorn shook his head. "No. They intended doing away with him anyhow, but later, after they'd got more dough. The plan, according to Cable, was to fill him full of liquor, put a bathing suit on him, and take him out in a motorboat and toss him overboard about five miles out. But Drew tried to fight Brady, night before last, and Brady brained him.

"The blond café gal picked up Drew on the beach that day he drove down from the town. He hung around that evening with her, had dinner with her, and then they began taking rides on the various gadgets. Finally the Old Mill, after she'd seen him flash a roll big enough to choke an ox. They got off at that platform in the Old Mill and the blonde took him into Clara Rubio's place. They drugged him, went through his clothing. His checkbook was on him and they saw his balance. They locked him in a room. Then from day to day they made him write out a check and sign it. Clara thought that checks going through that way would not draw any attention, whereas if she made out a check, say, for five or ten grand, it would draw attention. Each day they said to Drew, 'Now write out this check and we'll let you go.' So he did—but they'd come back next day for another.

"Cable was in love with Clara. She'd hooked him on the beach a couple of months before, found out she could use him. He'd be a swell pal to have at the bank. Steve and Jake agreed. So did Brady.

Of course, Clara was really Brady's gal. What you did, Jack, you broke up a vicious criminal ring. The State is finding out more every hour; they're accounting for at least five persons missing during the past year. Drew's the sixth. Sam the Mope was slated to be the seventh."

Sam gulped, put a hand to his throat.

"And you, Jack," went on Hammerhorn, "had a swell chance of being number eight. When hell began to bust that way, why didn't you call in the state police?"

Sam said, "Ha, de more hell, de better Jack likes it. I never seen de time hell could stop dat guy. I was owerjoyed account of I was able t' git dem troopers in when he needed dem, damned if I was not. Excuse de profanity, Miss Seaward. It's me ent'usiasm brings it out. But if it wasn't f'r Jack, I guess I wouldn't be here now." He dropped an embarrassed look on Cardigan, said, "Jack, you remember de time we played poker on dat Chicago train? You remember how you wouldn't play wit' de cards I had, but made me buy a new deck from de porter?"

"Sure. And you won twenty bucks anyhow."

Sam shook his head sorrowfully, laid out two tens on the bed. "Dem cards, Jack—I sold dem cards cheap to de porter when I got on de train, just in case. It's been on me conscience ever since, pal-o. Well, I got to git along."

He put on his hat and coat and ambled out of the room. In a minute he returned, shaking his head, saying, "Gimme back dem two tens, Jack. I can't do it."

Cardigan looked up round-eyed. "Can't do what?"

Sam held out a twenty-dollar bill.

"Take dis, Jack. Dem two tens I gave you is counterfeit."

THE DEAD
DIE TWICE

∎

BY FREDERICK NEBEL

ONE

THE POWDERED CORPSE

■

The crash could be heard the length of the block. The heavy glass-and-metal marquee over the side entrance of the Hotel Burley trembled under the impact, and an instant later the pajama-clad body of the woman rolled leisurely over the edge of the canopy and landed on the sidewalk.

A bellhop pushed open the plate-glass swing door, took one forward step, and stopped in his tracks with a grimace frozen on his face. Across the street a woman, her arms laden with bundles, let out a frenzied scream, dropped her bundles, and fainted into the arms of a total stranger.

For a minute, in the small area before the hotel's side entrance, things came to a complete standstill. A dozen persons stood transfixed, rooted to the pavement. Westward was the low hum of auto traffic on Park Avenue; eastward, the blatant racket of traffic on Lexington and the winking of colored neon signs.

Two cops came on the run through the lush summer night, and a mounted policeman trotted his horse smartly up from Park, his shield and buttons glimmering in the glare of an auto's headlights.

A couple of cars had slowed down and the mounted policeman, taking one look at the body on the sidewalk, wheeled his horse about and with sharp, peremptory gestures yelled for the cars to keep moving. One of the cops turned on the crowd that had streamed after him from Lexington Avenue; he raised his arms and bawled, "Get back. Beat it. Scatter." The other cop dropped to his knees beside the body, then looked up and said to the bellhop, "Call an ambulance." He stood up and there was a sickly look on his face as he muttered to the other cop, "Geez, Joe." The mounted policeman swung down from his saddle, left the reins hanging; the horse remained dutifully at the curb.

A man in civilian clothes, with a hard straw hat on the back of his head, bored his way through the crowd, broke out of it. He crashed into one of the cops. The cop spun angrily, then relaxed and said, "Hi, Sarge."

"What happened?" the plainclothed man asked.

"She took a header."

"And me just after eating."

The cars were stopping again. The mounted policeman set his jaw, went out into the street, and cut loose with a tart, impatient tongue. The bellboy who had appeared first at the door now reappeared, and behind him surged other bellboys, other people, men and women. A man pressed through to the street and one of the cops turned and put a hand against his chest.

The man said, "I'm the house physician."

The cop took his hand down and shook his head. "I guess you ain't gonna be a big help here." He gestured toward the body, but did not look at it.

"Good God," the doctor muttered.

"You and me both," said the cop.

"It's"—the doctor pointed—"it's Mrs. McMann." He looked up at the side of the building, gulped. "She lives on the fourteenth floor."

The cop said, "That's a long dive in any man's language," and kept his eyes away from the body.

The clanging of an ambulance gong rose desperately above the other sounds of the city.

Cardigan shouldered his way through the crowd jammed in the doorway and came down the three steps to the sidewalk. He was hatless and his shaggy hair bunched all over his head. There was a half-smoked cigar in his mouth and his big hands dug in his coat pockets, bagging them.

The cop said in an angry, jittery voice, "What do *you* want?"

Cardigan stood staring somberly at the body on the pavement, tongued his cigar slowly from one side of his mouth to the other. He seemed not to have heard the cop's outburst.

The cop shoved him. "Get back! Get inside!"

"Calm yourself," Cardigan growled indifferently.

The plainclothed man in the hard straw hat squinted across the sidewalk. "What you doing here, Cardigan?"

"House-dicking for one of our men, Abe. Googan—he got a gutful of bad banana." He took the cigar out of his mouth, dropped his voice. "I see Madge McMann took a run-out powder."

"Madge McMann!"

Cardigan put the cigar back between his teeth, nodded. "Flush McMann is now a widower. Pull your pants up, Abe. Your shirt's sticking out."

The ambulance gonged its way up the street, swung sharply in against the curb. A white-coated figure jumped down from the seat. He was a young man with a dry, tight smile. He sucked at a cigarette twice, tossed it away, said, "Not what you'd call a three-point landing, eh?"

The mounted policeman looked stonily at him. The two cops didn't think he was funny, either. The man in the hard straw hat scowled.

Cardigan said sarcastically, "Where do you find your gags, fella, in the gutter?"

Madge McMann, in salmon-colored pajamas . . .

The news spread through the hotel like an unleashed electric spark. It sputtered through the dining room, the kitchens, the basement; it clicked round the lobby, up and down the corridors, among the maids and porters and elevator operators; it skyrocketed to the roof garden, leaped from waiter to waiter, ear to ear. It reached Tommy Thoms's orchestra, and as if to thrust the tragedy farther away, the orchestra picked up speed. In a little while the ambulance sped away with the broken, pajama-clad body. A porter came out and mopped the sidewalk. The spark continued to sputter and flicker and the hotel management tried to catch it and keep it under control.

The door of Apartment 1404 was done in light gray enamel and the numbers were of chromium, like the knob. The corridor was like any other corridor in the hotel; if anything, it seemed quieter than the others—the management, eager to keep the hotel running smoothly, had seen to that. But it was different on the other side of the door numbered 1404.

Chadwick, the house physician, said, "She was ill. I've been treating her for a month. I stopped in to see her"—he looked at his watch—"four hours ago, at six o'clock. Her nerves were rather shot and she was in the habit of fainting dead away."

Abe Green, the plainclothed sergeant, had a searching, narrow stare fixed on the doctor. "Did you tell her to stay in bed?"

"I advised it," Chadwick replied, working the knuckles of his right hand back and forth across the palm of his left. He was a dark, heavy-set man, with short bristly black hair and coarse eyebrows that met above his nose. "I advised it principally because of her fainting spells. I didn't want to have her faint and— well, crack her head against some piece of furniture or—"

"Fall out a window," Abe Green cut in.

Chadwick nodded gravely. "Yes."

Abe Green turned and pointed. "She was in the bathroom and she took a bath—a shower. The shower curtain's still wet and there's a damp bath towel on the rack. She powdered herself all over, like women do, and then— Now look. Her slippers, or what maybe you'd call mules, are still in the bathroom—and there on the carpet in the bedroom you see the marks of her bare feet that had powder on them. They zigzag across the floor, unsteady, very unsteady, and go to the window. What d'you make of that, Doc?"

Chadwick frowned. "Possibly she went to the window to get air. She may have felt faint and—"

"Exactly!" broke in Abe Green, raising a gnarled forefinger and pivoting to impress the others in the apartment. "I just wanted to see if somebody else besides me added that up and got the same total. Okay, then. She took a shower, a hot one, and the steam in there, let's say, kind of got her—but she managed to dry off and powder herself. But she had to leave sudden—didn't have time to put her mules on—in order to get air. She got her pajamas on and then—" He threw up his arms, let them drop with simple finality.

"It figures. Or does anybody around here think she committed suicide?"

Chadwick shook his head vigorously. "Not that, certainly. I never saw anyone more eager to live. You see"—he lowered his voice—"she had a weak heart and was likely at any time to pop off—instantly. She knew that, but she wasn't afraid. She wanted to live intensely in the meantime."

The assistant manager of the hotel rubbed his hands together approvingly. He was a prissy-looking fellow with a dandified haircomb and a precious little mustache. "Everything sounds very logical," he purred delightedly. It was always better to have someone die naturally in a hotel; suicides and murders and things like that were horrible. "Yes"—he actually beamed—"it all sounds most reasonable." His eyes glimmered on Abe Green, on the half-dozen cops, the couple of newspapermen, the news cameraman. "I should like to send you boys up some champagne—"

Cardigan came big-footed in from the bedroom eating an apple and wagging his shaggy head sourly from side to side. "There's a few things around here that don't fit as smoothly as the paper on the wall," he grumbled.

Green narrowed one eye. The sergeant was a bony-faced man with a good head on his shoulders and a blunt but good-natured way of saying things; his sense of humor was on the rough side, but it was without acid, without malice. His homely face got lopsided with a half-grin. "Okay, Jack," he said. "Chuck your ideas at me and I'll bat 'em down and look 'em over."

Cardigan looked suspicious. "Listen, Abe—if you're going to go into a fan dance, I'll shut up."

The assistant manager cleared his throat, looked annoyed. "See here, Cardigan," he said. "I wish you wouldn't set out on a carnival of theories; put ideas, foolish ideas, in people's heads. After all, you are working for the hotel—"

Green interrupted with a wave of his hand. "Let him, let him. There's none of us masterminds, Mr. Pentmater. If I think Jack's screwy, I'll tell him so. Go ahead, Jack."

Cardigan, who had planted a dark, disapproving stare on Pentmater, now took a vicious bite at his apple and said to Green, "Come in the bedroom a minute." He turned and went in himself and the others followed; he pointed to the wide double bed, which stood in the center of the room, its right side toward the bathroom, its left toward the two windows. He said, "Human beings get in the habit of doing things a certain way. Madge McMann was in the habit of sleeping on the right side of the bed—in this case, the side nearest the bathroom. You can tell that—"

"Both pillows are rumpled," Abe Green cut in. "Being sick, and being alone in the bed during the day, she could be all over it."

"I don't mean about the pillows—I'm thinking of her slippers. Besides the mules, she had another pair of slippers—they're here on the floor at the right of the bed. McMann's, you see, are on the left. Now take a look at the bed covers. If you sleep on the right, and if you have a habit of getting out on the right side of the bed, you generally grab the right side of the covers and throw them back from right to left and toward the foot of the bed. These covers here are thrown back from left to right."

The assistant manager snorted. "Pure theory!"

"You call it that and I call it common sense. And here's a little more common sense." Cardigan turned to Green. "You figure that after that hot shower she felt faint, so faint, in fact, that she didn't have time to put on her mules. That might make sense, Abe, except for the fact that she had time to put on her pajamas. A woman don't go into a bathroom to bathe wearing pajamas. She takes them off in the bedroom and puts a robe and mules on, and after she's bathed she puts the robe back on until her body's completely dry."

Green pulled at his lower lip thoughtfully. "Maybe you know more about women than I do. But what are you trying to make out of it—suicide?"

Pentmater snorted again. "Suicide! Pah!"

Cardigan tossed the apple core into a wastebasket.

Doctor Chadwick shook his head earnestly. "I absolutely hold out against the suicide theory. I've seen this woman almost daily. I know the signs of suicide. She had none of them."

"Of course, of course!" cried Pentmater; and to Cardigan, indignantly, "I'd appreciate it if you would stop letting your fancy run away with you!"

Cardigan gave him a dark, disgusted look.

Pentmater spluttered, "And I must remind you again that you are here in the interests of the Burley Hotel—though one would hardly know it." He whipped out a perfumed handkerchief and patted his lips excitedly.

Cardigan snapped, "It happens that I knew Madge McMann when she was Madge Cassidy, and that I bounced her on my knee when she was nine and I was twenty. I knew her old man and her old lady, and her old man gave me my first job and her old lady mended my clothes and took care of me when I was sick."

Pentmater looked cold. He said, "That has nothing to do with your duty to the management."

"Oh, it hasn't? Well, let me tell you something, fancy man. You and the management can go plumb to hell if you think I'll shut up just because I happen to be pinch-hitting here tonight for our man, Googan. I know my duty here, and it don't include keeping my mouth shut when I feel I ought to talk."

Pentmater stood back on his heels, made a petulant gesture. "I'll speak to the manager. I'll have you removed."

"Speak to him, sister. And stop in the flower shop down in the lobby and buy yourself a daisy chain."

"Ha, ha, ha!" guffawed one of the cops.

"Hey, you," reprimanded Abe Green. "Cut it."

Pentmater pranced out indignantly, turned and came back to shake his finger hotly at Cardigan. "You'll see! There!"

Abe Green tried to be reasonable. "Well, look, Jack. Now if this gal was an old friend of yours, it don't figure—I mean, you trying to make suicide out of it."

"Did I say anything about suicide?" Cardigan shouted.

The third-assistant manager appeared and said, "Mr. Pentmater, I've come to report that Plavy, one of the porters, has disappeared."

"Well, what of it, what of it?"

"He had a passkey. The head porter said that Plavy started up to this apartment with a package about ten minutes before Mrs. McMann fell from the window."

Abe Green's eyes opened wide.

T W O

THE MISSING PORTER

■

The bar was down in the basement of the Burley—a small, clubby hangout, with paneled walls dressed in sporting prints. At eleven that night Cardigan drifted in and Bottles Hannahan, the bartender, folded a newspaper, took off his eyeglasses, and rubbed his carroty nose.

"Tough, that had to happen, Mr. Cardigan."

"Double rye, with water on the side."

"She used to come in here, that is, before she took sick, and she was a fine young lady. Not like some o' these dames that come in and get plastered from A to Zowie."

"She was the top," Cardigan said dourly.

Bottles sighed and wagged his fat bald head. Then he said, "When will Mr. Googan be back?"

"Couple of days."

"I hear he ate somethin'."

"A bad banana, he said."

Bottles looked professionally concerned. "I knew a gal once was crazy about bananas, Mr. Cardigan. She come from Iceland

and I met her at a friend's house. She never seen bananas in Iceland and she was crazy about them. Only the first time I seen her eatin' them I thought she was nuts. She didn't eat them the way we eat them.''

Cardigan downed his drink, said, "What d'you mean?"

"Well, the poor gal never had seen a banana in Iceland and—well, I guess you couldn't blame her. But, honest, when I saw her eatin' the skins and chuckin' the insides away, I says to meself, 'Montmorency, this dame is nuts.' '' He sighed sadly. "But she just didn't know, Mr. Cardigan. She thought the inside o' the banana was the pit and that you was supposed to chuck it away and eat the yeller part."

Flush McMann came slowly through the doorway and put his elbows on the bar, stared vacantly at his hands. "Scotch," he said. He was a big man, burly, in evening clothes. His hands were big, white, solid. His lips hardly moved. The point of his heavy jaw had a small cleft in it. His eyes were blue, droopy, dead-looking.

Bottles set a bottle and a jigger down in front of him and said in a hushed voice, "Yes, sir, Mr. McMann."

Cardigan turned and leaned with his back against the bar, his elbows hooked on it, one heel hooked on the rail. His voice came low, regretful. "Sorry, Flush."

McMann turned his head slowly, rested his dead eyes on Cardigan. "Hello, Cardigan," he muttered, and poured himself a drink; downed it fast and poured another, and stared brooding at his hands.

Cardigan said, "Ever see that porter, Plavy?"

McMann shook his head slowly, seemed preoccupied with other matters.

Cardigan turned round to face the bar. "Did they tell you I figured she didn't fall?"

"Yeah, they did," McMann said in a thick, sunken voice. He said somberly, "She's dead. That's all I can think about. I can't think about anything else—how, or why, or anything." He threw the drink down his throat. "She was getting well, too," he muttered bitterly.

Cardigan said, "I'd like to get my paws around the throat of the guy that did it." He drank, set down his glass. "I think I will."

"You stay out of this, Cardigan," McMann said dully, his eyes fixed on space. "She was my wife, and the guy's my meat. The cops'll get him, and when they get him I'm going to walk right into the police station, pull a gun, and let him have the works."

"If I get to him first, Flush—I'll hold him for you."

McMann paid for his drinks, turned and walked slowly, somberly out of the bar.

"He'll do it," said Bottles. "He don't say much, but he'll do it, Mr. Cardigan."

Cardigan left the bar five minutes later and when he reached the lobby he saw Abe Green turning away from the desk.

"Checking up?" Cardigan asked.

Green shrugged. "Just routine. You got to eliminate all possible chances. I just checked up on McMann to satisfy the inspector. The inspector never liked him. Flush checks okay. He came in the hotel here at eight, went up to the apartment and came down again at eight-twenty and went out. He left word here that his wife was sleeping, but that if she wanted him, or if the doctor wanted him, he'd be at the Orion Club. So I checked up at the Orion and Flush was there from eight-thirty till ten, when we phoned him about her death."

"Got a soft spot in your heart for Flush, huh?"

"We were kids together, Jack, and I was a little guy and Flush used to fight my fights for me." He wagged his head. "I was sorry, kind of, when he took to gambling."

Cardigan went on to his small office at the rear of the lobby and in a little while Meyer, a Cosmos op, walked in.

"Okay," Cardigan said. "You carry on here, Lew."

"You fell into some hot stuff, eh?"

"Feet first, bo."

"Well, I hope you don't sink in it over your head. Is there anything I should know about this layout?"

"Just the usual routine. Googan used to go through all the corridors at two A.M. with the time clock, so you might as well stick to custom. Try all doors and if they're unlocked, knock and tell whoever's inside to lock his door. Finish up in the basement, then check the vestibules for lush workers. And if you see a tall, fancy guy with pink cheeks and an oh-so-lovely walk, he's the assistant manager, Pentmater. If you feel like hitting him—don't, because I'm in bad as it is."

"Did he burn you?"

"He gets in my teeth like corn on the cob."

Cardigan picked up his lop-eared fedora and rolled out of the office. His blue serge suit could have done with a pressing and his soft white collar was out of line. The black tie he wore looked more like something that somebody else had thrown there as a joke. He wore no vest, his coat was unbuttoned, and his shirt was taut across his heavy chest and pinched in behind his broad belt.

He went down to the basement and cornered the head night porter and said, "What about this guy Plavy? How long's he worked here?"

"About six months."

"Where'd he come from?"

"His last place was the Hotel Seaboard. He worked a year there. Came here with good references."

"How old was he?"

"Oh, about thirty."

"I don't remember seeing him. What'd he look like?"

The head porter pointed to a large glossy photograph nailed to the wall. "That was taken last month by the hotel. It shows all us porters. He's second from the left."

"This guy?"

"Yeah. He was swell at drawing people with his pen—quicklike."

"Pretty husky," Cardigan said.

"Yeah, he is." The man indicated some drawings. "Those're his."

"Did the cops get his address?" Cardigan asked.

"Oh, sure."

"I'll take it, too."

The head porter gave it to him.

"He married?" Cardigan asked.

"No. He lives alone." The head porter wagged his head in a mystified manner. "I can't figure it out, no kidding. The guy was liked by everybody in the hotel. He was never late, he did his job good, and never made any trouble at all. He just must have gone nuts all of a sudden—you know, how a guy will." He scratched his head. "And what's more, he had his porter's uniform on and nobody—the bellhops, doormen, me or any of the other porters—nobody seen him go out. How the hell did he get out?"

"What was in the package he took up?"

"It was from Mr. McMann's tailor. A suit, I guess. You know, one of those big cardboard boxes."

"There was no cardboard box in the apartment."

"Hell, he couldn't have carried it out—somebody'd have seen it."

Cardigan nodded to the photograph on the wall. "You have incinerator shoots on each floor. He could have put on the suit—he's about McMann's build, according to the picture—and dumped the box and his own porter's outfit down the chute."

"Hell, I never thought of that."

"Did the cops?"

"They didn't say anything about it."

Cardigan went to 1404 and found McMann brooding over a bottle. By the look in McMann's eyes, he was pretty drunk. Cardigan said, "What kind of a suit was that one you had coming from the tailor?"

"Light gray, pencil stripe," McMann mumbled soddenly.

Cardigan looked in the clothes closet. "It's not here."

"Didn't come, I guess."

"It's what Plavy was bringing up. I figure he put it on in here in order to walk out without being noticed."

"Oh," mumbled McMann dully.

"What was the tailor's name?"

"Vincent Bush's the trade name."

Cardigan looked in the clothes closet again, saw the name Vincent Bush on the labels of a couple of suits hanging there. He turned and said, "Better lay off the bottle, Flush."

McMann made a feeble, heavy gesture of not caring. "I got to stay tight for days," he said thickly.

Cardigan muttered, "I understand, Flush," and left the apartment. When he reached the lobby Pentmater, the assistant manager, was bickering with the clerk at the cashier's window. Pentmater turned suddenly away with an expression of brittle petulance and almost smashed head-on into Cardigan. Instead of apologizing, he snapped, "A fine house officer you turned out to be!"

"I'm not a house officer. I was just batting for Googan."

Pentmater rasped, "What'll I do? I was to tell McMann tomorrow that if he didn't pay up we'd have to ask him to leave."

"What does he owe?"

"Six hundred and ten dollars. And he owes Dr. Chadwick over three hundred!" He bounced on his toes. "What am I to do?"

"Wait'll he sobers up."

"Pah!"

"Well, you asked," Cardigan said, and went across the lobby to a telephone booth and made a call. When he heard Abe Green's voice at the other end, he said, "Abe, this is Jack. You guys have probably been looking for a guy in a porter's uniform. . . . Well, try this one. Try finding a guy wearing a light gray suit with a pinstripe and a label reading Vincent Bush inside the inside pocket. . . . That's the tailor's name. Plavy took a suit up to the apartment, but it's not there and neither is the box it was in. My guess is that he put the suit on and chucked the box and his own outfit down the incinerator chute. . . . Don't mention it. Always glad to help a white cop."

He shoved out of the booth, lit a cigar, and sat down and thought things over for five minutes. Then he rose and shouldered his way out the side door. He paused for a moment to look at the spot where Madge McMann had lain on the sidewalk. His lips flexed, tightened. He scowled and walked over to Park Avenue and stood and watched the cars stream past. Southward, he could see the rows of lights stretch away, and the pale immensity of the Waldorf-Astoria—and beyond it the motor tunnels leading to the ramp. He frowned down at his cigar.

A cab pulled up and the driver said, "Taxi?"

"Yeah," Cardigan said, and pulled open the door.

THREE

48 IN THE SHADE

■

The Orion Club was in a quiet street on the upper West Side, near
Central Park West. The building was three-storied, granite-faced,
and had a large cathedral door. The door opened into a heavily
carpeted foyer furnished in antiques and with several oil paintings
on the walls. A couple of men stood around in tails and one of
them came forward as Cardigan entered.

"You must be in the wrong place," the man said.

"This is the Orion Club, isn't it?"

"Yes, but—"

"Then I'm in the right place."

"But evening clothes are required."

Cardigan twisted his hat and thrust it into his pocket. "If you
think I'm going to go home and put on evening clothes, mister, just
to talk to Steve Shade—" He broke off with a laugh, then said,
"Where is he?"

The man dropped his affected formal manner and asked, "Who
wants to see him?"

"An old playmate, Jack Cardigan."

"Listen, pal, if you're hitting the boss up for a loan, there's no use, because—"

"Get going and tell him I want to see him. If you guess as bad as that all the time, what a sucker you must be on the races."

The man glowered for a moment, then turned on his heel and left the foyer. Cardigan strolled around the foyer pretending to take an interest in the oil paintings. The muffled sound of string music came faintly through the heavy inner door. The perfume of women who had been in this foyer still lingered. In a couple of minutes the door opened and the man who had gone to carry Cardigan's message returned and said curtly, "This way."

Cardigan followed him down a wide-paneled corridor, beyond which men and women could be seen eating and drinking at tables. He turned and went up a circular staircase at the heels of his guide, crossed a wide, polished corridor, and was led into a large, elegantly furnished room.

"Okay, Bert," Shade said, with a gesture.

The man who had brought Cardigan turned and left the room, closing the door quietly.

Cardigan hooked his hat on the top of a carved Spanish chair, knocked ash from his cigar into a beaten copper tray that sat on the heavy dark desk behind which Shade lounged indolently.

"From rats to riches, eh, Steve?" Cardigan grinned.

"What's funny about that?"

"Nothing. How are your games doing these nights?"

Shade looked at the cork-tipped cigarette he was smoking. He was a lean man of about forty-five, with thinning sandy hair, a hollow-cheeked face, rusty, dry skin, a pair of pale, perfectly blank eyes. His lips were flat and bloodless and there was thin sandy hair on his bony wrists.

He said dryly, "If you came here to talk about my business, Cardigan, the answer is this—my business is my own business."

"What do you think of Madge McMann?"

He shrugged. "Tough. I never met her, so don't expect me to bust out in a rash of flowers."

"Know Flush pretty well, don't you?"

"In the business I'm in, why shouldn't I?"

Cardigan was wearing a thin, amused smile. "Came here a lot, didn't he?"

"I guess he did. How often, I don't know."

"Who was getting the gravy, you or Flush?"

"I don't know off-hand. Couldn't have been much either way, or I'd know."

Cardigan said, "I just stopped off at the Agency office and found we're handling the Triple State Insurance Company and I phoned one of the directors and he said Madge McMann was insured for thirty thousand dollars."

Shade took a pull at his cigarette. "What's that got to do with me?"

"I thought you'd be interested, in case Flush owed you some money."

Shade kept his cigarette between his flat bloodless lips and raised his pale blank eyes. "You been drinking?"

"I always drink. What's the connection?"

Shade got up and walked peacefully around the room, taking meditative sucks at his cigarette. He stopped and stared blankly at Cardigan, and then said in his dry, unhurried voice, "Well, I'm not interested."

He sat down at his desk, picked up a pencil, and began adding a column of figures.

Cardigan said, "You don't have to show off, Steve. I know you can add."

Shade tossed aside his pencil and stared blankly into space with a kind of patient resignation.

"It's this," Cardigan went on. "Flush is in debt at the hotel. That means he's in debt other places. Is he in debt to you?"

"No."

Cardigan watched the rusty, expressionless face for a moment, then said, "You keep books, Steve."

Shade looked up at him. "Well?"

"Suppose you show me McMann's account."

Shade replied matter-of-factly, "My books are private business and suppose you cut out the clowning and take the air. I don't know what you're driving at, but I never got beyond the sixth grade, so I guess it's over my head."

Cardigan leaned straight-armed on the desk, his eyes narrowed. "Just Flush McMann's account, Steve."

"No." Shade waved his bony hand. "It's a rule I keep, and I'm not going to break it now. McMann don't owe me anything. Take it or leave it. But don't expect me to prove it. I don't have to." He stood up, smoothed down the points of his white waistcoat, said in his level dry voice, "You can find your way out. Find it."

"Okay," Cardigan said, and turned and strode to the door. But he did not go out. He locked the door, pivoted, and headed back darkly toward the desk. Shade reached for an electric button and Cardigan threw his cigar and Shade ducked to avoid being hit in the face. The cigar bounced off his shoulder. Sparks showered and Cardigan came around and stepped on the cigar, on the sparks. Shade's eyes did not change expression, but in some undefinable way his rusty face looked strangely sinister.

Cardigan's voice was low, blunt. "I knew Madge McMann when she was so high, sweetheart, and there's a bad smell in the air somewhere. I don't know just where it is and if I have to step on a few sharpshooters like you to find it, I'll step on 'em. I ask you a simple question and you sit there like a lousy wooden Indian. Where's your book?"

Stony-faced, Shade said, "Do you know what you can do?"

"Your safe's over there," Cardigan said, pointing. "Open it and get out the book."

Shade's voice was almost laconic. "You can go to hell."

"I can but I like it here better. Listen, you—" He slapped his hand down hard on Shade's bladelike shoulder and took hold of a handful of material there.

"Take your hand off," Shade said evenly.

"Don't worry about my hand—I'll wash it afterward."

"You're trying like hell to insult me."

Cardigan said, "If a guy said to me the things I've been saying to you, baby, I'd kick his teeth down his throat. You're just acting cool, calm, and collected because you haven't the insides to get stinking mad enough to take a poke at me. What's holding you back? I'm on your territory and there's probably two dozen guys in the building'd pile on me soon as you raised a squawk. So what've you got to lose?"

Shade's face remained expressionless, but he said, "Boil all that down and what does it spell? Crap."

"You've got the lines, Steve, but I don't think you've got what it takes to back them up. You might roll the yokels in the aisle, but— Listen, I want that book," Cardigan cut in suddenly, savagely, his thick brows snapping together above his nose. He straight-armed

Shade against the wall with such force that a picture hanging there was jarred lopsided.

Shade's eyes jigged for an instant, but then returned to their normal blank expression. Cardigan blocked him, saying somberly, "I've got to remind you, buddy, that a gal I knew as a kid died tonight and not by her own hand. If I have to break your lousy neck to get that book, I'll break it. I'm not just on a case for the Cosmos Agency. I'm not just checking up for the Triple State Insurance. My heart's in this case, Shade, and your wooden-Indian act pains the pants off me."

The eye is not the only medium of revealing a man's fright. Shade's eyes remained level, blank; nothing could be read into them. But round his mouth there was a twist of fear, and a pulse was beating in his throat. Cardigan's hand shot outward, clamped on Shade's throat; he lifted Shade an inch off the floor and plastered him against the wall.

"The book," he said grimly.

Shade nodded, his face flushed with blood that welled suddenly beneath his dry rusty skin. Cardigan let him go and Shade stumbled to the safe. He coughed, hacked. He worked the combination with dry, nervous fingers. Then he turned the handle. Instantly bells began ringing near and far and Shade spun away from the safe, ran to the far side of the room, got behind a table. The bells kept on ringing.

Cardigan's lips curled. "You started those bells!"

"When I turned that handle," Shade said.

Fists pounded on the outside of the door and Cardigan wheeled toward it. His hand slid for his gun, but he checked his draw; he knew it would be suicide to show a gun in this place. Besides, the club was filled with people in no way connected with it—women, men, who had come here to eat, dance, gamble. The door burst in and whanged back against the wall and men streamed into the room, some with drawn guns.

Cardigan threw the light switch, plunging the room into darkness. He could hear the startled, angry outcries of the men. He strode toward the doorway, which was bathed in light from the corridor. All but two of the men had swept into the room. These hovered uncertainly in the doorway. Cardigan hit them with the speed of a trip-hammer, stepped between them as they fell, and vaulted over the banister. He landed halfway down the staircase, stumbled, and carried a man with him to the bottom.

Three men waited at the bottom. One of them swung a club as Cardigan rose and Cardigan shot his head to one side, dodged the blow, and heard the club bark against the newel post. Another man lashed out with his foot toward Cardigan's stomach, and Cardigan shifted, took the blow along his thigh, hit the man twice in the face with blows so close together that they seemed like one. Another man heaved a chair and Cardigan caught it in midcareer, kept it swinging, and then let it fly up the stairs at three men who were pounding down from above. It stopped all three of them. He slapped a smallish man contemptuously in the face and strode toward the foyer. A gang of five had reorganized and started after him and he had to break into a run. As he reached the doorway leading to the foyer he ripped off the heavy portieres, turned and flung them into the faces of the running men. The men's arms flailed, one of them tripped, and the others sprawled on top of him.

Women were running about in the foyer, jabbering and making small terrified outcries. One of them, her jaw shaking, held out her jewels to Cardigan. He never noticed this, so intent was he on reaching the door. He rolled the women out of his way. One of them, a hefty redhead, had a slipper in her hand, and was saying, "One of those guys you socked was my husband!" She brought the pointed heel of it smack down on Cardigan's head. It was like being hit with a wedge of wood. Cardigan's eyes seemed to pinwheel in their sockets. He waded through the women toward the door, heard the rush of men in the corridor. His hand slapped on the door and he pulled it open, saw two uniformed cops standing on the sidewalk below in listening, curious attitudes.

Cardigan shouted, "Police! Help!" He ran down the steps to meet them, pointed back toward the door. "A fight in there! A lot of guys fighting!"

The cops gripped their nightsticks and charged through the doorway. The redheaded woman was wildly flailing the air with her slipper and it connected accidentally with the ear of one of the cops. He swung and chopped with his nightstick and the redhead went down.

"Oh!" cried another woman. "You hit a woman!"

"Geez," said the cop, "I thought it was a guy with a red beard pointed toward the ceilin'."

*   *   *

Cardigan reached Central Park West and walked south, his tie far over to one side and his hat crushed down over his forehead. As he passed beneath a streetlight he looked thoroughly disgusted. He had not wanted to pull a gun in the Orion, and he knew that if he had remained they would have beaten him to a pulp. His only out had been—to get out, fast. Now he began to wonder if he had done right in going there in the first place. A wild hunch—a blind stab in the dark—that had come to nothing. Yet he could not get certain suspicions out of his head.

A panhandler shuffled up and said, "Say, chief, how about—"

"Beat it!" Cardigan snapped. But a few steps farther on he stopped, turned about, and said, "Here." He tossed a quarter that rang on the sidewalk, glimmered beneath a streetlight. The bum slapped it down with his foot.

Cardigan hooked a taxi and rode as far as the Burley. He looked in the office for Meyer, didn't find him, and went down to the bar. Meyer was having a beer.

"Hey," said Meyer, "that guy McMann is taking it pretty hard. He was in the bar here about an hour, drank five Scotches in a row, and I had to lug him up to his apartment. I couldn't make him understand about locking the door, so I left him on the bed and locked the door from the outside."

"Got the key?"

"Yeah. I was intending to take another look at him in a few hours."

"Let's have the key."

Cardigan went up to the fourteenth floor, keyed his way into 1404. One light was burning in the living room and a low nightlight was burning in the bedroom. McMann, fully dressed, lay sprawled on the bed in sodden slumber. Cardigan stood looking thoughtfully at him for a couple of minutes, then moved slowly to the bed. He reached over and cautiously drew a wallet from McMann's inside pocket, backed slowly into the living room, and stopped beneath the single burning light.

He found in the wallet two ten-dollar bills, a lot of club cards, a sweepstakes ticket, some of McMann's personal cards. But there was nothing that aroused his interest, except one card, an Orion Club card, with Shade's home address on back. Replacing the contents of the wallet he inadvertently dropped one of the cards into a wastepaper basket. He bent down, picked out the card and a rumpled ball of paper—leaving the basket empty. He remembered that on his last visit to the apartment the basket had been completely empty. He opened the rumpled ball and found that it was a piece of hotel stationery containing figures written in a scrawled, unsteady hand.

Hotel	$ 610.00
Liquor	115.00
Tailor	205.50
Doctor	315.00
Shade	48,000.00
Dresses	425.00
	$49,670.50

Cardigan thrust the paper into his pocket. His eyes fell on an automatic pistol that lay on the desk and he picked it up, weighed it in his palm, peered toward the bedroom door. He shook his head ruefully and laid it down again, then returning to the bedroom, he slipped the wallet back into McMann's pocket.

When he walked into the bar ten minutes later Meyer was paying up. Cardigan gave him the key.

"How's he?" Meyer asked.

"Dead to the world. I closed and locked the window and jammed the lock. Flush might take it in his head to follow suit if he feels low enough. I was going to take his gun away, too, but I changed my mind and left it. He might—well, it might come in handy."

He went up to the lobby and as he was heading for the door the clerk on duty called, "Mr. Cardigan."

"Yeah?"

"I didn't think you were in the building. Sergeant Green phoned about a minute ago and said I should tell you to come over right away to Thirty-ninth Street, between First and Second Avenues. I said you weren't around and—"

Cardigan cut him short with, "Thanks," and slapped his way through the swing door.

THE LEOPARD'S SPOTS

■

It was in front of a row of darkened garages, a dismal fag end of the East Side. Cardigan, coming around from First Avenue after having left his taxi at the corner, saw the cluster of automobile lights, the bulky shapes of men. There was an ambulance on the scene. Abe Green had his hard straw hat in his left hand and was scratching the top of his head with his right. The ambulance men were lifting a body on a stretcher. Green pointed.

"Plavy," he said.

Cardigan could see the light gray suit with the pinstripe, the quiet face of the dead man.

Green pointed up the block to where a light burned in front of an all-night garage. "Guy up there said he heard running feet and caught a glimpse of two guys streaking past on the other side of the street, one of them—this guy, Plavy, I guess—about twenty yards in the lead. The other guy yelled, 'Stop!' but Plavy kept on. The garage guy stood in his door and watched them fade away, but before they reached First Avenue he heard three shots." Green nodded to the ambulance. "Plavy was shot three times in the back. I was wondering if it was Flush did it."

Cardigan shook his head. "I just left him ten minutes ago, drunk and sound asleep. Did the garage guy get a look at the guy who was chasing Plavy?"

"Uh-uh. Too dark." Green put his hat back on. "Well," he said, "we wanted Plavy and we got him, but we ain't got him the way we wanted him, and the way we got him"—he shook his head—"don't make sense. I sure expected it was Flush that nailed him, but you say Flush is drunk and asleep, so that's out and now I got to go to the trouble of thinking hard again.

The ambulance doctor called him and Green walked over to the ambulance. Cardigan lit a cigarette and tossed the match to the sidewalk, and when he looked down, casually, an instant later, he saw that a piece of paper lying there had caught on fire, and in the small glow he saw some marks on the paper. He slapped the flame out with his foot, picked up the paper, and moved over in front of the headlights of one of the parked cars. Only a corner of the paper had burned and he saw that it was a piece of Hotel Burley stationery. On it was printed in ink the words, "Tips, June 9th," and beneath these words were seven entries in amounts ranging from ten cents to a quarter. Cardigan shrugged, turned the sheet over, and saw several pen-and-ink sketches.

Green called across the sidewalk, "Hey, I'm going over the precinct, Jack."

"Okay." Puzzled, Cardigan crammed the sheet of paper into his pocket.

Fifteen minutes later he walked into a bar on Forty-fifth Street, ordered a double rye, and drew the paper from his pocket. The sketches were all of the same face, drawn from various angles—a man's face, the hair inked in black. Somewhere, sometime, he had seen that face. He had another drink and continued to brood over the sketches, racking his memory. He shook his head, sighed, downed a third drink. And then his eyes started in their sockets. He remembered. Bert—the fellow who had first accosted him at the Orion and who had led him up to see Shade.

Cardigan went out of the bar like a blustering wind. He walked to Fifth Avenue, hopped into a taxi at the corner, and gave the address of the Orion. When the taxi braked sharply in front of it Cardigan stepped out, saw the place was completely dark—there was no glimmer of light anywhere in the building. He remembered the address he had seen in McMann's wallet—the Orion Club card with Shade's home address written on the back. He got back into the cab and said, "Shoot through the Park at the Sixty-sixth Street transverse and let me off at Park Avenue and Seventieth."

The cab entered Central Park at Sixty-sixth Street, but the east end of the transverse emptied into Sixty-fifth. The cab went north on Fifth Avenue and then over east to Seventieth and Park. Cardigan got out and stood on the corner taking quick, hard puffs at a cigarette. The avenue was almost deserted, only a scattering of autos moved. The lights of the tall buildings looked cool in the mellow summer sky. Cardigan crossed to the northeast corner of Seventieth, walked north several blocks, and then turned right.

He entered the large apartment building and walked down three steps into a low gray-and-chrome lobby that had square pillars of mirrored glass. At one end was a small black marble desk and on it stood a couple of phones. A clerk behind the desk was sorting mail.

"These house phones?" Cardigan asked.

"Yes."

Cardigan picked up one of them, turned his back on the clerk, took off the receiver but held the hook down with his left index finger. He said in a loud voice, "Mr. Shade's apartment." He waited a moment and then said into the mouthpiece, "Steve. This is Jack. I'm down in the lobby. I'd like to see you . . . Okay. I'll be right up." With the hook still held down, he slipped in the receiver, put back the instrument, and started off. But a few yards farther on he turned and called out, "By the way, what's Mr. Shade's apartment?"

"Ten-twelve," the clerk said.

An elevator car full of chromium and mirrors hoisted Cardigan to the tenth floor. It was not much of a walk to 1012 and in a minute he was plugging his thumb against a shiny pearl button imbedded beside the door.

Shade, in trousers and stiff shirt, but collarless, opened the door and though his mouth sprang open in surprise no sound emerged— for Cardigan was already denting Shade's stiff shirtfront with the muzzle of his gun. He stepped in, closed the door, and motioned for Shade to move down the inner corridor. The corridor was rather long, with a closed door at the end, but on the right, near the closed door, an open archway led into a vast living room with large casement windows framing the city and the sky. The room was empty.

Cardigan's voice was low, threatening. "You the only one in the apartment?"

"Yes."

"You want to be damned sure of your answers, Shade, because I'm feeling my oats."

He tapped Shade's pockets and pushed him on into the living room. Shade's rusty face was expressionless, wooden, and his eyes, pale, blank, moved across Cardigan's face in a curious manner that seemed to lack completely any hint of curiosity.

"This guy, Bert," Cardigan drilled on. "The bird that showed me up to your office tonight. What's his full name?"

"Novack."

"Where's he live?"

"I don't know."

Cardigan laid the flat of his left hand hard against Shade's face and said, "I told you to be sure of your answers."

Shade's face remained wooden, and though his eyes blinked under the impact of the slap, they did not shift expression. The only change showed in his dry, flat lips; they got a little flatter against his teeth and one corner moved minutely like a pulse beat.

There was a ruthless dark look in Cardigan's eyes. "McMann owed you forty-eight grand, Steve."

"Yes?" asked Shade dryly.

"I found a paper he'd been figuring on, putting down his debts on. Forty-eight grand for you. You lying tramp, you told me he didn't owe you anything!"

"And I told you, loudmouth, that what people owe me is my own business, and their business."

Cardigan's face was warped with contempt. "You can chuck those Sunday-school stories out the window. You didn't hold back because of any sense of honor about telling a man's debts—you held back because you didn't want me to know he owed you that much. I remember back along the years, Shade, when you ran gambling joints in Chicago, St. Louis—before you came up to the classy layout you're running now. If a guy owed you money in those days he paid it—or something happened to him or somebody in his family. A leopard don't change his spots, fella."

"Screwy as usual."

"If being screwy helps me step on rats like you, I'm glad I'm screwy. Now where does Bert Novack live?"

"I don't know."

Cardigan thrust his gun into his pocket and hit Shade with both fists. He hit him a third time and flattened him across a table. He picked him off the table and hit him twice more and sent him flying into a divan. Shade lay there like a deflated balloon. Through puffed lips he mumbled an address.

Cardigan hauled him off the divan, walked him across the room, and handcuffed him to the pipe of a radiator. "That's to keep you honest and—well, to keep you. I'll be back." He turned and strode to the door, took out the key, locked the door from the outside, and went down in the elevator.

He walked over to Lexington Avenue, turned south and flagged the first cab that came along. His bow tie had become undone, but he paid no attention to it. The crown of his hat was all out of shape—his hat was, as a matter of fact, on backwards, the brim turned down on his neck and up, above his forehead. The wrinkled cuffs of his shirt stuck completely out of his coat sleeves and one of his socks had rolled down to his shoe top.

An elevated train rolled by overhead as Cardigan got out at Third Avenue and Forty-second Street. He walked down Third to Fortieth Street and turned east. The street was dark, gloomy, and he had a hard time seeing the house numbers. He passed several garages, one of them open and with a dim light burning. He walked on, counting houses, until he came to a lean brick one of three stories, with a dull yellow door. Through the transom he saw a dim light burning in the hallway beyond. Alongside the door was a button with the word JANITOR printed beneath it. He pressed the button.

A scared-looking man in a ragged bathrobe opened the door and Cardigan said in a low voice, "Novack?"

"Hanh?"

"Where's Novack's room?"

"Go 'way. Don't live here."

The muzzle of Cardigan's gun rose and stared the man in the

eye. The man, shaking, backed up into the hallway. Cardigan followed him quietly—quietly closed the door. He did not lower his gun. He said in a somber whisper, "If you don't want to get mixed up in messy business, you'll tell me—and then you'll shuffle off to your room, stuff cotton in your ears, and keep your nose clean. Where's his room?"

The scared man pointed upward, whispered hoarsely, "Next floor. Number Five."

"Get."

The man turned and pattered off down the hallway, vanished into a room. Cardigan heard a bolt click shut.

He went up the dimly lighted staircase, reached the hallway above, and stood looking warily around at the doors. Number Five was toward the front. He stood before it, looked up at the partly open transom. He listened—there was not a sound. His left hand crept out and closed on the knob. The door, of course, was locked. He slipped a match into the keyhole to see if a key were on the inside, found one there.

Stepping back a pace, he gathered all his weight and strength in his left shoulder, lunged forward, and ripped the door inward. The flashlight in his left hand sprang on; its beam cut the darkness, swooped, steadied.

"Hold it, Novack," he growled.

Novack lay twisted sidewise on a bed. He was in shirt and trousers and socks; his other clothing was strewn over a chair. His hand was poised midway between the side of the bed and a small table on which a gun lay.

Cardigan dropped his flashlight on a chair in such a manner that its beam hung steadily on Novack. Then he reached up and pulled a light cord. An electric bulb sprang to life, flooding the room, and he turned his flashlight off and thrust it back into his pocket.

"Get dressed," he said, and took the gun off the bed table.

Novack's lean white face began to take on a cynical half-smile. "For a big guy, you sure get around fast. What's in your hair now?"

"You."

"Yeah?" Novack put his shoes on and laced them. "You sure gave me the surprise of my life that time. Why am I in your hair? I didn't bop you at the Orion."

"Be funny. Look at me bust a rib laughing."

Novack looked at him. "You must laugh on the inside of your face. The outside looks like a secondhand prune." He stood up, whipped a tie round his neck, knotted it smartly up into the crotch of his collar. "I'll never eat prunes again."

"Do you like grapefruit?"

"Crazy about grapefruit."

"Well, the chances are you won't eat grapefruit again, either."

Novack snapped his arms into his coat, was particular about parting and combing his hair. "Would it be too much to ask you why I'm being waltzed out of here?"

"Not at all," Cardigan said. "For killing a guy named Plavy, a porter at the Burley Hotel. And for killing—Madge McMann."

"Go on, it sounds interesting."

"I figure that just as you pitched her from the window this guy Plavy came into the apartment with a passkey to leave a package. The package contained a suit. He caught you in the act and you pulled a gun on him. He dropped the package and it fell open. You knew you were caught red-handed, but you didn't dare fire a shot there because that would've given the whole scheme away. So you made Plavy put on the suit he was delivering and you made him walk out of the hotel with you. You had plenty of time, because fifteen minutes passed from the time Madge McMann hit the sidewalk until anyone entered the apartment.

"You brought Plavy here and trussed him up, locked the door and went back to get advice from Steve Shade. Shade probably told you that the guy Plavy would have to be done away with—no other alternative—and you came back here to do it. But Plavy had worked himself loose and you met him, either in the house here or on the street, and he ran. Sometime during the time he was here he made a couple of hurried pen drawings—the guy was an amateur artist—and when he was found dead down in Thirty-ninth Street, the drawings were found, too. They looked like nobody but you."

Novack indolently lit a cigarette. "All sounds swell, except why the hell should I dump McMann's wife out the window?"

"Because you're one of Shade's boys, and because McMann owed Shade forty-eight grand and he wanted the money."

Novack put on his hat. "Come on. Take me over the precinct. You don't worry me at all. There's six guys at the Orion, including Shade *and* McMann that'll prove I was there when Madge McMann took her dive."

Cardigan's smile was chill. He motioned to the door and Novack strolled out. He took hold of his arm as they reached the sidewalk. "This way," said Cardigan, and walked Novack to Third Avenue, where he stopped a cab. "Hotel Burley," he told the driver.

"What's the idea?" asked Novack.

"What idea?"

"The Burley."

Cardigan laughed hollowly. "You took too much for granted, Novack, when you thought I'd take you to a police station."

Novack stared straight ahead, his brows bending, a queer glint in his eyes. The cab turned west and in a few minutes pulled up at the side entrance of the Burley. As they got out of the cab, Cardigan nodded to the sidewalk.

"That's where they picked her up."

Novack turned a white, numb face toward him. Cardigan grabbed him by the arm, walked him into the lobby, and on into an open elevator car. It rose to the fourteenth floor. They got out and walked down the corridor to 1404 and Cardigan used the bronze knocker on the door panel. Novack's eyes were round, quiet, mirroring apprehension. His face was dead white and one corner of his mouth was sucked inward.

There was the sound of a snap lock being turned and then the door swung and McMann stood there, in trousers and undershirt, a highball in his hand. He looked foggily at Cardigan and said, "You still up, too?"

Then he looked at Novack and a dull, listless, heavy stare came to his eyes. Cardigan pushed Novack through the doorway, pushed him on into the living room, and into a chair. McMann followed with lagging steps.

Cardigan said to Novack, "So you thought I'd take you around to a police station where you could hook a lawyer, eh? You'll talk here, mister. Right here. You'll talk your head off before I'm through with you. I've got Shade manacled to his radiator and I've got you—and Madge McMann is dead—and she didn't die by her own hand. And Plavy is dead—and he left behind him a sketch of you."

McMann screwed up his face, as though he found difficulty in understanding all this. Novack eyed him sidewise, furtively. McMann looked at the wall and, as though he had found an answer there, his eyes widened and a look of fierce determination set suddenly round his heavy jaw. His eyes swung round and blazed on Novack.

With a hoarse outcry McMann fell upon the desk, snatched up his automatic pistol, wheeled wildly and leveled it at Novack. Novack squeezed back into the chair, gritted his teeth, pressed his eyes tightly shut. Cardigan made a dive for McMann, yelling, "Wait till he talks!" but he stopped in his tracks, amazed by the small flat sounds that McMann's automatic was making. The gun was empty.

Realizing it, McMann stared down at it as though it were some foul, unclean object. With a fierce snarl he flung it the length of the room. Cardigan said, "Easy now, Flush," and McMann turned on him and hit him in the face. The shock of the surprise and the blow unrooted Cardigan and he hit the floor on his back. But he bounded like rubber and was on his knees, then on his feet.

McMann was roaring, staggering, trying to get under way. Cardigan saw a wild, unreasonable light in his eyes, and the awful grimaces on his face. McMann's big feet clubbed odds and ends of furniture out of the way. He reeled, swayed. Cardigan, a dark, bitter look on his face, jumped in front of him and barked, "Flush!"

McMann flung both fists at him, kicked out, picked up a bottle and heaved it. Cardigan ducked the lot. Then suddenly he stepped in, clipped McMann on the jaw and brought him down with a crash. He spun to find Novack speeding toward the door.

"Novack!" he roared. "Stop! Stop! Novack—" He fired low. Novack skidded helplessly along the wall and then dropped to the floor. Cardigan turned and looked at McMann. The big man lay where he'd fallen, low groans mumbling through his lips.

Abe Green was brooding over a small beer in the Burley bar. He muttered, "I'd never in the world ha' thought that of Flush McMann."

"He had his back to the wall," Cardigan said, "and he must have been a rat at heart. And he was scared stiff, because Shade wanted the forty-eight grand and he told McMann that if he didn't get it soon, he'd get something else—in the gut. When McMann went up to his apartment at eight he found Madge dead, lying there in bed. Her heart had given out. He told me all this when he came to, after I socked him—but you'll get it again in the formal confession. Well, there she was—dead. She was insured for thirty thousand, but thirty thousand, after he buried her and all, wouldn't be enough to pay Shade and the other people he owed. So instead of reporting her death, he went out and went up to the Orion Club. He was scared stiff that if he didn't pay Shade, Shade would have him knocked off. Shade was hard up, too, desperate for money. So McMann told him that Madge had died—told him that there was thirty grand due in insurance.

"Shade told him that wouldn't be enough—that he had to have forty grand himself by the first in order to meet his own debts. So then McMann said, 'There's a double-indemnity clause in the policy. Thirty grand if she dies naturally, sixty grand if she dies by accident.' Well, there they were, both desperate for money. So they called in Novack, who was really nothing more than a floorwalker around the Orion, and offered him a thousand to do the job. Novack accepted and McMann gave him the key to the apartment, and a few instructions.

"McMann knew that Dr. Chadwick would testify that Madge had fainting spells. So he told Novack to wet that towel and shower curtain, as if she'd taken a bath, and to spread powder on the bathroom floor. Then Novack was to pick her up, put her feet on the powder, and then toddle her across the carpet, leaving those footprints, as if she'd staggered to the window to get air. He never stepped into the bathroom himself after he spread the powder, so there was no powder on his own shoes to leave any marks.

"It all worked—until that poor guy Plavy happened to walk in. Well, you know what Novack just told you about that—he had to take Plavy with him to keep the cat in the bag." He swallowed some rye.

"There I had it all figured out that the hookup was between Shade and Novack and that McMann was just a poor widower drowning his sorrow in drink. Sorrow, hell. The guy was so scared, after things went wrong, that he tried to drink himself insensible. And when he saw Novack, when I brought Novack in, he just went haywire—figured that Novack was there to confess and tried to kill him. And he'd have killed me, too, if that gun had been loaded. You might say Madge died twice—once in bed and once out the window."

Abe Green took a drink of beer. "Why the hell was he toting an empty gun?"

"He wasn't. The last time I looked in his room it was loaded. And when I came down I told Meyer, one of our ops who was taking my place here, that I'd left the gun up there loaded, even though I had a feeling McMann might get blue enough to bump himself off. So Meyer, not wanting to have anything like that happen while he was on the job here, went up after I left and unloaded the gun."

"Sounds like a very conscientious guy."

"Well, not exactly. He likes to get a good night's sleep on these hotel jobs, and he wasn't taking any chances."

"Where's he now?"

"Sleeping."

"My god, didn't all that racket wake him up?"

"No. I woke him up and he told me about emptying the gun, but he fell right to sleep again. He'd had a stomachache earlier and took some powders to ease him. But he took sleeping powders by mistake."

Bottles, the barman, said, "It's my fault. I was meanin' to give him the gut powders and me the sleepin' powders, and the minute after I took what I thought was the sleepin' powders, I said to meself, 'Montmorency, there's somethin' wrong.'"